The Lucky Chip

Also by D.J. Ciccarello

Boys Like Kevin

The Lucky Chip

No Time For Duplicity

Boys Like Daniel

The Lucky Chip

*A Psychological Thriller of Betrayal
and Murder in The City of Sin*

D.J. Ciccarello

Dedicated to Spring and the enduring strength and resilience of motherhood.

"Luck always seems to be against the man who depends on it."

— Ukrainian proverb

SAM AND FRANKIE

(1963)

To be anywhere near 190 Hoover Street was dangerous, but Frankie was dealing with dangerous people. The meeting place was to be secret and the discussion between the two men private, but following Frankie there was easy. The uninvited figure hiding in the shadows could not help but inch forward quietly to better look at the two men and hear their conversation. Despite his reluctance to attend, Frankie Grant was there. He had no choice. A business owner like himself in Las Vegas could only decline offers from The Alliance so many times.

"Look, Frankie, I understand." He spoke empathetically as he leaned forward, calm and confident. "We all want to be kings of our castles. But even kings need allies. It's like treaties between countries. Agreements and accords. No king stands alone. We all need partnerships. You know, people we can trust for help when enemies attack. We gotta all stand together here, Frankie. Like a family, you know?"

"Mr. Giancarlo, I appreciate—"

"Please, Frankie, it's Sam," the well-dressed gentleman interrupted, smiling and leaning back in his chair. He brought his palms into his chest as if he were about to share a piece of his heart. "You're a success now, Frankie. We're family, so talk to me like a brother." He leaned back into the intimate yet intimidating conversation, his eyes fixed and focused on Frankie's apprehension.

The fat envelope lay in the middle of the table between the two men as they debated the concepts and merits of independence and interdependence, autonomy, and business interactions. Each had their own agendas and goals. Each also had their own instructions. They were playing a high-stakes game, and only one could emerge the winner this time. Frankie had already had one too many pushes, and neither the dealer nor the player had won.

Cigar smoke filled the stale air of the dimly lit room as Frankie hesitated. He finally reached for the envelope with his left hand and rose to shake Sam's hand with his right. He was both relieved and terrified as he did. Sam's investment in the new Casbah Hotel and Casino was now secure, and the two men's partnership was finalized. Sam dealt Frankie a hand he did not want, and although Frankie was holding the cash, Sam and The Alliance won the game. As they exchanged salutations before exiting through separate doors, the slender figure in the darkness slowly backed away from the silent vantage point in the shadows so as not to be discovered.

After Mr. Giancarlo exited the room, Frankie returned the envelope to the center of the table and sat down again. He savored the remainder of his cigar like a convicted man, relishing the last few minutes of his freedom. Frankie contemplated the weight of his action for twenty minutes. All circumstances have options, and all decisions have costs. Some people benefit while some people pay. Frankie was trying to decide which side of the coin the people he cared for would land.

Frankie Grant exited the door and walked toward his car, cutting through the chilly desert air befalling the City of Sin at night. The hour was late, and as he pressed the door handle's button and opened the driver-side door, he realized how hungry he was. Frankie wondered if his children were already in bed and if his wife had saved him some dinner in the oven to keep warm. She had, of course. She always did.

"Grant!" the voice shouted out.

As he turned, the first shot cut through the clear night air and hit Frankie in the stomach. The second and third shots cut through his jacket and shirt to hit him squarely in the chest. As Frankie tried to brace himself against the car door's interior handle with his right hand, his shoulder slid against the door panel on his way down. The fourth shot pierced his arm as the assailant walked toward him. Frankie was a big man, the kind of man who goes down to the ground slowly, reluctantly. He murmured something, struggling to reach into his jacket pocket. Something precious. But his struggle ceased when the fifth and then final sixth shot struck Frankie, and his head slowly fell to rest in the pool of dark blood forming under his large frame on the pavement.

After removing the precious something from Frankie's jacket pocket, the dark figure strode into the still-darker shadows cast by the adjacent buildings against the lights and glamor of the Vegas strip in the distance.

JACK AND EMILY

(Sixty Years Later)

The change in the plane's pitch was slight but noticeable to those attuned to their surroundings. "Ladies and gentlemen, we've begun our initial descent into Las Vegas. Please stow all carry-on items under the seat in front of you or in the overhead bin. All seatbelts should be securely fastened. Please pass all used service items toward the aisle …".

Jack swallowed the last of his beverage as the ice cubes in the plastic cup tumbled toward his face. He then reached to grab the near-empty water bottle to his right.

"Leave it," she said, listening to Adele's "Rolling in The Deep" through her earbuds. During the three-hour flight, Emily cycled through her playlist but repeatedly returned to the same song.

"Sorry, sweetheart, I thought you were done."

"I'll let you know when I'm done, Jack." Emily's gaze remained affixed out the window toward the hard ground racing toward her. She tried to refocus on the song's lyrics, shifting her weight and position in the seat to distance herself from the now frequent landing announcements over the intercom and the annoyance of conversation from the seat next to her.

"Hey, Emily, I want this weekend to be special. You deserve this. You've worked hard these past few years to keep things together."

Succumbing to the unavoidable, Emily turned away from the window and removed her earbuds. She gave her husband a glassy stare while tapping one thumb against the other atop her folded hands. "I wish you wouldn't do that, Jack."

"Do what?"

"Drink, Jack," Emily replied curtly. "Do you *really* think that's a good idea?"

"Em, it was only ginger ale. I'm fine, I promise. Don't worry." As Jack's hand reached out to comfort hers, she reached for the plastic bottle between them. Raising the spout to her mouth, Emily finished what water was left and handed the empty to him to pass to the flight attendant.

"Look, Jack," she said, placing her hand on his forearm in a small and increasingly rare offering of tenderness. "I know it's our anniversary. I appreciate the trip and concert tickets. You know I've wanted to see this show for a long time. I'm just," she paused, searching for the right words to use as the inner conflict between patience and resentment waged within her.

"Ladies and gentlemen, we have started our final descent. In preparation for landing, please return to your seats and fasten your seatbelts. At this time, tray tables must be stowed, and seat backs must be in their upright and locked position."

Emily welcomed the interruption of the announcement, waiting for the crew's message to end before continuing. "Jack, I just worry about things returning to how they were." Emily was still holding her earbuds in her hands, but she could hear the song's lyrics repeating in her head just the same. "And Vegas," she continued, "with its alcohol and bells and flashing lights. It all seems exciting, but appearances can be deceiving, Jack. I can't go through all of that again."

"I know, Em," he said, offering reassurance. "But I'm back on my feet. I have a new job. There's a lot to be grateful for. I'm fine, I promise. I'm not going to screw up again. Please don't worry. Just relax and let me take care of you for a change this weekend."

As Jack spoke, he observed how much Emily and Adele resembled each other. They were about the same age, as far as Jack knew, and both had parents from the UK, although Emily herself was born and raised in Dallas. Jack presumed that was the reason for his wife's mix of proper sophistication and tough Southwestern grit. Although he knew nothing of the singer's music, Jack guessed their strengths came from the same place of pleasure. Emily knew better, however. She knew every lyric to every song, their shared strengths from the same place of pain.

Emily wanted to believe and trust her husband, but the past two years had been difficult. His unemployment and subsequent alcohol abuse and depression had taken a toll on their marriage, stretching her tolerance to its limit. In her mind, divorce looked imminent, at least until he finally pulled himself out of the dark hole and cleaned up his act.

Jack knew just how close he came to losing her. The close call profoundly impacted him and became his most powerful motivation to change. He knew he couldn't survive without her. Jack also knew he had to become a man again. Emily *was* strong, but every man needs his pride, too. He intended to win back her trust again. Jack needed her to respect and admire him again. Maybe then she could need him as much as he needed her. He was confident he could win her love back, too.

Trust, respect, admiration, need, and love. All interwoven

threads in the tapestry of deep relationships. Trust lays the foundation, respect builds integrity, admiration fuels desire, need fosters dependence, and love binds them together, creating a resilient and enduring bond between two people.

"Okay, Jack," she said, accepting his hand and offering him a reluctant smile to let him know everything was okay. "I'm good," she continued. "It's going to be a great weekend, and we'll have a good time."

The landing announcement continued in the background as Emily and Jack looked at one another, each confident they knew what to expect and had the situation under control. "…flight attendants will pass through the cabin one last time to pick up the remaining service items. We will be landing shortly. Thank you."

THE BELLMAN

Hotels lower the thermostat of guest rooms before visitors arrive, especially in the desert, where the heat and temperatures fuel irritability, and sweat is barely distinguishable from tears.

"This room is pretty nice, don't you think, Em?" The couple faced one another on opposite sides of the king mattress as they decided what to unpack or leave in their carry-ons. "Did you bring your phone charger?" Jack asked.

"Of course I did. You didn't bring yours?"

"No, I guess I forgot it. Can I use yours for a minute, please?"

To lessen her annoyance, Emily avoided eye contact with her husband, choosing not to make cutting remarks about how he should be more attentive when he packed. Instead, she remained focused on removing the clothes from her case as she tossed her charger over the bed in his direction.

Rechecking his bag, Jack saw a glimpse of the object flying in his direction. His reflexes were quick but not quick enough to catch the unexpected toss. The charger flew by Jack's hands and grazed the lampshade beside him before hitting the wall and falling behind the nightstand.

"Wow, wild pitch. I missed that one. Sorry, Em."

Jack kneeled on one knee and wedged his hand between the wall and the back of the nightstand to retrieve the charger. He felt another familiar but unexpected object with his fingertips as he did. Jack struggled to push and squeeze his hand farther into the crevasse until he could pinch the object between his index and middle finger, retrieving the hidden item and the phone charger.

"Hey, what's this?" The envelope looked yellowed with age, like a rare find new homeowners discover in attics or behind walls demolished in preparation for remodeling. Jack moved toward the bedside lamp for a better look and noticed the envelope's flap tucked inside, the glue edge still unsealed. The envelope's letterhead read 'Casbah Hotel and Casino,' typeset in red letters in the upper left-hand corner.

"What did you find there, Jack?" Emily was not yet interested enough to look up from the contents of her suitcase but alert enough to notice Jack's stillness and silence—that simple awareness of his quiet was enough to raise her wariness. Emily learned, over time, to be suspicious when Jack seemed obsessed and focused on something new that did not fit into their routine. Recognizing the signs was all part of the recovery process.

"It says, *To Sofia. I'm so sorry. Frankie,*" he replied. The writing was cursive, written in ink with fine penmanship, in a manner no longer used today with modern technology and keyboards, penned with exactness in the style once taught in school when handwriting was important. Jack repeated the words to himself, *To Sofia. I'm so sorry. Frankie.*

"Hey, there's something inside." Jack's grin grew wide. He felt energized and awake with adrenaline-fueled anticipation, like a child stumbling down the stairs with grogginess before noticing all the presents under the tree on Christmas morning and sprinting to rip them open all at once.

"Don't open it, Jack." He now had Emily's full attention as he studied the envelope in his hands, flipping it over and sideways to inspect it from all sides. "It doesn't belong to us," she added.

"It's okay, honey," he replied. "It's in our room."

"It says Frankie. You are not Frankie, Jack." Emily was about to suggest they turn his find in at the front desk on their way to dinner, but she was too late. Jack's curiosity had already untucked the back flap of the envelope as its contents slid out and into the palm of his hand.

"Wow, it's a $500 poker chip! Look at this, Em."

"Jack, why did you open that? You know that doesn't belong to—."

The polite knock on the room's door interrupted Emily's harsh disapproval. The couple glanced at one another as if asking if the other knew who might be knocking or why—perhaps wondering which would move first to answer the knock. Emily finally swept her hand across the air, motioning to Jack to get the door. There was another polite tap, and Jack slipped the purple chip into his pants pocket while laying the old envelope atop the dresser on his way toward the door.

A tall and well-dressed man met Jack. "Pardon me, Mr. Harper," the bellman said, "but I have a gift for you and Mrs. Harper. May I come in?" The elderly gentleman spoke in a courteous and professional tone, a manner you would expect from the well-trained staff at luxury hotels, yet becoming increasingly uncommon in the modern world.

Jack observed the small room service cart next to the gentleman and opened the door wider, motioning him to enter. "Oh yeah, of course. Come in."

"Thank you, sir," he replied, bowing his head as he entered the room and walking past Jack toward the foot of the bed near where Emily stood. He acknowledged Emily with the same respectful nod and politely said, "Mrs. Harper." The bellman glanced toward the bed between the couple's half-unpacked suitcases. "May I?"

As the bellman placed the tray on the mattress, Jack noticed he didn't ask where to set the tray in the room; he thought that observation odd. On his way to the bed, he had bypassed the desk on the opposing wall and the small coffee table in the center of the junior suite.

"A gift to celebrate the occasion, Mr. and Mrs. Harper." A bottle of Perrier-Jouët, chilled and half submerged in an ice bucket with a red napkin twisted around the bottle's neck, occupied one-half of the tray. Two champagne glasses and red heart-shaped chocolates on a petite dish sat on the other half.

The bellman gestured toward the bottle as if about to offer to open and pour them a glass. Emily anticipated his intent and instinctively waved her hand over the tray. "Oh, no. Not right now. But thank you." Her instinct was keen when it came to men and their intentions.

"But of course, Mrs. Harper," he replied, stepping back into the center of the room where Jack was standing.

The bellman and Jack exchanged pleasantries for a few minutes. The bellman asked how they enjoyed their trip thus far, hoping their flight into the city was pleasant, if not issue-free. He inquired about their grand plans for their stay, offering to assist should they need suggestions on where to eat or require reservations made. He had, after all, lived in Las Vegas for most of his life.

Emily watched the two men as they spoke, occasionally glancing toward the champagne and chocolate hearts before

11

returning her attention to their conversation. They were the same height, over six feet tall, with healthy lean physiques. They both had long and strong jawlines. The bellman was clean-shaven, whereas Jack sported two-day stubble, trimmed with straight lines and a neat appearance. Both men combed their gelled hair back with a part on the left side of their head, although the older man had far less hair left than Jack. At thirty-four, Jack still had a full, thick head of dirty blond hair showing no signs of thinning. He was handsome, and Emily sometimes kidded him about his strong resemblance to the actor who played Eric Northman on "True Blood." She wondered if the bellman had been as handsome back in the day, some forty or fifty years ago, as far as she could tell.

After tipping his imaginary hat in Emily's direction as an act of courtesy, the bellman began walking toward the door, accompanied by Jack as he reached into his pocket in search of the small fold of bills he carried for the occasional tip on trips like this. Jack felt the round chip in his pocket as he did, clenching it within his grasp to keep it safe and concealed.

Just before opening the door, Jack stopped and asked, "Say, you said you were raised here in Vegas, didn't you?" He glanced back at Emily, who had returned to her unpacking.

"Mostly, sir, indeed. I've been here a great many years."

"Then you may have heard of the Casbah Hotel and Casino?" Jack asked, quickly glancing again in his wife's direction before returning his full attention to the tall gentleman and his response.

The bellman raised one hand to his jaw and chin, rubbing them in deep concentration while looking down toward his polished shoes before answering. A relaxed smile fell on his face as he looked back up at Jack. "Yes, sir, I sure do. I remember the Casbah. Gosh, I haven't heard that name in years." He explained the Casbah was a hotel on the old strip. "Must have opened in the early '60s, I think. It's long gone now, though. Changed owners a few times," he continued. "Torn down years ago to build the new library or some office building, I think."

"Interesting," Jack replied, glancing a knowing grin in Emily's direction as she finished placing her clothes in the dresser drawers and closed her suitcase. He felt proud to have uncovered some information about the mysterious chip. It was like a boy digging up a coin in his backyard, washing it clean of the dirt concealing its identity, to discover the mint date preceding his birth year. The chip was older than Jack was, uncovered in a lucky find behind his nightstand.

"Well, I'll leave you two to it, then. Good luck."

"Luck?" questioned Jack. "Oh, we're just here to see a show. Not the gambling types, but thanks anyway."

The bellman acknowledged with a nod and accepted the folded five-dollar bill from Jack's outstretched hand as he closed the door.

"Well, he was odd," Emily said as she poured herself a glass of champagne from the bottle she had just opened, crossing her arms as if protecting herself from a sudden chill. She thought Jack's effort to arrange the delivery upon their arrival was sweet. Perhaps Emily had been too hard on him during the flight. Maybe she should take Jack's advice, lower her guard, and enjoy herself this weekend. Perhaps she should begin to trust Jack again instead of worrying about him relapsing or succumbing to the temptations of the city. Emily raised the glass to her lips and took small sips as Jack took the poker chip out of his pocket, returning it to its yellowed envelope. He folded the envelope neatly into squares and slipped it back into the right pocket of his trousers.

"I'll give it to the front desk when we go downstairs for dinner," he stated.

"Come here, you." Emily hugged Jack above his shoulders, still holding the now-empty champagne flute. He welcomed the hug from her, hugging her tightly around the waist and drawing her in, relieved she was finally relaxing into the weekend. "Thank you for the champagne and chocolates," she whispered into his ear. "That was very sweet of you," she added, kissing him on his neck before lowering herself from the embrace.

Jack looked down toward his wife, still holding her waist, captivated by her approving smile and the golden blond hair she so often swept away from her face and tucked behind her ears. She meant the world to him, and the thought of losing her once devastated him. But with their troubles behind them, Jack was confident their weekend celebration would finally put any lingering tensions to rest.

"When did you arrange it?"

"Oh. Um. When I booked the room," Jack replied, quickly deciding that was when he would have arranged the room service delivery since Emily had been by his side since arriving in Las Vegas hours ago. *It's obviously a gift from the hotel*, he thought. That would be Jack's first, harmless little mistruth of the weekend.

Back in their room, after a large steak and exhausted from the workweek, the weekend's planning and preparation, and the flight to get there, Jack and Emily fell into a restful sleep.

EVILYN AND SOFIA

(1962)

The first light of dawn illuminated the kitchen and its hectic morning routine. As Evilyn stood at the stove, four slices of toast shot into the air. Her movements were smooth and efficient, flipping pancakes and scrambling eggs with practiced ease. The aroma of coffee and breakfast filled the room, a comforting constant amid the family's energetic and lately chaotic mornings.

Even while cooking breakfast for her family, Evilyn's all-American beauty shone through with wholesomeness and sophistication. Her heart-shaped face, framed by shoulder-length blond waves, was stylish and perfectly coiffed to accentuate her high cheekbones. Her complexion, fair and smooth, glowed with natural warmth and elegance.

"Sweetie, help your sister butter her toast, please," Evilyn calmly asked her ten-year-old son, Richard, who quickly put aside his comic book to butter Lucy's toast as his mother requested. As she served the eggs and pancakes onto each of the four plates at the dinette table, Evilyn glanced toward the swinging kitchen door and called out. "Frankie, breakfast is ready." Richard returned to his comics, and Lucy picked up one of her pancakes and took a large bite after folding it like a taco.

"Daddy, breakfast is gonna get cold," Lucy called out.

"Going to, honey, not 'gonna,'" Evilyn corrected gently, a smile tugging at her lips.

Frankie appeared in the doorway, already dressed in his suit jacket, face drawn with exhaustion. He bypassed the table and headed straight for the coffee pot. "Morning, kids," he mumbled, managing a weary smile as he made his way to the counter.

"Morning. You're just in time for pancakes," Evilyn announced, her voice bright as she washed the breakfast pans at the sink. She turned to him, softening her tone. "Here, let me get that for you. Sit down and eat breakfast with the kids."

Frankie kissed her cheek before walking to the table, ruffling his son's hair affectionately as he passed. Richard looked up and acknowledged his father with a muffled 'morning' before returning his full attention to his comic book. Lucy was too busy finishing her pancake tacos to notice much else.

"Finish up and brush your teeth," Evilyn instructed her children. She would clear the table and have the dishes washed and placed in the drying rack before driving Richard and Lucy to school, as she dutifully did each weekday morning. But before doing so this morning, she lovingly voiced her concerns to Frankie. "You were up late again last night. I heard you walking around. Is everything alright?"

Frankie didn't meet her eyes. "Yeah, of course. It's just work. You know how things go this close to opening, darling."

Evilyn nodded, drying her hands on the dishtowel opposite Frankie, her gaze laden with unspoken worries. "I know, but the hours you're putting in, Frankie. It's starting to show. And our finances—"

Frankie interjected with a forced cheerfulness, "It's all going to pay off, Evie. I promise. It might seem like we're in a tight spot, but everything will be fine once the casino opens."

Evilyn hesitated, the usual reluctance to press him warring with her need to voice her concerns. She continued softly but firmly this time, "But what if it doesn't work out? What then, Frankie? We're stretching ourselves so thin."

"Evie, it will work," Frankie reassured her, masking his concern. "We've come too far to doubt now. I need you to trust me a little longer. Everything's under control, I promise."

Evilyn looked at her husband, her expression a mix of love, worry, and resignation. She had expressive hazel eyes, a mix of green and brown that sometimes looked golden in the sunlight, conveying warmth and earthiness to Frankie when he looked into them. Evilyn's eyes reflected her adaptability, suggesting a balance between logic and emotion. Her eyebrows were finely arched, adding to her composed and elegant appearance.

Evilyn wanted to offer help and to be more involved. Pushing wasn't her style, though. She could see the stress etching itself deep into him. He was gaining weight and having trouble sleeping. Frankie worked seven days a week for months and was out late most evenings. His usually upbeat personality was all but gone, only surfacing when forced, like when he entered the kitchen earlier to greet his children. Frankie was tired, and although his prior business ventures had all been taxing, they had all been successful. This time, however, felt different to her.

Evilyn sighed and reluctantly backed down. "Okay, Frankie. We're all with you. Just try to slow down and don't keep things all bottled up inside yourself, alright? We're a team, remember?"

Evilyn had always been supportive and would have made a fine businesswoman had she not married Frankie and started a family.

Valedictorian in high school and a college graduate, she happily traded her potential career for the title of wife, mother, and PTA President. She volunteered regularly at the local hospital and other charities. She managed food drives to feed underprivileged families and bake sales to fund school supplies. Evilyn was caring but cautious, responsible yet respected.

Evilyn removed her apron and hung it up, revealing a classy blue drop-waist swing dress and pearl necklace she wore today to cook breakfast and run errands after dropping the kids off at school. Standing around 5'8", she had a slender and graceful figure, often dressing in the sophisticated fashions of the time—tailored dresses and skirts that complemented her poised, ladylike manner. Her overall presence was one of quiet confidence, with a soft yet clear voice, adding to her aura of approachability and charm. Evilyn was from an affluent family with a proper upbringing, and she intended to provide the same safe and appropriate environment for her husband and children.

Frankie nodded, offering a smile meant to reassure her and himself before turning his attention to his children as they burst into the kitchen through the swinging door separating the kitchen from the rest of the ranch-style home. He wondered how the door stayed on its hinges, being pushed from one side to the other and back again, constantly changing directions to allow people passage to where they wanted to go or to swing back to stop them dead in their tracks.

As she shepherded the kids through the kitchen's back door, Evilyn turned back to Frankie with a smile. "It's roast beef night. Love you."

***

The expansive space was already humming with activity when Frankie arrived at 7:45 a.m.. Carpenters, electricians, and painters

18

moved around one another in a coordinated dance of productivity. Rows of slot machines were being positioned diagonally atop the freshly laid carpet as the sounds of hammering and testing filled the dim but colorfully lit area. The site reminded Frankie of his time serving aboard the USS Franklin D. Roosevelt as a young enlisted teenager just after the war ended. He was an original crewmember of the ship, but the Roosevelt was commissioned too late to see actual combat; thus, Frankie never did either. Still, the thrill of working below in the ship's hanger, abuzz with activity around the tightly packed planes and equipment waiting their turn on the exterior lift for transport up to the flight deck, was no less exciting. His new casino floor reminded him of those two years at sea. Only this time, Frankie would captain the carrier-sized operation instead of taking orders from others.

Frankie took the stairwell up to the 'Eye' where he found several phone messages and neatly written notes beside his coffee cup and the fresh-brewed pot of coffee. The Eye was Frankie's nickname for the viewing room above the soon-to-be-completed casino floor, or what the industry called the 'eye in the sky.' Filled with closed-circuit TV monitors and one-way glass, security personnel would soon observe gambling activities and staff below without being seen themselves. Frankie considered the Eye his command room, like the Bridge above carrier flight decks where the captain commanded the vessel and oversaw flight operations.

The activities and progress below pleased Frankie, sweat beads still glistening on his forehead from walking up the stairs as he sipped the third cup of this morning's caffeine. He could see his dream coming together, and for a few brief moments, he didn't focus on his financial, operational, or regulatory approval issues. Frankie only saw success as he looked at the bustling activity below. In the middle of the commotion, holding blueprints and paperwork and directing workers, was Sofia, his assistant.

A few minutes later, Sofia bolted through the Eye's door like a raging tempest of energy filling the room. "Quei lavoratori sono degli idioti, lo giuro! (Those workers are idiots, I swear!)," she said before noticing Frankie standing by the glass. "Banker hours?" she added once she saw him. A confident but frustrated aura surrounded Sofia, her Italian heritage evident in her demeanor and fiery spirit.

"It's not even 8:00 a.m.," he shot back. "Easy."

"No, no-easy! These contractors are dragging their feet, and we're behind schedule." Sofia was much more than Frankie's assistant, making coffee and taking phone messages. She meticulously oversaw the final touches of the three-story, 100-room hotel and casino buildout. She offered Frankie suggestions when there were limited options and emotional support when his worries arose. Sofia was now driving the schedule, coercing the vendors, and pressuring the workers.

"Grazie," Frankie replied in his mid-western, overly Anglo accent. "I don't know what I would do without you."

Sofia was fiery, but she was also highly competent. In her thirties, she was a potent mix of beautiful toughness. Her breast-length, jet-black hair framed her attractive Southern European facial features. Those features could be tender and inviting or callus and aversive, depending on which was required. Sofia usually wore black, even during daylight hours or in the heat of summer. Black was her heritage; the color was her signature. The only things Sofia varied in her dress were her neckline and hemline. She chose them carefully, depending on the task at hand.

Sofia straightened her fingers and raised her stiff hand in a half-salute motion as she exclaimed, "Fallire, ovviamente (Fail, obviously)." That's what Sofia thought Frankie would do without her. He would fail. She rested her hands on the table in the center of the room. She looked at Frankie as he stood by the viewing window, holding his cup of coffee against the casino floor backdrop behind him. "It's going to be a great place. It's the perfetto time. Look at all the success around us. The Dunes and Riviera, l'Hacienda e lo Stardust. We're next, Frankie. The Casbah."

Frankie listened to Sofia's words of confidence as the sparkle in his eyes returned to his tired and worried face.

***

Carmine's was a quiet restaurant on the city's outskirts, not too far from the strip but far enough away to be discreet. They never advertised, so the tourists didn't know the establishment was there, and the locals knew better than to frequent it. Carmine's catered to an exclusive and select clientele, individuals who wanted a few hours in the evening to let their guard down and relax in a simple, understated environment where they could eat an authentic meal. Carmine's was neutral territory and only open in the late hours of the evening. You didn't go there to make deals or to get noticed.

Frankie had only dined at Carmine's a couple of times and had only recently risen to the social stature of being welcomed there. His fortunate timing and success as a real estate developer were gaining notice from newspapers and citizens in Las Vegas. His building of the Casbah was gaining interest from the people who owned and ran the city. Carmine's was the perfect place for Frankie and Sofia to meet for a late-night dinner after working the long day together.

Sofia sipped her wine while watching Frankie finish the last of his porterhouse. "Frankie, ascoltami (listen to me)," she said, waiting for him to wipe his mouth and lay his fork and knife on the plate in a crossed position, fork prongs downward like taught to do as a child. He leaned back in his booth seat while 16 ounces of expensive beef settled in his middle-aged businessman's belly. She looked at his plate and quietly sighed. *Stupido (Stupid),* she thought to herself. Crossing his silverware instead of placing them parallel to each other with the fork prongs facing upward indicated he was dissatisfied with his meal. Everyone knew that, or at least in Sicily, they did.

Sofia leaned in, her voice low but intense with determination. "Frankie, listen to me. We have to be realistic." She observed his expression darken as if they had had this conversation many times before and knew what she was about to say. Still, she continued. "*La Alleanza* (The Alliance) still has a stronghold on this city, Frankie. There's no way to work around it. We need their connections. We need their protection. We need funding to finish. Don't be stubborn, Frankie. We need to work with them."

Frankie leaned into her words with his jaw clenched in reluctant frustration. "I won't do it, Sofia. I won't get involved with them. I refuse to compromise my integrity. I'll find a way, a clean way, to get us across the finish line." Sofia spoke in 'we' while Frankie spoke in 'I,' but they were both determined to see the Casbah open. They were also both intent on being successful.

Sofia sighed. Her dark eyes and gaze searched his face for any sign of wavering during the uncomfortable pause. When she scooted a few inches closer to Frankie in the half-circled booth, by some accounts closer than mere business colleagues should, Sofia tilted her head and smiled before softening her tone. "Frankie, amore mio (my love), I understand your reluctance. I do. But this isn't just about us anymore. It's about the bigger picture, the world we're living in. *La Alleanza* controls everything—the unions, the politicians, and most of the hotels and casinos on the strip. You know this, Frankie. We can't afford to ignore this."

Sofia wasn't wrong. Las Vegas was quickly transforming into the country's gambling and entertainment powerhouse. The mob, who had considerable control over businesses, especially casinos, using them for skimming operations, heavily influenced the city. As Vegas rapidly grew, newer and larger casinos opened while the older ones expanded or renovated. It represented a glorious cycle of materials, labor, and financing requirements, not to mention tourists and locals eager to wager their portion of the booming US economy. Post-war expansion, government spending on infrastructure and defense, the space race, and technological innovation put money in people's pockets. Consumer confidence led to higher spending on automobiles and housing. Even tax cuts helped stimulate the economy.

Money flowed, and the various crime syndicates were right there to do their part and take their cut, just as they had been for three decades. The Kansas City family had the Tropicana. There were the Balistrieris from Milwaukee and The Cleveland family with its Desert Inn. The Chicago Outfit was the largest with its investment in the Stardust. The way things worked was considered an open secret by residents, local authorities, and federal agencies.

In the center of it all was The Commission, the governing body or council for the American Mafia. The Commission resolved disputes, distributed territories, and regulated the activities among the different families to prevent conflicts and ensure business ran smoothly—businesses like racketeering, money laundering, gambling, and loan sharking. The Alliance, the Commission's Las Vegas arm, operated Carmine's, where Frankie and Sofia sat debating their future.

Within a whisper's distance from one another now, Frankie and Sofia shared a tense moment of silence. The distant sounds of wine glasses clinking, the kitchen preparing late-night meals, and the muffled voices of other conversations and laughter shielded them from the tension of total silence. Their conflicting ideals and boundaries cast a shadow over their relationship.

Frankie squared his shoulders to his assistant and reached to cup her hands within his. Firmly and with a newfound resolve, he said, "I appreciate you, Sofia, but I won't budge on this."

Sitting back, Sofia withdrew her hands from his embrace. She reached for her glass and took a last sip of wine, turning her shoulders away from Frankie to look ahead instead. She surveyed the room, assessing how many tables were businessmen, how many were married couples dining in solitude together, and how many might be husbands cheating on their wives with their mistresses.

Frankie also felt the disconnection, but the sensation was more blunt with him. He lacked Sofia's keen observation skills or ability to make assumptions or deductions about the people around him based on their behavior and interactions. Frankie had never had to cultivate cynicism or awareness of human nature as she had to. And then he thought about Evilyn at home and wondered if she had kept some roast beef warm in the oven for his return from a long day at work. She had, of course. That was what Evilyn did.

CASH AT THE CASBAH

(Present)

J ack waited for Emily downstairs in the lobby while she finished dressing. He watched people bustle about, some checking into the hotel while others checked menus and prices outside of restaurants as they decided which Saturday buffet line to choose. Many people were already gambling, either tired leftovers from the night before or fresh hopefuls as today's contenders. The atmosphere was an odd early-morning cocktail: the smell of pancakes and bacon, the sound of plastic discs clanking together, the bells and buzzers of the slots, and the feel of the ribbed texture of the chip's outer edge concealed in his pants pocket. Jack ran his fingertips around the grooved edge in a circular motion, round and round, as the chip calmed his nerves and called to his vulnerability.

Jack knew exactly how Emily felt about gambling. She was no risk-taker, never had been, not even a raffle or lottery ticket. Her parents opposed gambling on religious grounds, viewing betting as morally wrong and sinful. Emily wasn't as devout as her parents. Still, as a former family law attorney herself, she had seen the detrimental effects gambling addictions had on families: the financial strains, the relationship problems, and the mental health issues. She felt gambling exploited people who could least afford it, and there was no way she would surrender control of her financial fate to games of chance with odds heavily stacked against her from the start.

Jack wasn't as strong as Emily. He couldn't help but caress the old chip in his pocket. He imagined how many fortunes had been won at the high-roller table over the years with the purple chip as part of a lucky man's stack. Jack knew the chip had no real value today. The Casbah was long gone, and the chip's only value was sentimental. He had already decided the relic was nothing more than a souvenir to remember their Vegas anniversary trip by the time he came downstairs earlier and ditched the old envelope into the first garbage can he passed.

[Be down in 15 min.] Emily texted.

[okie] Jack replied.

With fifteen extra minutes, Jack began roaming the casino floor, watching people lose their money while he waited for his wife. *Better them than me*, he thought with self-assurance. Jack was also relieved; Emily seemed to have settled down and relaxed like he had asked her to during the flight. Their room was great, and they had a good time at dinner the previous night. Even the surprise delivery of champagne and chocolates worked in his favor, and Jack couldn't be more pleased with how the weekend was progressing.

That's when the object in the distance caught Jack's eye. It was smaller than the others around it, not as bright or loud as the others, but unique and authentic, lit with a vintage color palette that spoke to him. Jack's skin tingled as he carefully strolled closer. With each step, the sounds and distractions of the rest of the casino's busy morning slowly faded into the distance until there was nothing else but Jack and the Cash at The Casbah slot machine.

It was too much of a coincidence, not unlike reaching deep behind a nightstand to retrieve a phone charger that should not have fallen there, only to find an old envelope containing a vintage five-hundred-dollar poker chip.

Jack slowly scanned the sea of other slots surrounding him to confirm the machine was the only one of its kind, and it was. The slot machine had no video screen with advanced graphics and animations offering multiple pay lines, intricate bonus rounds, or free spins. This slot machine was straightforward and old school, with physical reels displaying fruits, bells, and the occasional BAR symbol. Its odds were fixed and printed directly on the machine's front. The Cash at The Casbah looked like a long-forgotten remnant sitting next to the modern giants powered by complex software with their bewildering arrays of screens, lights, and features. Its only modification seemed to be the addition of a black box to accept dollar bills instead of coins and to print pay-out slips. Jack looked around again to see who was in the general area and perhaps confirm Emily wasn't. She wasn't. Jack was alone with the coincidental slot machine and the lucky chip in his pocket.

Jack won the first time he inserted a dollar bill and pulled the handle. Cash at The Casbah had no push-to-spin buttons. The heavy pull lever felt more authentic, anyway. The slot machine felt just as Jack thought Vegas should feel.

He bet his new winnings and pulled the handle, winning once again. Four dollars now won on a single dollar. Jack wagered his winnings once more, and again he won. Each time Jack pulled the lever, the spring-loaded gears turned, and the metal reels rapidly spun until, one by one, they stopped to display a matching combination of symbols. Jack was on a streak, doubling his winnings each time.

When Emily texted to say she was on her way down, Jack hit

the cash-out button. When the machine printed the voucher for $256, Jack snatched the paper and shoved it deep into his pants pocket, nestled now with his newfound chip. A gratifying relief swept Jack as he turned and walked toward the bank of elevators where his wife would soon descend. He slowed his pace, recognizing how hurried his stride had become, and took a deep breath to ease the unaccustomed smirk of confidence on his face. His winning happened so fast. His winning felt so satisfying.

***

Hand in hand, Jack and Emily walked to Café Americano for a light breakfast. Jack had initially chosen Bacchanal, known to have one of Vegas's best buffets, but Emily wanted something lighter after the heavy meal the night before. Once seated, she ordered vanilla almond granola yogurt topped with blueberries, pomegranate, banana slices, and strawberries. Jack convinced her to add a side of avocado toast they would share since this might be her only meal before the concert. Jack had a larger appetite that morning, ordering a Classic Benedict served with breakfast potatoes and an add-on short stack of buttermilk pancakes with chocolate chips.

"Wow!" Emily commented when the waiter walked away with their order. "Maybe we should have gone to the buffet instead?"

"No, this is great, Em." Jack's hazel eyes sparkled above his wide grin. He wanted to share his excitement about the winnings with her but did not dare. No, he would use his winnings to treat her to a nice dinner or buy her a gift, keeping the source of the cash to himself. Emily was only beginning to relax and trust him, and Jack wasn't about to risk that now.

"I can't wait to see Adele tonight," she said, reaching across the small table to grab Jack's hands and hold them in hers. "I'm so excited," she continued. "Thank you for the tickets, Jack,"

Emily added with tenderness absent for quite some time.

"You're welcome, Sweetheart," he replied.

"Say, did you give that envelope you found to the front desk?"

"Yeah, I got rid of it."

"Good," she commented. "I love you, Jack."

"I love you too, Em." He could feel the round disk in his pocket but wasn't lying to her. Emily asked about the envelope, and he had gotten rid of it. Her question was specific, and he answered the question directly. Jack had no intention of betraying Emily now, after working so hard to get his life back on track and salvage their relationship. A rush of relief swept over Jack as the waiter politely intervened to place their breakfast plates in front of them.

When they finished eating, Emily told Jack she wanted to lie by the pool for a while to get some sun. "I want to get some color on my face before tonight's show," she said. "Want to come with me?"

"No, you go ahead. I'll walk off breakfast first and see where the theater is. I'll see you out there in a minute."

"Okay, but don't be gone long. And no gambling, Jack," she added, giving her husband a playful nudge before heading toward the elevators and their room to change into her swimsuit.

Jack chuckled. "Don't worry, Em. I'll be right behind you."

Dr. Norman and Casey

Each time Jack's phone vibrated in his pocket, he ignored it, focusing instead on what was in front of him. A pause followed each sequence of eight vibrations, then another but different, shorter vibration, signaling a voicemail as each call went unanswered. Jack would not have been allowed to answer phone calls, anyway. But when the cell phone vibrated for the fourth time, he grudgingly stood and conceded his seat at the table, picking up his small but growing stack of chips. Jack had won or pushed every hand of blackjack played in the half-hour since promising Emily he would join her at the pool momentarily. The next vibration was a text message.

[Jack, where are you?] Emily texted.

[on my way] he promptly texted back.

Jack quickly cashed in his chips and shoved the folded bills into his pants pocket, nestling the cash safely alongside the slot machine's credit voucher and his lucky chip. He glanced toward the Casbah slot machine in the distance as he walked the maze-like paths through the irregularly arranged gaming areas to get to the center aisle leading back to the elevators and pool access hallway. Jack did not want to look in its direction. He purposely tried to avoid looking that way. Still, Jack soon inserted the paper voucher from earlier in the morning and pulled the long metal lever again. Four cherries, and once again a winner.

Why hasn't anyone else found this little gem? Jack wondered as the rush of dopamine filled him with excitement and delight. Despite his winning, however, he is cautious this time. Instead of doubling each bet, Jack decided it best to wager in small amounts and did so five and ten dollars at a time, winning each time the cylinders stopped spinning. Knowing he shouldn't be gambling, the streak was a complicated combination of gratification and guilt. Jack also knew he couldn't lose. *Just this once more, that's it.* Jack's mental bargaining helped ease the discomfort of his conflicting emotions. He was well aware that Emily was waiting for him. She could even have come into the casino looking for him. Still, Jack was no longer looking over his shoulder or cautiously surveying his surroundings. He knew she was outside and wouldn't enter the casino in pool attire. He had time for just one more spin.

It was a magical succession of bets, pulls, spins, and wins. Jack's gaze became a trance as the cylinders of symbols rotated rapidly next to one another. Slouched forward, his eyes wide and unblinking, he stared at the mesmerizing array of colors and images as they spun. Jack was oblivious to anything around him, keeping one hand on the betting button while the other pulled the lever. Each pull set the reels spinning anew, accompanied by the mechanical whirring and chiming of the Cash at The Casbah slot machine. His focus was intense as adrenaline coursed through his veins, which was when Jack saw it. They were just brief glimpses at first; the numbers |1||9||6||3| displayed repeatedly. When the numbers appeared to become stationary without the four cylinders ever coming to a stop, however, time warped and distorted around Jack—seconds blended into hours, days, weeks, months, years, and decades as Jack drew inexorably deeper into the Casbah's hypnotic spell.

Lights flashed while bells chimed as Jack focused on the rotating yet stationary digits. The illuminated images on the plexiglass front of the old slot machine changed each time the patterns of lights changed. Jack saw reflections of the old Casbah sign light up for the first time. He saw flashes of Frankie, happy and triumphant, as crowds clapped and congratulated him. Jack watched as Frankie held something in his hand while cutting the ceremonial ribbon. Jack saw Frankie's good luck charm, the poker chip specially made to mark his successful opening of The Casbah Hotel and Casino. Jack saw *his* lucky chip in Frankie's hand and saw *his* success in Frankie.

The spinning cylinders abruptly stopped when Jack's phone vibrated again. His eyes rapidly blinked as he shook his head, dispelling the lingering remnants of 1963. He took a sharp breath of conditioned air and heard the sounds of the casino surrounding him again. This time, Jack answered the call.

"Mr. Harper?" the male voice asked.

"Yes, this is Jack."

"Mr. Harper. Hi, this is Dr. Norman with Village Boarding. We've been trying to reach you about Casey."

"Casey?" Jack was confused at first. He walked away from the immediate cluster of gaming machines toward the quieter perimeter of the gaming floor, taking a few seconds for the sounds of chance to transition into the words of concern on the call.

"Yes, Casey, Mr. Harper," the veterinarian repeated. "I'm afraid Casey became ill this morning."

"Well, what happened? How ill is she?"

"We're not quite sure yet, Mr. Harper, so we'd like to do bloodwork and run some tests if that's alright with you."

Casey had always been more than just a dog to Emily, adopted as a puppy after the couple married. The golden retriever's soft, pale fawn coat was a constant source of comfort to her, especially during the worst period of Jack's depression when he slept on the sofa most nights. Emily often rested her hand on Casey's back or stroked her fur, finding a sense of calm in the dog's steady presence. To Emily, Casey was a loyal companion, offering quiet reassurance when she needed it most.

It was Jack, however, with his flexible schedule while unemployed, who usually took Casey in for her vet appointments or boarding before the couple traveled out of town. Village Boarding had Jack listed as their contact and had already left several messages for him. From the edge of the casino floor, Jack's eyes remained trained on the Cash at The Casbah's distant wager button.

"Yeah," Jack finally replied after a long pause. "Let me. I'll tell you what. Let me, um, let me call you guys back. I need to discuss this with my wife." Jack nodded, acknowledging the urgency, before ending the call.

Jack slid his cell phone into his back pocket and buried his hands deep into his front pockets, where he felt the folded bills and his lucky chip. He held the chip tightly, rubbing the edge ridges with his thumb in a circular motion around its circumference, round and round again. The action helped him focus as he paced the immediate area where he stood. Jack pinched his bottom lip between his teeth, debating whether to tell Emily about the call. He suspected she would want to return home immediately if he told her now. Casey was, after all, Emily's baby and always had been. Realistically, however, the illness was probably nothing serious. Jack hoped to wait to see if the dog's condition improved. Her illness probably would. If the past two years had taught Jack anything about recovery, it taught him patience and optimism are key. He would bet now on both.

Walking toward the exit, Jack combed his slicked hair back with his left hand while still clutching the chip firmly with his right inside his pocket. He took a deep breath as he walked, puffing his cheeks before slowly releasing the air as he cut through the large room on his way to his wife. Jack imagined Casey in the vet's office, laying on her favorite blanket they always took with them when dropping her off for a stay, not feeling well and wondering where the people she loved most were. It is a horrible feeling to be left alone with one's illness.

What Jack worried about more was Emily. If he told her about Casey's condition and they flew home early, the airfare, hotel, and concert tickets would have all been a waste of time and money. Emily deserved to see the singer she admired and the concert she had long wanted to see without worry or concern. This trip was, after all, for Emily. The weekend was his gift to her, and leaving now would negate his hard work and planning.

Jack drew another deep and calming breath as he picked up his pace. *Patience and optimism,* he repeated to himself, were both essential attitudes and qualities for individuals finished with their recovery.

THE PHONE CALL

(1963)

Frankie sat on the barstool, his back turned away from the padded counter as he faced the nearly completed casino floor. Most slot machines and tables were in place. A few finishing touches remained in the casino, with a few more required in the building's upper hotel floors. Frankie should have been happier than he was.

"Another of the usual, Mr. Grant?"

Frankie swiveled around and rested his elbows on the bar. "Yes, Max. Thanks." The glass shelves behind the bartender were already half-stocked. It would not be long now, probably only a few weeks, until the casino would bustle with people and players as the newest gaming establishment on the strip.

"Here ya go, Boss." Max was loyal. Frankie had known him for years from other establishments, and he was lucky to have convinced Max to leave his security and clientele at the Stardust to take a chance on the Casbah. Frankie once had the same type of loyalty from Sofia. However, since their late-night dinner when he told her a partnership with The Alliance was out of the question, their relationship now seemed strained. Frankie told her he would find another way, but now he wondered if his

35

relationship with her wasn't jeopardized. Frankie did not believe he could open and run the casino and the hotel without her.

"Everything good, Mr. Grant?" Max asked, unpacking boxes and washing new glassware.

"Yeah. All good, Max, thanks." Frankie wasn't all good, though. He pinched the excess skin under his neck with his right hand while holding the neat whiskey with his left. Frankie's worry revealed itself each time he wrinkled his brow or strained a fake smile, which was made worse by his difficulty sleeping and Evilyn's constant suggestions to slow down and take better care of himself. Evilyn didn't understand, not like Sofia did. Evilyn was the love of his life and the mother of his children. Sofia was the driving force behind the casino and the woman who stoked the fire of success in his belly. Evilyn was conservative and concerned; she was meatloaf and pot roast. Evilyn considered the Casbah a risk. Sofia was stimulating and confident; she was a medium-rare filet. Sofia deemed the Casbah a reward. Sofia understood, but it was becoming more challenging for Frankie to extract her creative ideas while suppressing her opinions and viewpoints.

Frankie stared at himself in the mirrored glass behind Max and through the bottles of liquor lined on the shelves. He rubbed the back of his neck while confliction simmered into frustration at his inability to discern what he wanted from what he needed. Evilyn, the children, his status in the community, and his image as a family man were all important. Opening the Casbah, his business relationships, personal success, and finances were all important. Everything was important, but so was making a decision. He spent the past weeks repeatedly weighing his options, reluctant to commit for fear of choosing the wrong person or course of action, for fear of making the wrong bet. Frankie wanted to be the house, not the gambler.

Staring at his reflection, he tapped his index finger repeatedly against the rim of the glass. "I'm sorry, what?" Frankie asked Max, unable to focus on anything but his internal conflict. When one hesitates too long, decisions are made for them.

"Sir, a call for you," Max repeated, placing the rotary phone on the bar top while stretching the spiral cord to offer Frankie the handset. "Boss, from the Eye," Max said, gesturing the handset upward and behind Frankie as he offered it to him again to take.

"Grant here."

Max continued to wash and dry the new lowball glasses, his head downward toward the task while keeping his eyes fixed on his boss. Max could also see Sofia up in the Eye, peering down at them, one hand on her hip as the other held her cigarette as if she was gauging Frankie's reaction to the call she had just transferred downstairs to him. Max could see Frankie's expression blanch after about thirty seconds into the call, asking the person on the other end of the line if they were 'sure.' Frankie's voice grew louder and irritated as he asked them 'why.' Irritation escalated to anger when he demanded an 'explanation.' The matter made no 'sense' and certainly wasn't 'acceptable.' Frankie stood and turned around, his back to Max now, and glanced up at the Eye and Sofia, who was still looking down at him. *How could this be happening now, just weeks before the grand opening?* He stared up at Sofia again as she smoked her cigarette and stared back at him, his thoughts scrambling to understand. The call lasted no more than two minutes when there was a 'click' on the other end. Even Max could hear the click, and when he did, he saw his boss swing around to face the bar again, knocking the barstool he had been sitting on to the floor.

"Boss, everything—?" Before Max could finish the question, Frankie let out a guttural roar, smashing the phone's handset against the bar top. Once, twice, three times. Each had a windup and force harder than the previous until, on the fourth blow, the handset's high-impact bakelite casing shattered, sending the receiver and internal wiring flying across the bar top. The caller's words and Frankie's pulse were pounding in his ears as adrenaline pulsed through his stout body. The years of hard work, the months of stress, and weeks of anxiety were now spilling out unto the bar top like a breached dam, unleashing a flood of pent-up emotions, drenching the polished wood in a deluge of anger, exhaustion, and despair. Frankie was tightly clutching what remained of the handset, his knuckles white from his constricting grip.

Max had never seen Frankie this angry and stepped back, the bar towel still in hand. He wanted to step forward and wipe what remained of Frankie's spilled whisky glass but did not dare. Sofia also stepped back, away from the floor-to-ceiling glass of the Eye above, fearing Frankie's rage would radiate up to where she stood like the radioactive waves radiating outward from one of those atomic blast tests routinely conducted deep in the desert not far from the city itself. Like Max, Sofia had never seen Frankie lose control like that. She also knew control was needed now.

DEALER'S CHOICE

(Present)

The pool area starkly contrasted the cooler and darker hotel lobby, taking Jack's eyes a few minutes of squinting to adjust to the brightness of the Nevada sunshine at noon. He debated stopping by the room first to get his sunglasses or to change into his swimsuit. Still, an hour had already passed since first telling Emily he would be right behind her. It could have been longer; Jack wasn't sure. Breakfast with her seemed so long ago, before the blackjack table, the visions in the Casbah slot machine, and the vet's call about Casey. It had been too long; Jack knew that, walking straight to the pool instead of stopping to change. As his vision adjusted to the intensity of the sunlight, he surveyed the surroundings and finally spotted Emily in the distance. She was standing and appeared to be collecting her belongings.

"Em, hey!" he called, weaving his way through the maze of lounge chairs. Jack wasn't sure what type of greeting he would get from Emily. He was also unsure what to say to her as he swallowed hard to soothe his dry throat and mentally prepare for her likely foray of questions or criticisms.

"Jack, where have you been? You said you were on your way, and you said that over—"

"I know Em, I'm sorry," he interrupted. *Better to beg for forgiveness,* he thought to himself. Jack would have never gotten permission. He rattled off a half-dozen untruths that could have plausibly occurred but hadn't. "I'm here now, Em. Sit back down. Let's get something to drink."

"Jack, I've already been out here for—"

"Come on, babe," he interjected again, pealing his polo shirt over his head and sitting in the chair she held for him next to her lounger. "It's so nice out." Asking Emily to sit back down was a gamble. Jack would be a stationary target for her interrogation of his whereabouts and activities during his absence. Still, it was the only thing he could quickly think of to delay the inevitable questions. Every second gained was another second Jack had to anticipate and internalize a response.

Emily laid her towel on the lounger and sat down to face Jack. She leaned back and listened to him explain his delay, his voice carrying the melody of sincerity, his eyes flickering with what she hoped was genuineness. Still, a whisper of skepticism brushed against her hope, a gentle reminder of past tales that lost their way in the light of truth. She observed him, not with the sharpness of accusation but with the quiet discernment of someone who has learned to listen beyond words. She longed to dispel past doubts and wholeheartedly embrace trust again. As Jack spoke and smugly smiled, she took his words and expressions all in, navigating the delicate balance between belief and suspicion.

Emily leaned into Jack, looking upward into his eyes while taking his hands and holding them tight within hers like the grip of a lie detector machine's cables strapped to the test's subject to measure their pulse and breathing patterns. "Jack," she asked, "have you been gambling?"

Jack bolted upright but did not pull away from her grasp,

widening his eyes and shaking her hands up and down as you would do to a child trying to coax them onto a scary ride at the fair. "Come on, Em," he replied, "of course not." Jack's mind immediately flashed back to when Emily asked him the same question two years ago. She told him then she wouldn't continue putting up with the problems his drinking and gambling addictions caused. She wouldn't endure that again, no matter how much she loved him. Their marriage would have been over had he not cleaned up his act. That was Emily's red line. It was also Jack's wake-up call. He shimmied his chair closer to her with unwavering eye contact. "I swear, absolutely not, sweetheart," he repeated with conviction and assurance.

That was Jack's final chance to come clean—his point of no return. Small truths might have scratched the fragile trust between them, but big lies had the potential to cut too deeply ever to heal. But what happened in the past did not matter now. Jack's past troubles no longer defined him. He was a winner now, and he would show everyone, especially Emily, that he was back on top. He was in control of his actions, and he was in control of his fate. Jack could and would have it all. He was also confident that, in the end, Emily would see his control, too.

When Emily broke her grip on Jack's hands, she slowly ran her palms up and down Jack's forearms in comfort. He was athletic and muscular, and she liked that about him. She observed how the high noon sun cast shadows across his chiseled facial features and well-defined chest. She needed him to be as strong emotionally as he was physically to regain his place of equality in their relationship. Emily also needed a break, a chance to return to the role of an attractive woman and desired wife. She was tired of playing the overbearing guardian and cautious caretaker.

"Okay, Hun," she softly spoke. "I'm sorry. I shouldn't have asked that." Emily smiled at her husband, her fortitude weakened by the heat and her desire for normalcy. "Thank you for being honest, Jack. I love you."

"Aw, Em," he replied, leaning forward to cradle the back of her neck and pull her into his kiss, undaunted by the phone's vibration in his back pocket as Village Boarding called again.

CALMING THE STORM

(1963)

Frankie called out for Sofia even before opening the door to the Eye. She was waiting for him as he entered, facing the door with her back to the wall of windows she had just stood before to watch him at the bar. "Did you know about the call?" he asked, agitated by the rapid climb up the stairs and her composure despite his frantic approach.

"Yes, of course. The call came here, which I transferred down to you."

"So you knew it was the Gaming Commission? You knew they pulled my fucking gaming license out from under my fucking feet at the last minute?" he bellowed, still sweating and short-breathed from his hurried climb to question her.

"So they said," she answered calmly, purposely sauntering across the room to face him. "That's why I sent the call to you, Mr. Grant."

"Oh, don't *Mr. Grant* me, Sofia," he snarled, still visibly rattled by the call. "Who the fuck do they think they are?"

"They're the Nevada Gaming Commission, Frankie. They can do as they please. Or should I say, they can do whatever that

43

bastardo (bastard) Giancarlo and his thugs pay them to do."

"You think Sam Giancarlo is behind this?" Frankie asked. He had caught his breath but continued anxiously pacing the room while rubbing the back of his neck. "Why? Why interfere if he wants a piece of the pie?"

"Don't be *stupido* (stupid), Frankie!" Sofia vehemently replied. "He doesn't want to break us. He wants us to need him. To force us to partner with him." With each word, Sofia became more passionate and began pacing with Frankie, chasing him, consuming the space between them. "I told you from the beginning," she reminded him. "We need their connections, support, and protection. No one operates without their partnership here. *Nessuno* (nobody)!"

"Sofia," Frankie snapped back. "I'm not getting into bed with those guys. It's not going to happen."

Sofia turned and flung her arm, slicing the air like a swordsman drawing his foil from its sheath. "Well, the Casbah is not going to happen either," she replied. "There is no casino without a license and no hotel without a casino." Sofia was unrelenting in scolding Frankie for putting them in this position after all her hard work and the money sunk into the venture. She chastised him for not taking her advice from the beginning. She dismissed his ability to handle the hard decisions required to become a success in the casino business as inadequate.

As Frankie listened, he grew silent and vulnerable through her tirade, like a sailboat with its mast torn off in a violent storm, now tossed about at the will of the storm's wind and driving rain. As much as Frankie did not want to be subject to it, he admired the passion and strength of Sofia's determination. Her passion and strength had served him well until now. Sofia was so unlike Evilyn at home. Frankie loved them both. He needed them both.

Sofia's deluge stopped. Silence filled the room like a vacuum of pressure, as if the wall of the hurricane had just passed to enter the storm's eye. She stared at Frankie, calm in the storm, a vacuum of fear, daring his response. But Frankie had none. He knew she was probably right about The Alliance's involvement in his gaming license and inability to obtain it alone without their partnership. There wasn't another major hotel or casino in Vegas operating independently, so why did he believe he could? A sudden clarity came to Frankie during the calm as Sofia stared at him and waited for his response. She saw weakness while he felt resolve.

Frankie knew he could no longer suppress and control the great storm. But he still needed Sofia's help. Frankie knew he could not keep his family, have Sofia as an assistant and mistress, and run a clean business without The Alliance's interference. The clarity and acceptance were liberating, and he willfully let go of believing he could have it all. Frankie grinned as he slowly raised his head to make eye contact with Sofia. His sudden clear-headedness must have appeared welcoming to her, either as resignation or vulnerability.

"Darling," she said, moving closer to him and touching his chest with her palm as if healing his heart. She came closer still, her head almost resting on his shoulder as she spoke softly into his ear. "I can fix this all for you, *il mio amore* (my love)."

With Sofia's head resting firmly on his shoulder and her long leg and high heel raised and wrapping around his inner thigh, Frankie stared straight ahead with resolution through the big glass windows into the casino floor.

"Frankie," she whispered. "Keep your promise. Divorce your housewife and marry me. Make me your partner in the Casbah. We can have everything. You promised me, *Amore*."

"I will, baby," he replied, gazing steadfastly through the Eye's windows onto his casino floor. "Set something up with Sam."

With Sofia's head nestled against Frankie's shoulder and pressed firmly against the fabric of his suit jacket, Frankie felt the gentle tightening of her cheeks as a smile blossomed across her face.

PARADISE PALMS

Richard yelled, "Come on, Dad!" as he ran onto the playground ahead of his father. Months had passed since Frankie spent real time with his children, but he allowed himself a few hours with Richard on this sunny Saturday morning. Evilyn and Lucy were already at the elementary school's bake and book sale event. Sofia was at the Casbah reviewing punch-list items with contractors. "Watch, Dad," Richard called out as he traversed the monkey bars, hand over hand, from one end to the other.

The morning felt relaxed despite the sudden reversal of his gaming license approval. Frankie had been a businessman all of his life and understood politics and leverage. His experience taught him every setback came with a solution. He had a network of connections, bankers, and business owners. Any obstacle was solvable in business by either force, reciprocity, or payoff. Frankie also had Sofia, at least for now.

Frankie enjoyed watching his son play, now on the teeter-totter with another boy his age. Without knowing one another, the two boys found instant harmony in their up-and-down motion. Their fun was a dance of cooperation, with each boy intuitively understanding when to push and when to yield, and their movements synchronized in perfect balance. Laughter filled the

47

air as the teeter-totter became a vessel of trust and camaraderie, demonstrating the values of give and take, of supporting each other, literally and metaphorically, through the highs and lows. Watching Richard play reinforced Frankie's decision never to leave Evilyn and his children, not even for the sexy woman who fueled his burning fire and promised him success.

"Beautiful day, isn't it, Frankie?" the voice from behind asked. The words sounded more like an authoritative statement than a curious question, interrupting Frankie's moment of absorption in the ease and joy of family life at the playground.

Frankie turned, offering the stranger a courteous yet cautious smile as he assessed the origin of the unfamiliar voice. "Yes, nice morning," he replied, recognizing the gentleman dressed in the tailored suit and fedora hat, overdressed for a casual weekend morning at the subdivision's park.

"Sam Giancarlo," the familiar visitor offered, extending his hand to Frankie.

"Yes, Mr. Giancarlo. Frank Grant. Please call me Frankie." Sam already had. "Nice to finally meet you," he added. He knew Sam Giancarlo, although he had never been introduced to or personally spoken to him. Everyone who was anyone in Las Vegas knew of Mr. Giancarlo. Frankie had been to galas and benefits and saw him with his entourage from a distance. Sam's influence was well known, and his reputation preceded him.

"It is an outstanding community. Isn't it, Frankie? I partnered with Paradise Development to build this place just a few years ago. Just a pile of sand back then, and look at it now: homes, shopping, the Stardust Golf Course. Even this playground."

"You live in the neighborhood, Mr. Giancarlo?"

"Oh, no," Sam replied. "Not far from here, though. I'm a

traditional kind of guy, myself. This contemporary or mid-century modern design stuff, with its curved streets and cul-de-sacs, isn't for me. It's nice though, don't get me wrong. It's a nice place to raise a family. You like it, right Frankie?"

"Dad, did you see how high I went on the swing?" Richard asked as he ran up to interrupt the two men. "Can I get some ice cream?"

"You must be Little Richie. Nice to meet you," Sam said as he again extended his hand to greet the younger Mr. Grant.

"I'm not little. I'm ten," Richard replied, watching the stranger as he produced two quarters from his pocket before his father could respond to his son's request.

Sam chuckled. "You are absolutely right. You're not little at all. Here you go, Big Richie." Sam placed the two quarters into the youngster's palms and watched him tear off toward the pavilion.

"Thanks, mister!" Richard shouted as he ran away.

Frankie's mind raced, searching for answers. *Why was Sam Giancarlo here on a Saturday morning? How did he know Richard's name? Why was he so slow to react to Sam introducing himself to his son and giving Richard money for ice cream without even so much as glancing at him for permission or approval?* Frankie felt emasculated by Sam's presence, having strolled up and effortlessly disrupted Frankie's quality time with his son.

"Good kid you got there, Frankie."

"Yeah, he is, Mr. Giancarlo," he replied. "So, what brings you by here on a weekend? I've already asked my assistant to arrange a meeting for us to chat, but—"

"Yeah, yeah," Sam interrupted. "Look, Frankie, you gotta lose the broad, okay? She's a woman and a pushy one at that.

Gentlemen conduct business out here. She's not good for business. She's got a smart mouth, and people don't appreciate smart-mouthed broads. Do yourself a favor, Frankie."

Frankie raised a hand to interrupt Sam but quickly diverted it into his pants pocket instead. He was surprised at Sam's comment. Sofia had encouraged Frankie's partnership with The Alliance from the beginning, so why did Sam take such a harsh position on her? What did Sam know about Sofia that he didn't?

"Frankie," Sam continued, "far be it from me to intrude on a man's affairs, but this fling you got going on with Sofia, it's not good for you. Affairs, divorce, kids," he continued, "It's not good for business; for public opinion."

Frankie began sweating in the bright sunlight with the muffled sound of children playing in the background. "Do you know anything about the delay in getting my gaming license, Mr. Giancarlo?" Frankie asked directly.

"Yeah, I heard about that, Frankie. It's not a problem. It's probably just a mistake or misunderstanding, you know? Nothing we can't have fixed right away."

Frankie's eyes narrowed and squinted in the sunlight as he mentally asked himself the questions to which he already knew the answers.

"The important thing is that you understand how crucial family is, Frankie—both blood family and business family. We don't want to hurt our families, do we, Frankie? We protect the family. The family helps us all prosper, to live in nice places like this, and send our kids to good schools."

"Listen, Mr. Giancarlo, what's it going to take to …"

"Frankie, please," Sam interrupted once again, his hand raised to waist level as if instructing Frankie to slow down or gently patting a little boy on top of the head, telling him everything would be alright. "There's plenty of time to iron out details. It's Saturday, Frankie. Relax with your kid. I got your back." Sam turned his wrists as he spoke, so his palm was now faced upward, like a priest in Oran's posture guiding his congregation through an Our Father prayer during mass. "We good?"

"Yes, of course," Frankie responded.

Before he could say anything else, Sam turned away from their conversation and opened his posture to welcome the young boy returning. "Hey, big Richie is back!"

"Dad, you want a bite?" Richard offered the remaining half of the cone to his father, but as Frankie gently waved his son's offer off, he accidentally brushed Richard's hand, sending the remaining ice cream and cone tumbling toward the ground.

"Dad!"

Frankie instinctively lunged for the falling cone, but it was too late. His son's generous offer now rested atop the foreign grass and native desert dirt as he apologized to his son.

"It's fine," Sam introjected, reaching into his pocket and producing a one-dollar bill. "Here, son," he said, handing Richard the cash. "Now you can buy two more."

"Wow," Richard exclaimed, his eyes widening at seeing the crisp bill offered to him.

"No, that's okay," Frankie declared. "Thanks, but that's too generous. We've had enough ice cream for one day. Return the bill to Mr. Giancarlo, Richard."

"But Dad, you knocked it …"

"Your Dad's right, big Richie," Sam said. "But you hold on to it for next time." Sam stood straight again and looked at Frankie, extending his hand. "Glad we ran into one another this morning, Frankie. Talk soon, then."

Sam turned and walked back to his car, where the second gentleman dressed in a suit stood, hands folded in front of himself until Sam got close enough for him to open the backseat door.

Looking up at his father, with the crisp dollar bill still in his hand, Richard asked, "Who's that, Dad?"

Frankie told his son to fold the dollar and put it in his pocket. "Come on, son. It's time to go home." He placed his hand on Richard's shoulder as they began walking. "Remember to put this in your piggy bank when we get home. Don't let your mom find that dollar in your pocket on wash day."

BACK TO NORMAL

(Present)

Back in their room, Jack watched his wife from the middle of the room as Emily looked through drawers for something comfortable to wear.

"The spa had an opening at 3:00 p.m., so I booked a massage, Jack. Is that okay?"

"Yea, of course, honey," he replied, stepping toward her from behind.

"You want me to call and see if they have anything available for you?" Emily called out, not realizing how close Jack was. He quietly wrapped his arms around her slim waist and gently pressed his chest into her back, firmly holding her from behind like she used to allow him to do.

"Oh, Jack," she uttered, startled by his touch. He held her firm, and she exhaled and relaxed into his embrace. With one arm around her waist, Jack used his other hand to tuck her blond hair behind her ear, planting small and kind kisses on her neck. Emily allowed it, tilting her head toward her opposite shoulder, exposing more of her soft neck and ear. She eased into him fully as he cradled her and ever-so-gently swayed from side to side, rocking her like one does to soothe an infant when troubled.

"Jack, I'll be late."

"We've got plenty of time, Em," he whispered into her ear. Jack's kisses migrated from her neck to her jawline, each deliberate and infused with intent. He savored the texture of her skin as she smiled under his attention, responding to his touch with a soft sigh communicating trust and longing. As Jack held her, his chest against her back, Emily lowered her hands. She moved them behind her, exploring the contours of Jack's thighs through his trousers, communicating her emotions better than words could.

Jack's heart throbbed with a powerful urgency, prompting him to hold Emily even tighter if such a thing were possible. Emily nestled into the strength of his embrace, feeling its security and promise. Her eyes were closed, but her deep breathing and sensual touch revealed layers of long-denied affection and vulnerability. Emily was very close to touching it, discovering its round and rigid outline beneath the material of his slacks.

And then Jack remembered the chip in his right pocket. He quickly released his loving embrace and spun Emily around to face him, grabbing her hands and kissing her deeply and desperately until she gasped, pulling away from the long, unexpected kiss.

"Jack?"

"I'm sorry, Em. I love you so much and had to kiss you."

"I'm not complaining, I just …"

"You need to get ready for your massage," he interrupted. "We can finish this later, after the show."

Emily smiled, her cheeks glowing light pink with pleasure. She leaned forward and rested her head against Jack's chest and his rapid heartbeat for a moment, sighing in satisfaction.

Jack patted his wife on the back and leaned away from her. "Go get ready," he urged.

"Just need to rinse the sunscreen off," she said, standing on her toes to reach up and peck Jack on the lips.

Jack sat, his heart still racing from the adrenaline of holding Emily so close for so long, their deep and passionate kiss, and his narrowly avoiding her detection of the chip.

Her voice floated through the open bathroom door, casual and clear, purified by the sound of the falling water from the overhead rain shower. "I'm going to call to check on Casey."

"Why?" Jack replied.

"I checked the webcam several times this morning by the pool and didn't see her anywhere."

"Casey's fine, Em. I spoke to them this morning." Jack could hear the shower handle turn and the falling water dissipate to a trickle. "I saw her twice on camera, too," he added, "playing with the other dogs."

"That's odd," Emily replied as she walked back into the room with only a towel wrapped around her wet hair.

Jack watched her glide across the room to the stack of casual clothes she laid on the bed to wear to the spa. Her body was beautiful. She was fit and toned. Her attention to her health and fitness had not wavered throughout his spiral into depression and hopelessness. He wanted to leap up and pounce on her like a starved, ravenous lion, greedy for gratification. He yearned to claim his prize and breed his lioness, but the more he admired her, the hotter the chip in his pocket felt until, all at once, he thought he might leap up in anguish instead of lust.

"What?" Jack asked, sensing she said something.

"I said, why did you talk to them? Did you call the vet?"

"Oh," he replied, the pain gone as soon as he focused on her words instead of his desire for her. "No, they called me." Jack cleared his head and concentrated on not lying while avoiding the truth. "They wanted to know if we wanted them to bathe Casey before we picked her up. I forgot to tell them one way or another when I dropped her off."

"Oh, makes sense." Emily sounded relieved as she finished dressing. "What did you tell them?"

"Yes," Jack responded. "I told them to take care of it. That's why you didn't see her when you checked earlier, I bet."

Emily gathered her things and looked at her watch. "I should be back by five-thirty. What are you going to do?"

"Probably just go to the gym and workout, or the treadmill. Too hot outside for a run."

"Okay, meet you back here, then. Don't be late." Emily kissed Jack's cheek on her way out. "Love you."

"Love you too, Em."

Jack waited a few minutes before calling Dr. Norman back. He tried several times, each call going to the office's voicemail. Jack then looked at his watch—three o'clock. "Shit!" he shouted, remembering the two-hour time difference between Las Vegas and Kansas City. Today was also Saturday. Jack called again, but this time left a message.

***

Exiting the elevator, Jack paused at the top of three steps leading down to the vast carpeted floor. A cacophony of sounds and blinking lights struck him with an almost physical force, the air abuzz with contagious energy wanting to pull him in. The atmosphere was a vibrant allure, a siren song Jack knew all too well. He stood there as each flash of the colorful lights washed over him, tapping into a deep, almost primal excitement, one he swore off but still felt irresistibly drawn to.

Emily was just thirty minutes into her spa treatment as Jack stood there. Other hotel guests exited the elevators and walked past him to the casino floor. Some approached him on their way to the elevators and their rooms. Activity surrounded him as he stood affixed atop the uppermost step while reminding himself of his countless promises to Emily. He had come to Las Vegas for her, not for himself. He had come to Las Vegas for a concert, not to gamble. He told himself he could handle the proximity of temptation without succumbing to its allure, despite his earlier flirtation with the Cash at The Casbah slot machine. The fresh memory of his easy wins and the sounds below echoed like a chorus of victory in Jack's head to test his resolve. The casino floor spread below him, a canvas painted with opportunities for confidence and elation.

Jack placed one foot in front of the other, landing on the second step, and felt a familiar thrill course through his veins. One more step down and an adrenaline rush of possibility flooded his senses. With another final step down to the casino floor, the tantalizing promise of fortune was now within Jack's reach.

Moving deeper into the casino, the lure of the games tightened its grip. The roulette wheel caught Jack's eye, its hypnotic spin mirroring the tumult in his mind. The clattering of the ball bouncing across numbers held a sort of poetry for him; each tap was another possibility, another what-if. Standing there, he felt the urge to place just one bet, to feel the weight of chips in his hand, the thrill of risking everything on a single spin.

But Jack resisted and, with clarity, refocused his gaze on the people around him. He saw faces lit by the glow of hope, eyes wide with excitement or narrowed in concentration. Jack saw desperation, too, the kind tugging at the corners of some gamblers' smiles. It was a desperation he knew in himself. The casino was a temple to possibility, and every person there was a devotee. Despite knowing the dangers and the potential for ruin, Jack felt a kinship with those people, a pull toward the camaraderie of the hopeful.

From his vantage point at the mouth of the casino floor, Jack could see his slot machine off to one side: dimly lit, lonely, and waiting. Each step toward it was a self-negotiation between the memory of his warm embrace with Emily in the room a half-hour earlier and the growing warmth of the chip in his pocket. *Just one pull*, its presence reasoned. But Jack just stood in front of the machine, clutching the printed winnings voucher from earlier in the day and the old token from another era in his pocket. He felt the weight of what was at stake, of what he was risking. He knew he stood on a dangerous threshold, a reminder of a past self he was both drawn to and desperately needed to run from.

"Mr. Harper," the polite voice stated from behind, neither a question of identity nor an introduction of presence. The gentleman cleared his voice in a refined, sophisticated manner and repeated himself. "Pardon me, Mr. Harper."

Startled from his reverie, Jack turned to the figure beside him and instinctively withdrew his hand from his pocket, releasing his tight grip on the voucher and chip. "Hey," he said, his voice tinged with surprise and a flicker of alarm at being recognized. But as recognition emerged, his initial shock softened. Of course, the bellman who delivered champagne to his room the previous night. He worked there. *The voice was only the bellman.*

"Excuse me if I startled you, sir," he apologized. "I trust you and Mrs. Harper are having a pleasant stay?"

"Yes, great. Thanks."

"I see you are admiring one of the old originals. I know you said you were not one to partake in gaming, but I suppose strolling the floor and taking in the energy is enjoyable."

"Yes. Yes!" Jack replied. "She doesn't seem to get much attention way over here." Jack's chuckle, seasoned with a dash of nervousness, exited his mouth without warning and sounded odd once released. *He knows I'm talking about the slot machine, right?* Jack wondered.

The bellman respectfully smiled, allowing Jack to compose himself. "And the weekend anniversary celebration is going well, Mr. Harper?"

"Yes. Thanks." The words reverberated in Jack's mind—*anniversary celebration.* Yes, they were there to celebrate. Jack's gift of the trip and the concert tickets tonight were proof of that. But their anniversary? Jack unexpectedly felt panicked and hollow, like a man sitting at a restaurant on a date who realized he had left his wallet at home halfway through the meal.

"Very well, Sir. If there's anything we can do, please don't hesitate."

The bellman humbly nodded and backed away when Jack added, "Well, actually, there is something I could use your help with." Jack thrashed for ideas like someone unexpectedly thrown overboard into frigid waters, reaching for a floating life preserver. "A gift," he added. "For Emily."

"Ah, but of course. Excellent idea, Mr. Harper. Perhaps a nice piece of jewelry for Mrs. Harper? Something unique and appropriate for the occasion."

"Yes," Jack replied. "Exactly what I was thinking." Jack had the new voucher for his slot winnings in his pocket and some cash from the blackjack table, now worth nearly forty-one hundred dollars. His original winnings from a single-dollar bet, two hundred and fifty-six dollars, quickly doubled four times over with his last four wagers before meeting Emily by the pool earlier. There was no way he could hide or explain so much cash. Besides, a gift for her from his winnings was the genesis of his wagering. Jack's actions were only out of thought for Emily.

"We have some excellent shops in the hotel's Galleria. Tiffany & Company or Cartier? Perhaps even Harry Winston? Is now a good time for me to assist, Mr. Harper?"

"Now? Are you allowed to do that?"

"Why, of course, Mr. Harper. Your anniversary is a special occasion, and you are a special guest."

Jack looked at his watch. He had at least an hour and a half before Emily would return, so he allowed the bellman to escort him to the shops. Jack was confident Emily would love whatever he selected. She would appreciate his thoughtfulness in choosing and presenting the anniversary gift to her before the concert.

THE GIFT

The cut aquamarine stones set in platinum and encircled with smaller brilliant diamonds were stunning. The bellman recalled his mother having a pair of similar earrings, telling Jack they were among her most cherished possessions. The salesperson called them 'vintage,' remarking how the sophisticated setting and translucent color would compliment Jack's wife's eyes, according to how Jack described them and the cellphone pictures of her he shared. They no longer made jewelry like this, the salesman informed him.

"Brilliant, Sir. I believe Mrs. Harper will be very pleased."

"Yes, she will," Jack responded to the bellman, fixated on the clear pale blue stones with their round brilliant cut of 58 facets refracting the showroom's bright lights aimed toward the showcases.

"Do you plan to give them to Mrs. Harper over dinner before the show tonight?" asked the bellman.

"Over dinner? Yes, exactly."

"Then may I suggest," the bellman continued, "you allow us to present Mrs. Harper the gift after the entrée. Covered on a silver platter, of course. We often present in that manner for proposals. It is very romantic, if I may say so, Mr. Harper."

Jack imagined Emily's surprise and the attention his gesture would receive in the restaurant. "Yes, I like the idea," he enthusiastically agreed.

"May I ask how you would prefer to handle the payment today, Mr. Harper?" the salesperson inquired.

"Yes, of course. How much, please?"

"The exquisite pair is eighty-two hundred dollars, non-inclusive of tax, of course."

Jack took a moment to process the cost as silence fell between the three men. There was no question in his mind these earrings belonged to Emily. They were as perfect as she was, created to be clear and to radiate light and purity. They would rest on her ears and whisper his eternal love to her. They were a symbol of his success and proof of his worth. They were also like a new automobile that a dealership lets you drive home overnight for a test drive. Once the neighbors see the car in your driveway, your ego will not allow you to return it.

Jack looked at his watch again. The purchase was no longer a question of their value or whether they were affordable to the couple. Jack wasn't even concerned about what Emily's reaction might be. The decision was simply a matter of how he would pay for them—the gift cost over twice the value of the winnings voucher from the slot machine in his pocket. Using a credit card was out of the question. Text notifications immediately followed large purchases, and this one would tip Emily off to his grand gesture.

"Sir," the bellman suggested as if he could hear Jack's internal deliberation. "Since Mrs. Harper's earrings are a surprise, perhaps we should charge them to the room to be settled at check-out?"

The salesperson immediately interjected, "That's a rather unusual arrangement—." His words trailed off as the bellman locked eyes with him and gently tilted his head forward in approving guidance. "But of course, Mr. Harper, we would happily accommodate any arrangement you desire."

"Yes, settled then," he said. The bellman outstretched both palms to Jack, offering to receive the precious gift. He closed the black felt box and placed it in his suit jacket pocket for safety until the presentation a few hours later. "Congratulations, Mr. Harper."

A knowing smile spread across Jack's face. Just one small task remained before he could return to the room to prepare for dinner, setting the stage for the most memorable evening of Emily's life.

***

Jack's heart quickened as he approached the row of blackjack tables, drawn to the hypnotic rhythm of the cards being shuffled and dealt. The clink and clatter of chips changing hands had its rhythm, too, and the special chip in his pocket longed to join the arrangement. He looked at his watch again, noting he had forty-five minutes to spare. Jack only needed one winning hand. Just one double-or-nothing wager from the voucher in his pocket. That's all he needed to pay for the earrings. That's all Jack needed to give his wife the best anniversary gift she would ever receive. Still, a single wager was too risky. Even Jack knew that.

He walked past rows of blackjack tables packed with players until he reached the last table farthest from the central aisle, the busy casino's motorway moving people between hotel rooms, shops, restaurants, and sections of gaming stations. This table in the corner was also conveniently in front of the cashier's cages, handling cash-outs, chip exchanges, and currency exchanges. It's a well-known marketing design, forcing people to walk past all the playing fields to get to cashier's cages and then back past them again. It's like walking through a gambling minefield not once but twice. Jack felt safe back there, watching the dealer's skilled hands flick cards to each player with the soft rustle of their bets placed across the green battlefield of winners and losers.

Safety and confidence make convincing allies, encouraging Jack to stroll to the cashier's cage to exchange his forty-one hundred dollar voucher for a short stack of orange, thousand-dollar chips and a single black chip worth one hundred dollars. He could use the black chip to tip the dealer once he had played a few hands and earned what he needed to clear the tab at checkout. He planned to check out himself in the morning, using the cash, while Emily was upstairs doing her final packing and preparation before leaving.

Returning to that last table, Jack watched a few hands from behind the seated players. Their faces were a mixture of concentration and anticipation until one brave soul in the middle of the half-round table decided he had lost enough, standing and quietly walking away. Jack had watched a few of his hands from behind and judged him an amateur from the very start by the way the young player hit or held when his and the dealer's face cards said he should have done the opposite.

"Come join us," a voice from Jack's immediate left said. He turned to see a heavy-set, middle-aged man dressed in shorts and a loose-fitting short-sleeve shirt extending his hand toward the now-empty chair. "Name's Mike. Maybe you can bring some luck to the table," Mike chuckled.

As Jack settled into the empty seat, the soft green felt of the table beneath his fingertips sent a shiver of excitement down his spine, awakening the lucky chip in his pocket with warmth and approval. The dealer also greeted Jack with a friendly smile, her fingers deftly shuffling the deck as she prepared for the next hand.

"Name's Jack," he said, returning Mike's introduction.

"Good to have you join us," a voice from the chair to Jack's right said with a Latin accent. The well-dressed man with graying hair did not introduce himself by name, but he, too, wore a friendly, welcoming smile. "From the look of those orange chips, I'd say you've already got Lady Luck on your side," he added, gesturing to the thousand-dollar chips Jack had just placed on the table in front of the padded armrest.

The other players at the table joined in amusement, their camaraderie infectious. The dealer continued shuffling the cards as she allowed Jack to settle in and the table to relax and forget about their previous run of poor luck.

"And who's this lucky gentleman joining us?" an elderly woman with a raspy voice asked, her eyes twinkling with amusement as if she was just now processing the previous introductions and comments at the table.

Jack grinned at her, charmed by her age and demeanor. "Name's Jack. And I'm just hoping to catch a lucky break."

"Well, Jack, welcome to the party," she replied. "I'm Sarah, and this is my husband, Tom."

Tom nodded in greeting, his expression friendly but reserved.

"Always nice to have a young new face at the table," Sarah added, filling the void of her husband's silence.

These were all indications of good timing. The previously cold table was no doubt overdue for a change of luck. Jack was also more comfortable with a smiling female dealer than with one who was a curt and grim male. He was more secure with a female in authority, knowing how to use his good looks and charm to his advantage. The other players added to the advantage of positive energy with their friendliness.

With introductions and pleasantries uncommon to a blackjack table now complete, cards for a new game were dealt. Jack looked at his watch—thirty more minutes. He then peeked at his face-down card, an Ace underneath the Jack of Diamonds card already showing, a natural blackjack, which he immediately overturned to reveal—a 3:2 payout on his single orange chip bet—a quick fifteen hundred dollar win. The dealer promptly slid another orange and a single purple chip across the green felt toward Jack and collected his cards before continuing with the rest of the hand for the other players.

Jack's immediate blackjack win added to the upbeat atmosphere of his new friends.

"You've got the Midas touch, Jack!" Mike exclaimed as Jack stacked his new chips.

"I don't know about that," Jack replied modestly, with a grin. "Just a lucky start, I guess."

Jack's second hand was almost as good, splitting a pair of tens and doubling his wager of one orange chip on each pair. His second card on each split was a Jack again, contributing to an eventual dealer bust and each player at the table winning with elation. Jack couldn't shake the feeling something more than luck was at play. Perhaps fate had brought him to this table for a reason. These strangers were not just fellow players but friends destined for him to meet.

"Mr. Jack with his jacks," Sarah rasped. Her husband, Tom, nodded in approval while Mike clapped. The well-dressed Latin man with gray hair smiled and murmured something resembling awe or admiration in Spanish.

Jack considered his next wager as the dealer paused play to load the previously used and discarded playing cards into the automatic shuffler. He needed just one more win with a single orange chip to cover the price of Emily's gift, but as the Casbah Chip in his pocket grew warmer, so did Jack's confidence. A small crowd formed around their table, perhaps waiting for a chair to open at the hot table, and Jack's new friends began a low but supportive chant of "Black, Jack. Black, Jack." He felt bathed in support and companionship for the first time in a long time. He was again in control—a winner, no longer satisfied with getting by or normalcy.

Jack did not recognize what he had done until his fingertips retreated from the entire stack of orange chips in his ante pile halfway between himself and the house. Everyone around him cheered at the bravado of the new player who could not lose, and the attention made Jack uneasy. Instead of betting just one chip, he had inadvertently slid his entire stack toward the dealer.

"Thank you," the Dealer uttered, signaling everyone to lower their tone as she began dealing the new round of cards.

Jack's up card was another Jack, matching the value of every other player's face card now showing, including the dealer's.

"Let's go, Jack!" Mike yelled, breaking the hush engulfing the table as the dealer did her work. The sudden and uncomfortable shout of enthusiasm sounded like a canyon echo reverberating off the casino walls. Jack glanced up at the dealer, and as he did, his eyes glimpsed Emily, scanning the crowd in his direction. Her expression was of someone startled as she slowed her pace and stopped in the busy pedestrian aisleway from the spa to the hotel room elevators. Jack instantly tried to process whether his wife had spotted him or was looking for the origin of Mike's loud and ill-timed shout of his name. Jack instinctively lifted himself off the stool to duck and, in doing so, touched the table in front of himself in a grasp for balance. The gesture was a signal to hit. All the other players had already signaled their intention to stand, and the dealer's eyes were trained on Jack when he touched the table.

Another face card lay atop his hole card, still face down—a King of Spades.

When Jack raised his head, his hands still grasping the padded rail of the table, his proud stack of orange chips was gone. There was no sign of Emily in the distant aisleway behind the dealer. The lucky chip in his pocket was cold, and all he heard from his new friends and the crowd around the table was the unfortunate "aw" for his unfortunate hit when he should have stood.

Stunned, Jack stepped backward, away from the table. Another enthusiastic and confident player took his place as if Jack and his winnings had never occupied the space. With dull eyes, he glanced around without really seeing anything. *It can't be possible. I don't understand.* Everything was fine until he had caught a glimpse of Emily nearby. Jack now understood. *It was her.* She never wanted him to have the chip. She was against the notion of keeping the chip from the very start. Jack felt betrayed.

THE GRAND OPENING

(1963)

M aison Lafitte was one of Las Vegas's most exquisite and coveted restaurants. The establishment was also Evilyn's favorite. When, on rare occasions, a night of fine dining was appropriate, Maison Lafitte was always Evilyn's first choice. Though known for its reputation for exclusivity and giving a long stem rose to each lady dining there, Maison Lafitte excelled at a level of sophistication and quality in cuisine and dining experience matched by no other fine dining establishment in the city. Its location was also on the opposite side of Vegas from Carmine's and did not specialize in serving oversized steaks with loaded baked potatoes, their skins over-salted and over-sugared. Unlike Carmine's, people went to Maison Lafitte to be seen and heard. The difference was the documented truth rather than the speculative viewpoint.

"Frankie, I'm so proud of you," Evilyn said. "Tomorrow is going to be such a big day for you."

"A huge day for us both, Evie."

"Are you nervous?"

Frankie replied with a confident no. "Sofia and the crew have everything planned. We're all set. I'm ready."

Evilyn smiled and rubbed her husband's arm, repeating how proud she was of him.

"Good evening, Mr. and Mrs. Grant. It's a pleasure to have you dine with us tonight. Would you care for a cocktail to start your evening?"

"Just a glass of white wine for me, please," Evilyn replied.

"I'll take a Manhattan, thanks. Maker's Mark if you have it."

"Very well, Sir. Madame. Any appetizers to begin your—"

"We'll look over the menu," Frankie interjected. "Thanks." The waiter silently acknowledged with a nod while backing away from the couple before turning to retrieve their cocktails.

"You know, dear, Sofia is so competent and does so much for you. You should do something special for her when everything has settled down."

"She's well paid," Frankie replied. "Especially for a woman in this business." He looked at his wife and smiled, studying her face while replaying her words in his mind, racing through the possibilities of what Evilyn might know but likely didn't. Evilyn had only met Sofia once, briefly, and knew far less about the woman who worked for her husband than Sofia knew about her. "I just wish the kids could be there tomorrow," he said to change the subject.

"Frankie, Dear," Evilyn chuckled. "Tomorrow is a school day. Plus, a casino is not a place for children. It will be so hectic there, anyway. No, they can look at the newspaper article the following day if there is anything."

"Sir. Madame," the waiter announced as he placed the white wine and Manhattan on the table. Frankie welcomed the interruption. "Have you had a moment to explore our selection of appetizers for this evening? Perhaps I may assist you in making a selection?"

"No, I'm sorry, we haven't looked at the menus yet. We've been chatting. My apologies," Evilyn politely responded before Frankie had a chance to.

"But of course. Please enjoy your cocktails."

Frankie and Evilyn looked at one another and smiled.

"He's not rushing us," she said. "He's just trying to be helpful, dear. Try to relax."

"I am relaxed, Evie. I brought you here, didn't I?" Frankie smirked. "We could have gone to The Golden Steer or Bob Taylor's."

"Dear, I can't help but wonder if you ever tire of those dreadful steak houses with vendors and businessmen in those dreadful business meetings. It seems quite routine and taxing. Especially on your waistline," she added, giving him a playful poke in his gut.

Frankie reached over to hold his wife's hand. He did feel relaxed, especially considering the importance of tomorrow's grand opening, with its complicated logistics and the number of influential people attending. His gaming license had been the last hurdle cleared once the Gaming Board approved the license as quickly and irrationally as they had withheld it. Everything after just fell into place. "I love you, Evie. You were my first love in high school, and still are. You and the kids."

And then memories of his brief time visiting a European port as a young seaman in the Navy flashed before his eyes.

***

The city was alive with anticipation as the grand opening of the

Casbah Hotel and Casino approached. The desert sun hung high in the cloudless sky, casting a bright and hopeful hue over the bustling streets of tourists, residents, local politicians, and business leaders, half of whom had come specifically to attend the noontime event on Las Vegas Boulevard. The temperature was a comfortable sixty-five degrees, perfect weather for April and those flocking to witness the unveiling of Frankie Grant's latest venture, a shimmering new jewel in the heart of the Vegas strip.

Inside and upstairs in the Eye, Frankie put his suit jacket on and adjusted his collar and shirt sleeves. He checked the time on his Bulova—Eleven-fifteen. Frankie watched his employees below, dashing about the casino floor in last-minute preparations for the doors to open and crowds to swarm the building for their first look at Las Vegas's newest gaming house. Max was busy polishing the bar top one last time while his attendants prepared for the rush of lunchtime guests to whom they would soon serve celebratory cocktails. Servers in Moroccan-styled costumes began bringing out round trays of hors d'oeuvres from the kitchen. Their attire incorporated the rich colors and patterns characteristic of traditional Morocco but with a significantly reduced fabric, more attuned to the iconic and revealing costumes worn by Playboy Bunnies.

"Nervous?" Sofia asked from behind as she brushed his shoulders swiftly from his neck to his arms to remove any lint or creases on the tailored suit jacket. As she did, Frankie jolted forward, away from her touch.

"Evilyn will be here any minute." He felt apologetic as soon as he uttered the words, yet said nothing more. His reaction was a nervous and unnatural reflex for Frankie at work. His home and work worlds, along with their inhabitants, rarely collided. Today, Frankie would have to manage both in close proximity to one another.

"Ah, yes," Sofia replied, walking around to face Frankie. She increased the space between them to a respectable work-relationship distance. "The housewife at our grand opening." Sofia wore one of her knee-length black dresses, which was sophisticated and chic, suitable for the festive atmosphere of a daytime event as important as this. Today, however, she wore a necklace handcrafted by local artisans in Palermo, Sofia's hometown. Her grandmother gave the gift to her when she turned sixteen to commemorate her transition from childhood to womanhood. The necklace was silver, with tiny white pearls and polished red coral stones from the Mediterranean Sea. Dangling from the necklace was a Trinacria, a symbol of Sicily with the head of Medusa at its center.

"Sofia, don't," Frankie kindly asked in an instructive tone. "Let's just get through the day."

Sofia knew Evilyn would be attending for some time. She expected it. Evilyn was Frankie's wife and had to be there. She knew today was not the day, and now was not the time. Frankie had to be at his best in front of the press and everyone else in just half an hour. Sofia was brilliant and knew the importance of this moment. Still, her eyes betrayed frustration and resentment as she looked at him. Sofia couldn't help but replay the events leading them to this place.

She had been Frankie's loyal assistant for years, rising through the ranks of the real estate development firm with hard work and determination. But somewhere along the way, their professional relationship crossed into something more, something forbidden yet intoxicating. Their relationship had deep roots, like the ancient olive trees gracing the sun-drenched hills of Sicily, steadfast through the winds of change.

It happened innocently late one evening, well past office hours. Frankie had been pouring over the financials of the deal he was working on. Sofia stayed behind to assist, her presence both a comfort and a distraction. The atmosphere was thick with unspoken words and lingering glances, both aware of the line they were inching closer to but neither daring to cross it—until that night.

Frankie rubbed his temples, trying to ease the day's tension as they worked in the conference room. Sofia placed a hand on his shoulder from behind as she reached for some papers on the table. It was a simple gesture, but the warmth of her touch sent a current through him. He looked up, and their eyes met for just a moment. The distance between them dissolved as she moved closer, the scent of her perfume filling the space between them.

Without thinking, Frankie stood and reached out, his hand brushing against her cheek. It was an innocent touch, but the spark it ignited was anything but. Before either of them could second-guess their actions, Sofia closed the gap between them, their lips meeting in a kiss that was as unexpected as it was inevitable. The world outside ceased to exist as they lost themselves in the moment.

Frankie pulled away just as quickly, the reality of what they had done sinking in. He ran a hand across his thinning head of hair, his thoughts racing as he tried to process what had just happened.

"Frankie, I—" Sofia started, sensing his sudden discomfort, but Frankie shook his head and cut her off.

"Let's not... talk about it," he said, his voice low, almost pleading. He knew their actions were dangerous, but a pull between them was undeniable.

That late night at work changed everything. What had begun as a moment of weakness turned into a series of stolen glances, secret smiles, and shared touches that gradually grew bolder as they danced around the boundaries of their professional relationship. When Frankie left the firm to start the casino project, he insisted she come to work for him. They both knew the risks, but the thrill of their illicit connection was too familiar and tempting to resist. Frankie knew Sofia had the experience and skills he needed. Sofia knew Frankie had things she wanted as well.

A smile appeared as Sofia eased into a more relaxed stance. "Frankie, my darling," she whispered, closing the gap between them while reaching into her right dress pocket to retrieve something. She took Frankie's right hand and placed something in it, closing his fist around the object and tightly squeezing his hand closed with both of hers. "For luck," she whispered, "a symbol of your success."

"Sofia, please, not ..."

She silenced him with a finger to his lips, uttering a soft 'shh' and blowing Frankie a soft air kiss.

Frankie opened his palm and looked down at the gift—a purple five-hundred-dollar poker chip with the words Casbah Hotel and Casino around its inner rim. He grasped the gift in his fingertips and held the chip up. "Thank you, Baby."

"Go now," she said, pushing at Frankie's elbow to turn him and usher him toward the door. "Go knock 'em dead, *mio amore.*"

Evilyn was waiting for Frankie outside, under the tent set up for dignitaries to the side of the casino's entrance, meant to shield them from the mid-day sun and the unlikely event of rain. Red and gold ceremonial ribbons stretched directly in front of the entrance doors. Sofia had selected the colors just as she had planned and scheduled most of the other details of the event. She intended the red ribbon to symbolize luck, excitement, and energy, aligning well with the vibrant atmosphere of the casino. The gold represented luxury, prosperity, and success, which she expected from Frankie and the Casbah.

Frankie joined Evilyn, exiting the building from a series of hallways and corridors to a side door. She radiated elegance and charm in a designer dress that hugged the feminine curves not usually found in the body of a mother of two in her late thirties. Together, they were the couple of the hour, the epitome of hard work and wholesomeness. He was a successful businessman, and she was an efficacious mother and housewife. Together, they made the rounds, shaking hands with Mr. Gragson, the mayor, Mr. Cahlan, the editor of the Las Vegas Review-Journal, and Mr. Jones, president of the Chamber of Commerce. Frankie and Evilyn exchanged quick quips with reporters over the loud randomness of crowd noise and car horns from passing cars. They waved at pedestrians who stopped to examine the commotion. They thanked those who came up to them to congratulate their grand opening, among them Sam Giancarlo, whom Evilyn had never met.

But inside, amidst the glitz and glamor of the decorated main floor, tension simmered beneath the surface. Sofia paced anxiously, her high heels clicking against the polished marble floor of the casino's lobby. She glanced at her watch again for what may have felt like the hundredth time. She knew she should be out there, by Frankie's side, basking in the spotlight of their effort and success. But Evilyn was there, forcing Sofia to remain hidden from view, a secret kept in the shadows, at least for now. Frankie and Sofia's affair had been a carefully guarded secret known only to them and a few others who disregarded their indiscretions— except Sam Giancarlo, who vehemently opposed it. But now, with Evilyn by his side and in the spotlight, Sofia couldn't help but wonder if Frankie truly cared for her.

Lost in her thoughts and pacing, Sofia almost didn't hear the crowd erupt into applause outside. Her heart sank, realizing Frankie and the dignitaries had just cut the ribbon, smiling for the cameras with oversized scissors glinting in the sunlight. None of them deserved to be out there more than she did. Certainly not Evilyn. Sofia had sacrificed so much for Frankie, devoting herself to his service. Yet, here she was, relegated to the sidelines while Evilyn received credit for their success.

Sunlight filled the lobby as the doors opened and the crowds rushed in. Cheers from outside echoed through the casino. Sofia turned toward the light's warmth and took a deep breath. With a warm smile, she began welcoming the first wave of guests to the Casbah Hotel and Casino.

***

Frankie was exhausted by the time 10:00 p.m. rolled around. The opening earlier in the day was a success by anyone's account, even exceeding Frankie's expectations. Ordinarily, he would have just gone home to tuck Richard and Lucy into bed. Today, however, was extraordinary. Everyone wanted their piece of the celebration. When Sofia informed Frankie of Sam's desire to meet him at Carmine's later that evening, he was reluctant and declined. When she relayed Sam's message of urgency, Frankie reluctantly agreed.

"Good evening, Mr. Grant," the courteous maître d' greeted. Signaling to his right and into the bar area, he continued, "Ms. Ferranero is expecting you, sir."

"Oh, no," Frankie corrected, "I'm meeting Sam Giancarlo this evening." Frankie gazed past the gatekeeper of the establishment, around his shoulders, and into the main dining floor, looking for Sam.

"I'm sorry, sir, but Mr. Giancarlo is not dining with us this evening," the maître d' politely restated.

"Frankie," the firm and feminine voice called from the bar.

"Sofia, what are you doing here?" he questioned as he walked toward her. "Where is Sam?"

"Darling, come, sit, have a drink with me. Let's celebrate our achievement today."

"No, Sofia," Frankie demanded, still standing exposed between the restaurant's foyer area and the bar entrance. "What's this about?"

"It's about us, Frankie," she replied. "It's about the Casbah and our future." Sofia had changed her dress. She now wore a lower neckline, and while still black, the dress had a lower hemline. The dress was more of an evening gown befitting a late-night dinner at Carmine's. Her heels were higher and less practical than the shorter ones she wore throughout the busy day, running around ensuring the staff was flawlessly performing and the guests were well attended to. What was unchanged on her was the necklace her grandmother had given her all those years ago. Sofia was still wearing the enchanted gift around her neck. She reached out to touch his elbow, to sway Frankie into entering the bar with her, and to join her at the table she had selected for them to celebrate. As she did, however, he jerked his arm away.

"Not now, Sofia!" he demanded.

"Then when?" she retorted, her voice growing louder with each exchange.

"Sir, please," the maître d' suggested as he tentatively approached the pair from his host stand.

"Sofia, STOP!" Frankie shouted. The hour was late, and he was too tired to rehear the words his mistress wanted to repeat.

"Stop or what?" she roared back.

There was a palpable shift in the atmosphere. Once dynamic and bustling, the restaurant's ambient noise faded into the background, replaced by an uneasy silence as nearby diners became aware of the unfolding exchange.

The maître d' once again tried to intervene. "Sir, is everything alright?"

"No, it's not fucking alright," Frankie shouted back, not meaning to turn his frustration toward the guardian of reservations, upholder of Carmine's standards, and chief steward of the dining experience.

"That's right, Frankie," Sofia yelled. "It's not fucking alright."

The initial discomfort among Carmine's patrons and staff became a mixture of curiosity, concern, annoyance, and perhaps even sympathy as Frankie and Sofia's voices escalated and their emotions ran high. Diners became accidental spectators to the private drama unfolding before them. Conversations at tables ceased as people, many of whom knew Frankie and some of whom had attended the grand opening earlier in the day, observed the scene while exchanging furtive glances and murmurs among themselves. The clinking of utensils and glasses momentarily stopped, adding to the sense of suspended animation.

Carmine himself, summoned from the focus of his duties, rushed out from behind the kitchen doors to politely but firmly aid in the immediate resolution of the disturbance. "Mr. Grant, I'm sorry," Carmine apologetically requested. He then turned to Sofia. "Miss, please." He clutched Sofia's elbow with his left hand and beckoned a path cleared straight to the door with his right. Their movements made clear to everyone she was to exit the fine establishment immediately. The two large bouncers, never referred to as such, swarmed the scene almost before the commotion began. The two gentlemen, ever-present and always assumed to be part of Carmine's security presence, were there to ensure Sofia's safe and swift removal. Carmine understood his clientele's need for privacy, safety, and discretion.

"You're fired!" Frankie informed Sofia as they escorted her

past him to the exit. His tune was calming now, with control restored.

"Pagherai per questo, Bastardo! (You'll pay for this, you bastard!)," she shouted at him, struggling to turn and direct her words at him. "There are things you don't know!"

As Sofia transited through the doors, Frankie could hear her last outburst. "You'll regret this, *Bastardo!*"

THE CONCERT

(Present)

J ack and Emily were greeted by an aura of sophistication and elegance the moment they approached the entrance of The Elysian. Its grand entrance of tall, sleek columns framed a modern glass façade, giving them a glimpse of the chic interior beyond. A spacious foyer adorned with classic Greek artwork and stylish modern furnishings welcomed them as they stepped inside. Soft ambient lighting cast a warm glow against the couple crossing the polished marble floors and past the contemporary but plush seating upholstered in rich fabrics.

"This is beautiful, Jack. Nice choice," Emily remarked as she smiled and looked around, taking in the ambiance and experience. Usually, Emily would research and choose the trendsetting restaurants, appreciating the up-and-coming chefs and preferring to dress up for the culinary experience. Regarding dining, Jack preferred the tried and true, easy, no-fuss, casual, and convenient options. This weekend, however, was all about pleasing Emily and giving her what she wanted and deserved. Jack aimed for her experience to be idyllic and perfect, so metaphorically, The Elysian was the ideal choice.

"Hi. Jack Harper. Six forty-five reservation," he stated,

discreetly passing a neatly double-folded fifty-dollar bill from his palm to the palm of the maître d', hoping to secure a favorable corner table by the window. In their hometown, a twenty would have done the job nicely, but this was Las Vegas on a Saturday night. Jack wanted to take no chances on a center table in the back near the kitchen or a table next to a rowdy group of Las Vegas visitors here for a convention or family reunion. "We've got a show at eight-thirty," Jack added.

"Certainly, Mr. Harper. Please follow me." The maitre d', polished and impeccably dressed in attire befitting the upscale ambiance of the restaurant, warmly welcomed the Harpers as he subtly slipped Jack's offering into his pocket. Jack motioned Emily to please step ahead, like a gentleman, as the maître d' escorted them to the quiet table nestled in the restaurant's corner overlooking the artificial lake and fountains outside. Exquisite floral arrangements on stands throughout the dining room, against the backdrop of soft music, contributed to the elegant ambiance. There was even a tiny but bright pin light from above, aimed directly at the center of the table, which Jack thought would be perfect for highlighting the sophistication of the contents of the black felt box she would open when he presented the gift of love to her.

Once settled and with time to scan the menu, they each ordered an artisanal cocktail and a few small plates from the tasting menu. Emily thought it best to keep her selection light before the show, and Jack thought it best to keep his choice quick to allow enough time after dining to impress her with his gift. The Colosseum, serving as the venue for Adele's concert, was a brief five-minute walk from where they sat.

"I have to say, Jack," Emily softly mentioned. "I was initially concerned." She was half-finished with her second Vanilla Pear Bellini. Jack sipped a Coke on the rocks, switching after having just one Smoked Old Fashioned.

"Concerned about what, Em?" He moved his chair closer to hers so they could face the fountains and lights of the strip outside together.

"You know, concerned about coming to Vegas. I was worried about how you might handle it."

Jack looked into her eyes and gave her his full attention.

"As excited as I am to see Adele, I didn't want to deal with any," Emily paused briefly, "you know, problems."

Finished with their small plates and the table promptly cleared, Jack extended his hand toward Emily's and lovingly cradled it. "I know, Em. I understand. But I'm fine. We're fine."

Emily returned his reassurance with a smile. "Thank you, Jack. You've been wonderful. It's been a relaxing and perfect day, thanks to you." She leaned to her right and kissed her husband with openness and appreciation. He gently squeezed her hand and kissed her back with disguise and relief. The chip in Jack's pocket grew warm with resentment and remembrances.

"Should we get the check and head over now?" Emily asked.

Jack sat upright and looked at his watch—nearly eight o'clock. *Where is that bellman?* He scooted his chair back to its original position, allowing enough room for the bellman to approach the table and set the small silver platter with its covered dome between them, just as they had planned. Jack looked around the room, anticipating the bellman's approach at any moment but having to settle instead for their waiter. Jack signaled for their check. "We've got time, Em. Let's sit here and finish our drinks."

"Okay. Just a minute, please. I don't want to be late, and we need to find our seats and—"

"I know, Em. I love you, Sweetheart."

"Aw, I love you too, Jack." Emily rarely referred to Jack in euphemisms when speaking directly to him. Unlike most other couples, she never used endearing terms like 'Dear,' 'Sweetheart,' or 'Baby.' Emily always called him 'Jack,' direct and perhaps less overtly affectionate. That was how Emily's parents spoke to one another, rarely expressing any form of intimacy. They perceived such terms of endearment as insincere. Emily valued honesty and preferred straightforward communication rather than overly sentimental or cliché language. There was a time early in their relationship when she did, but now it was a forgotten practice.

Jack looked at his watch again and once more surveyed the dining room. There was no sign of the bellman or his anniversary gift to Emily. Jack only saw the waiter bringing their check to the table and felt the chip hidden in his pocket returning to life. He opened the padded bill presenter and studied the check, allowing the waiter enough time to take a few steps back. The waiter turned and left after Jack gave him the universal glance, signaling the request for more time. *He will be here any moment,* Jack thought. But time was running out. Jack slowly removed his credit card from his wallet and placed it in the bifold card holder, studying the check again and working for every second of delay gained before placing the holder on the edge of the table.

"I'll be right back, sir."

"Jack, it's eight-ten. We need to go."

The waiter was too efficient and returned to the table with Jack's card and receipt to sign sooner than he wanted and later than Emily desired.

Jack looked around one last time before adding the tip and laying the bifold presenter on the table, "The Elysian" embossed in gold on its front cover. The perfect opportunity had passed.

Jack would have to get the earrings from the bellman as soon as he could after the concert. As he saw Emily indicate she was about to scoot her chair back to stand, he jumped up and stepped behind her to pull the chair back, as gentlemen do.

***

"You look stunning, sweetheart," Jack repeated to Emily as they walked to the venue. He wanted to glance to his left and scan the perimeter across the large casino floor. The slot machine was nearby, but he knew to avoid looking in that direction. Now was not the time.

"You clean up pretty well yourself, Mister," Emily replied, holding onto Jack's arm as he escorted her to the end of the short line. Jack was right; she looked beautiful wearing her one-shoulder satin dress with a smocked waist and a layered skirt. The dress was royal blue, and Emily had seen Adele wear one very similar to it. As soon as Jack surprised her with the concert tickets two months prior, Emily instantly knew this was the dress she wanted to wear to see her idol. The aquamarine earrings would have indeed looked fabulous with Emily's dress.

With each step closer to their chosen line's ticket entrance, Emily stepped closer to her icon. She had been a fan of Adele's music since her first album sixteen years ago when Emily was turning twenty. Emily and Adele were the same age, and her love of Adele's music predated Jack. The song also predated her understanding of the heartache and sadness behind the lyrics of the first album, as well as Emily's understanding of love.

"Jack, I'm so excited!" There was a bounce to her step as she held on to his elbow, an unbridled excitement he rarely saw in her, a happiness she had not shared with him since his dark period began. Seeing Emily enjoy herself without worrying about him or remembering what he had put her through made Jack happy, too.

College sweethearts and happy newlyweds with promising young careers almost became just another familiar story about a young thirtysomething couple collapsing under the weight of a husband's middle-age crisis. But that was in the past. Jack had succeeded in slaying his demons and rescuing his wife from their grip. Clarity of who rescued who waned as Jack delighted in his accomplishment in making Emily happy again.

As the concertgoers ahead of them passed through the ticket checkers and turnstiles one by one, Emily could hear the pre-show music from within permeating outside the doors of the Colosseum where they waited. They were songs from the first album she fell in love with all those years ago. The songs were not on the concert's set list tonight, but they were songs Emily was familiar with and knew in her heart.

It was their turn next. Jack reached into the chest pocket of his blazer, where he kept the tickets for safekeeping. He presented them to the ticket checker for scanning. Ordinarily, Emily would have kept the tickets in her purse. She was the spouse who naturally kept all the essential documents when they traveled, except for the routine contents of Jack's wallet. Emily had asked to hold on to the tickets several times, but he insisted he would take care of them. Tonight's dinner and show was his treat to her, and he intended to be the man treating his wife out to a night she would never forget. He earned and deserved at least that much.

The scanner emitted a sharp and dissonant beep. As the attendant scanned the second ticket, the barcode gun again flashed red and signaled the same tone of denial, not pleasing to the ear. The second attempt at scanning both tickets produced the same harsh and unpleasant result, conveying a sense of rejection. The rapid third attempt result was no different.

A flush of adrenaline tingled through Jack's body as a sudden coldness hit Emily's core.

"Something wrong?" Jack asked the attendant, his eyebrows drawing together as he leaned in to decipher what the barcode gun's message was suggesting.

"I'm sorry, sir," the young man said. "Do you mind stepping aside while I call for assistance, please?"

"Scan it again, please," Jack asked.

"What kind of assistance?" Emily interjected as she alternated her glance between the attendant and her husband and back to the attendant again. She stood firmly at the head of the increasingly long line of ticket-holders.

"One moment, please," the attendant repeated as he radioed someone in authority. Jack attempted to reach for the tickets to look at them as though he could read and interpret the barcode to clarify the situation, but the attendant stepped backward away from Jack and held them firmly.

"What's going on, Jack?" Emily asked over the fluttering in her stomach, hyper-focused on analyzing what was happening.

"Nothing, Sweetheart. It's fine, don't worry," Jack replied, feeling judged by the ticket handler.

Within moments, a middle-aged man dressed in the same vest and bowtie as the attendant arrived. A brief sidebar between the two ensued; both backs turned to Jack and Emily to shield their hushed discussion. Emerging with the tickets in his hand, the manager tried scanning the tickets himself. The results were the same each time: a red flashing bar and a sharp and dissonant beep of rejection. He then scrutinized the tickets closely, using a pocket magnifying glass reminiscent of those used by jewelers. It took just seconds for the manager to carefully and expertly inspect every detail of the tickets, from the intricate watermark to the fine print.

The manager took several steps to the side and politely invited the couple to do the same and join him. "My apologies," he whispered to Jack and Emily in a hushed pitch, "but these tickets appear counterfeit."

"Counterfeit?" Jack snapped back in a harsher tone than needed. He tilted his head and paused, skeptical of the manager's words, jumping to resentment at the implied accusation. "What do you mean, counterfeit?"

"Jack?" Emily responded, her tone shifting from confusion to suspicion.

Jack now felt judged by Emily as well.

"Yes, sir, counterfeit," the manager insisted. "As in, they are not legitimate."

"That's not possible. Recheck them, please," Jack defiantly demanded.

"Jack, where did you get these tickets from?"

Jack was becoming agitated. He turned his attention away from the manager and toward Emily, raising his hands to define the space between them as if to halt her concern and questioning. "Em, the tickets are fine. They're real." Jack now felt judged by the growing and anxious line of people behind them as some switched lines, anticipating a longer and ongoing discussion.

"I'm very sorry, sir, but we cannot allow you in with these tickets."

"There's been some kind of mistake," Jack insisted. "The tickets are fine. We've come a long way and spent a lot of money to be here. It's our anniversary, damnit! We are going to see this show."

The manager stood firm as their debate over the authenticity of the tickets drew the attention of other concertgoers nearby. Jack's reactions also attracted the attention of security personnel, two of whom now stood beside the manager.

"What the hell is going on, Jack?" Emily could hear the pre-show warmup continue beyond the doors for which she was now not allowed. She recognized the melody as Adele's first big hit, "Chasing Pavements," in which a woman is trying to be optimistic about a relationship all but done, questioning whether she should give up on him or continue to try to make the relationship work. When it was apparent they would not attend the concert, Emily turned and walked away.

"Em, wait!" Jack yelled, pausing his dispute with the manager to follow his wife instead. With a few hastened strides, he caught up to her and reached for her elbow, hoping to slow her down. "Hold on, please."

Emily turned and recoiled her elbow from his touch. "What the hell, Jack?" The couple now stood in the middle of the space between The Colosseum's entrance and the gaming floor of Ceaser's Palace adjacent to the venue. The sounds of the slot machines and people rustling about them now quashed any sounds of Adele's old hit about love and regret from the venue.

"I swear to you, Em, the tickets are good. I bought them online. They're legit." Then, the cell phone in Jack's hand lit up and chimed with a new text. "Shit, it's the vet again."

Emily looked perturbed by Jack's behavior, checking his phone over a text message as they discussed what had just happened and knowing how upset she was. Emily's reaction to Jack's inconsiderate action paused. She tilted her head and squinted her eyes, looking directly into his. "Did you say 'the vet, AGAIN'?"

Emily's rewind of Jack's statement and sudden halt of any debate over the validity of concert tickets was no less unexpected and startling to her as the words clumsily and nonchalantly rolling out of Jack's mouth were to him.

"Why is the vet texting you at this hour, Jack? What's wrong with Casey?"

"Em, nothing's wrong with Casey."

"Jack, you haven't even opened and read the text yet!" she barked back. "Nine o'clock here means it's eleven on a Saturday night back home. What's going on, Jack?" Emily's disappointment and shock over the concert tickets quickly shifted to uncertainty about the vet's text message, concern for Casey's well-being, and skepticism over what Jack knew and was not telling her. Emily was shifting back into her former attorney role. She had Jack on the witness stand, smelling blood from his slip and drilling him with rapid-fire questions and shifting emotions to break him and draw the truth out.

Jack stammered. His mind raced, searching for the proper responses as people walked around them. A mixture of sounds from the crowded gaming floor filled the space between them: talking, laughter, excitement, bells, chimes, and whistles. Jack was seated in a passenger airliner as it abruptly broke apart in mid-air, plummeting uncontrollably through the sky toward the ground. People and carry-on luggage circled him as rushing air and screams of passenger terror surrounded him. Jack was strapped to his seat of lies, plummeting violently toward his demise. There was a long way left to fall.

"Listen, sweetheart, there's something else."

"What else *could* there be, Jack?"

"Don't get mad, Sweetheart. I didn't want to tell you before the show. I wanted you to have a good time tonight."

"What, Jack? What is it? Just tell me."

"It's Casey. The vet called earlier and—."

"Casey? What about Casey? Earlier when?"

"This afternoon. A little while ago, I don't know. I didn't want you to get upset like this."

"Well, I am upset, Jack!" she shouted. "I should be upset. What's wrong with Casey? What did the vet say? Why in the hell didn't you say something earlier? You told me you saw her on the webcam, and she was fine."

Jack told Emily about the call from Dr. Norman and Casey's sudden illness, his suggestion of running tests, and their costs. Jack informed her he had instructed the vet to do everything necessary. Jack tried to explain his motive for withholding the news from her. He did not tell her for her benefit. He did not tell her so she could enjoy the show.

"You're such an asshole, Jack!" Emily shoved her palms against Jack's chest as she cried the words, no longer caring if she made a public scene. She pivoted away from him with a resolute turn and stormed off.

Jack had never seen Emily this angry before, even in the depths of his drinking and depression phase. He knew better than to follow her now. Jack believed she needed time to cool down as he watched her march from him through the casino toward the elevator banks. Adele sang it in "Chasing Pavements": a lying man, a confrontation and argument, a woman who storms out, and a man who doesn't follow the one he is supposed to love.

Jack then saw the bellman walking in measured strides toward where he stood. He was holding a black felt box and had just passed Emily on his way to Jack.

OPPORTUNITY LOST

(1963)

Nearly a week passed since the confrontation between Frankie and Sofia at Carmine's on the evening of the Casbah's grand opening. Sam Giancarlo heard about the quarrel and contacted Frankie the following day, lending his support in any way Frankie needed it. He also reiterated his position that Frankie firing her was about time. It was for the best, yet a shame the spectacle was so public and on neutral grounds at Carmine's.

Sam contended delicate business and family matters were best handled quietly and discreetly. Frankie agreed and apologized to Sam for his former employee's actions and disturbance. Frankie also apologized to Carmine for the same. Carmine apologized to Frankie for not quashing the disturbance as soon as it started and for allowing Sofia to lie in wait at the bar to ambush Frankie in the first place. Carmine contended his staff should have known better, even though Frankie and Sofia had been seen there together in the past, and there was no way for Carmine's staff to have anticipated why Sofia was there. Still, the men all felt wronged by Sofia and found comfort in reaffirming their alliance.

Even a few of Carmine's patrons reached out to Frankie the

following day to apologize for what they witnessed and offer their support and congratulations for the Casbah's opening. There was ample embarrassment to go around and a generous number of apologies made. Most of Las Vegas's business and political elite had either witnessed or heard about Frankie and Sofia's altercation. Everyone except Evilyn, rather. She dutifully tucked the children into bed the evening of the quarrel and was spared the ripple of social gossip in the following days by her naivete of the event's occurrence.

Evilyn wasn't the only person removed from any embarrassment or apologies related to the incident. It was not that Sofia could be embarrassed by her actions or by forcible removal from Carmine's. She had long ago bartered away any capacity for embarrassment in exchange for being a strong, independent woman who could fight for what she wanted or deserved. Nor would Sofia ever apologize for such an altercation. Those exchanges were made long ago in Sicily when times were tough, and she had to make irrevocable choices as a young woman— choices superseding embarrassment and prohibiting being apologetic. Yet, in the week following the altercation at Carmine's, no one had any contact with Sofia. Sofia was as absent as Evilyn was oblivious.

"Boss, we're running low on half a dozen brands," Max called out to Frankie as the new casino operator whisked past the central bar during one of his many daily rounds around the Casbah.

"Send one of the boys down the street to a liquor store with some cash if you have to. I'll call the distributor later," Frankie shouted back without stopping. He wouldn't have time to make the call later, however, and he probably knew he wouldn't. Frankie was already working 20 hours a day, sleeping in his office in the Eye most nights. The pace of opening week was maddening, with what seemed like twice the activities as the staff had endured preparing the new establishment for opening. What had been an army of carpenters and installers to coordinate and push was now new employees and staff members, vendors, suppliers, and various regulatory personnel from a dozen different authorities, not to mention the thousands of customers themselves coming in and out and moving about the casino every day.

The report was similar in each area of the hotel and casino Frankie passed. Some slot machines on the casino floor were not operating despite being checked and double-checked during installation. On any given day, one or more table dealers might call out sick or not show up for their shift. The same applied to guest service personnel at the check-in desk or concierge services, maids to clean rooms, and laundry room personnel to wash towels and sheets and dining room linens. The restaurant was a mess with a new chef, newly created menu items, prep and cook personnel not yet battle-tested in their new kitchen environment, inexperienced wait staff, and missed food and beverage deliveries. The on-floor bars, the gentleman's lounge, and the nightclub hosting the live entertainment of singers, comedy shows, and magic acts were all experiencing the same type of hurdles and setbacks.

Frankie expected opening week challenges and glitches, or at least that's what he told those outside the operation, such as his investors, friends in the business community, and wife. He learned this as a young Seaman E-3 in the Navy during his first assignment aboard the newly constructed USS Franklin D. Roosevelt. The carrier was built and launched at the New York Naval Shipyard in Brooklyn. Frankie participated in its acceptance trials and shakedown cruise at sea. The officers and enlisted crew spent months familiarizing themselves with the ship's systems, conducting training exercises, and addressing issues when they arose. Once fully commissioned, they deployed across the Atlantic to the Mediterranean for their first tour.

Although Frankie expected these challenges, he told the Casbah's management and staff something different. All these issues meant lost revenue, which was not sustainable or tolerated. Guests not yet checked in can't begin to spend their money. Gamers who can't find open tables staffed with dealers or working slot machines to wager at can't spend their money. Diners who can't be seated to order food or whose favorite cocktail isn't available can't spend their money. More importantly, sustained issues would result in bad reviews or damage the establishment's reputation.

Frankie was determined to succeed, but where was Sofia when he needed her? Why had she insisted on pressuring him on his partnership and relationship promises? Why now, just as the Casbah was opening and all their hard work was about to pay off? Frankie was a real estate developer, but Sofia had the expertise and experience of managing a hotel and gaming operation. Frankie knew how to get projects financed, but Sofia knew how to get things done.

That first week of operating the Casbah was like trying to stay alive on the beaches of Normandy on D-Day. The week-long battle without his most crucial second-in-command left Frankie worn and exhausted. Everything took him three times the effort and time it took Sofia. Frankie desperately needed reinforcements.

Sam offered Frankie some help by sending his consigliere, or top advisor on business matters, along with a few of his caporegimes, or lieutenants, to help resolve some of his staffing issues. Frankie was hesitant. He didn't want to expose too many of the start-up week's issues or allow The Alliance to become too embedded in the details of the Casbah's daily operations. Each time Sam's crew visited, Frankie cleverly threw insignificant tasks at them or pointed them in directions of minor consequence. Gangsters don't like to work hard anyway, so they could put minimal effort in and walk away feeling helpful.

Evilyn also pitched in to help her husband when she could, between her civic obligations, volunteer work, and caring for the children before and after school. She also expected the Casbah to place unreasonable demands on Frankie's time in the beginning, so putting her feelings regarding casinos and gambling aside, she did what she could in Frankie's office to help by filing paperwork, answering calls, and taking messages for him. Evilyn was no Sofia, but she did have Frankie's best interest at heart, and her only personal agenda was her husband's welfare. Evilyn did not enjoy being at the Casbah. Still, as any mother would do, she was more than willing to sacrifice for the good of her family.

"Where again did you say Sofia was?" Evilyn would ask her husband.

"She's taking time to visit family," he would respond. "She worked pretty hard to get us to this point," he would add. "She needed a break."

"And when is she returning?" she would ask, still unaware of the incident at Carmine's. Evilyn had limited contact with other staff members at the Casbah, having avoided the casino floor altogether. Those she spoke to in the Eye would never have discussed rumors of a personal nature regarding their boss.

"Not sure," Frankie would answer as he ran off to tend to another issue and avoid any further inquiries.

Frankie was exhausted and frantic during the first week and considered telling Evilyn the truth. Any threat from Sofia appeared gone now, but so was the feminine support she provided. Frankie still needed that support to feed his confidence and caress his ego. He considered turning to Evilyn during the opening week when he felt powerless and consumed by self-doubt. If he just explained the altercation with Sofia at Carmine's, her unreasonable demands for him to make her a partner, and her unthinkable desire for him to leave his wife and family to be with her instead, Evilyn would understand the threat Sofia posed, and why he had no choice but to fire and banish her. Frankie came close to confiding in Evilyn and telling her the truth about everything. Trusting his wife was Frankie's second chance. He didn't take it. With his new lucky chip tucked safely in his vest pocket, Frankie kept rolling the dice and keeping his streak alive. Frankie wanted everything: his success and his stature, his wife and his family, his virtue and his secrets.

CASA DEL MAR

The climate and scenic landscape of Santa Barbara reminded Sofia of her childhood. Like Palermo, Santa Barbara enjoyed a Mediterranean-like climate with mild, wet winters and warm, dry summers. Santa Barbara had lush vegetation, including palm trees, olive trees, and citrus orchards, similar to what Sofia remembered in her hometown. She was most fond of Santa Barbara's seaside setting, with its stunning views of the Pacific Ocean surrounded by the nearby Santa Ynez Mountains. The scenery was very reminiscent of Palermo's coastal landscape.

Sofia had visited this small, family-owned retreat in the past. She called Casa Del Mar a retreat because that's what she did when she stayed there in the past. She preferred to think of the location as a quiet and secluded place to rest and relax rather than a place to withdraw or pull back from a battle. Case Del Mar was both.

Casa Del Mar was more akin to an intimate inn with beach apartments built in the 1920s, too far off the beaten path for its time and blessed with abundant acreage and gorgeous ocean views because of it. One would think they were in a Mediterranean villa with red tile roofs, white walls, and architectural archways. The intimate 21-room inn had narrow walkways lined with flowers and palm trees leading to gurgling fountains where guests could sit and relax to watch the large orange sun retreat into the waters of the blue Pacific. These days, a buyer wouldn't be lucky enough to stumble onto such a bargain. It was rare for original owners to keep it in the family for four decades rather than accept one of the frequent offers from real estate developers to sell it for a quick and handsome profit.

Casa Del Mar was the first place Sofia thought of when she was released on her own recognizance by the police outside Carmine's. Casa Del Mar was a world away from the hustle and bustle of Vegas, yet a relatively short seven-hour ride by Greyhound to get there. By chance or not, Casa Del Mar was also a convenient twenty-five-minute cab ride to the University of California, Santa Barbara.

Against the backdrop of an entire lifetime, a relatively short time had passed since Sofia lived in Sicily—less than two decades, in fact. So the breeze of memories flowed easily across her skin and through her hair as she sat and gazed out upon the Pacific, recalling what it was like to be innocent and vulnerable.

As Sofia watched the late afternoon sun glisten against the water's surface between the shore and the horizon, she caressed the Trinacria necklace her grandmother gave her shortly before her death. She and her grandmother Nonnina would spend hours together each day walking the narrow streets, searching for fresh produce and seafood in the local markets. They later used their daily finds to prepare meals for themselves and Sofia's parents. Nonnina taught Sofia how to knit, sew, and embroider clothes each Sunday morning after attending the Church of San Giovanni degli Eremiti.

Nonnina imparted many other lessons to Sofia. She taught the young teen how to be strong and, when strength wasn't enough, how to rely on ancient practices and rituals. Nonnina explained not everything in life was clear or absolute; some truths extended beyond mere intellect. While words like 'magic' and 'witchcraft' might seem fanciful in books, the conjurations and incantations handed down by their ancestors were genuine and powerful.

That was Sofia's old life, of course, before the Allied bombing of Sicily took her family away from her.

After successes against the Axis forces in North Africa, Palermo was the next target for the Allies as a natural route to mainland Italy. The bombings began in June, followed by massive amphibious assaults in July. By the end of the month, Mussolini was deposed and arrested. The Allied conquest of Sicily and the surrender of Italy in the war took a little over a month. Sofia lost her parents, her grandmother, and her way of life in as little time.

Most of Palermo's residents welcomed the Americans, even though many of their fathers, sons, and brothers fought against their new liberators as Italian soldiers. Sicily had a long history of conquerors and liberators: the ancient Greeks and Carthaginians, the Romans and Germanic Vandals, the Arabs and the Normans, the Swabians, the French Angevins, the Spanish Aragonese and Hansburgs. Through them all, however, the people of Sicily remained Sicilians, first and foremost.

With the Americans came reconstruction. Palermo became a city of recovery and rebuilding after suffering significant damage during the war. Still, Sofia remembered the shortages, the rationing, and the loneliness without her family. She was orphaned, not quite an adult, yet far from childhood. She cultivated the skills to survive in her hometown's bombed buildings and streets. Sofia vowed then never to become a victim of circumstance again.

With the Americans came prostitution. Desperate to support themselves and their families in the face of widespread poverty and unemployment, some Palermitan women turned to prostitution. Many had never been involved intimately with any man. But for some, the aftermath of war, economic devastation, and social upheaval left few options for survival. Some of these women were Sofia's classmates and friends, but Sofia found another way. The young orphaned Sicilian would service the American soldiers and sailors by helping to satisfy their second most sought-after vice, entertainment and gambling.

The Sicilian Mafia, or Cosa Nostra, had been active in Sicily for centuries before the war. They were involved in politics, business, law enforcement, and every other aspect of Sicilian society. While the Allies fought the Germans and Italians, the Cosa Nostra exploited them. The war allowed the Cosa Nostra to expand and consolidate its power and control over Sicilian society. The war provided opportunities for the Cosa Nostra, and the Cosa Nostra provided opportunities for Sofia. Rather than prostitute herself as many of her friends had to do, Sofia learned the skills required to manage and operate the brothels and gambling houses for her new employers. That's where Sofia learned the value of loyalty and the cost of betrayal. That's also where Sofia met a handsome young American sailor on shore leave in occupied Palermo.

Quiet reflection did not come naturally to Sofia, even at Casa Del Mar, as she watched the evening sun sink below the distant horizon. She was born a feisty go-getter with Sicilian fire coursing through her veins. Even as a child, she had things to do, problems to solve, and opportunities to take advantage of. When these tasks, issues, and opportunities were not naturally present, Sofia had a honed talent for creating them herself. Still, even superheroes sometimes need to retreat to their secret hideout, away from the world's chaos, to recharge their powers and strategize their next moves.

Sofia's Surprise

B right beams of sunlight reflected off the Cadillac's windshield, flashing across the front curtains of the living room as it turned into the Paradise Palms driveway. Richard and Lucy ran to the window and, in unison, shouted the announcement of their father's early arrival home. It was the first time in nearly two weeks that Frankie had arrived home before sunset. After weeks of tireless work, Frankie was determined to get home today before dark to eat dinner and spend a quiet evening with his family.

"Dad," Richard greeted his father enthusiastically, running up to him and taking his briefcase from his hand. "Want to throw some ball outside?"

"Daddy's home," yelled Lucy, directing her announcement toward the rear of the home as Frankie swooped her up into his arms and kissed her on the cheek, patting his son on the head simultaneously while making his way into the foyer toward the kitchen.

"I'm back here, dear."

"In a minute, son," Frankie replied to Richard, putting Lucy back down. "Let's say hello to your mom first." He could smell the faint aroma of dinner wafting through the air, mingling with the warm glow of afternoon sunlight spilling into the foyer from the front of the house. But as Frankie took the first steps into the kitchen and Evilyn approached him, he froze.

Evilyn kissed her husband on the cheek and, with the always-welcoming smile of a hostess whose home is always open to other ladies stopping by unannounced for a cup of coffee or tea and gossip in the afternoon hours, said, "Look who's here."

Frankie stood there in disbelief, his breath caught in his throat as each piece of the scene came into focus through his tired eyes—the kitchen, the dinette table in the center of the room, two white cups and saucers, lipstick remains on the rims of each cup. The voices of Frankie's children became faint and faded away as if time had slowed. The pounding of his heartbeat became louder and faster in his ears. He felt lightheaded and wanted to believe his fatigue or the desert heat was causing a mirage in his home. Frankie's thoughts scrambled to understand what was happening, trying to think back to the last moment they were together and the final words spoken between them.

"Well, I guess that answers my question," Evilyn stated.

"Evilyn?" Frankie asked, still staring at the figure seated at the dinette table in what was usually his seat at the head of the table. How he spoke his wife's name sounded like a question, a confused request for clarification, and an apprehensive warning, all at the same time.

"When I asked you when she would be back. From vacation," Evilyn replied. "I guess we know now."

"Hello, Boss." Sofia calmly handed Evilyn her empty cup for a refill. "I've heard things have been hectic."

"You don't know the half of it," Evilyn added as she poured the tea and patted Frankie on his shoulder, passing him to return the kettle to the stovetop. "Get you something to drink, dear?"

Frankie struggled to process the gravity of the situation—his secret world colliding with his reality at the most unexpected place and time. His gaze moved from Evilyn in the kitchen to Sofia at the table and back to Evilyn again, sensing the tension in the air while his brow furrowed in concern. *What is she doing here? What did she tell Evilyn?* Surprise, disbelief, nervousness, anxiety, and worry cycled through Frankie's mind; emotions like the spinning wheels of a slot machine, wondering where the wheels would abruptly stop.

"Sofia," finally forcing the words out of his mouth, "what are you doing here?"

"Frankie," Evilyn playfully scolded, as if calling out one of her children for saying something mean to the other. "We've been having a nice chat. Sofia has been telling me all about her trip. Come sit with us, dear."

Frankie moved toward the table with apprehension, grabbing onto the back of the empty chair Evilyn had just patted. He struggled to comprehend the presence of his mistress in their home, conversing with his wife as if the most natural thing in the world. Frankie didn't sit. Sitting would leave him too vulnerable. Sitting would also suggest his approval for Sofia to stay longer. Instead, he again altered his gaze between the two women and asked, "Is everything alright?"

"Everything's fine, Boss," Sofia replied, smiling and looking rested and confident. "I just can't wait to get back to work."

Frankie's mind raced as he searched for his next words, his throat dry and constricted as if he had collapsed right there on Evilyn's kitchen floor with Sofia's shoe pressed against his windpipe. But before Frankie responded, Sofia rose.

"I'm sorry, Evilyn," she said, her tone laced with guilt.

Frankie wanted to shout out. He considered lunging toward the manipulative woman who had no right to be in his home with his wife and children. Frankie wanted to stop Sofia before she could do any more damage than what she had probably already done. Sofia was nearly eye level with him and only feet away on the other side of the table.

"But it's time to go," Sofia continued. "Thanks so much for letting me drop by unannounced and for the tea. It was so good to finally spend some time with you chatting." Sofia chuckled. "I spend so much time working that I forget to have a personal life." She looked at Frankie and smiled.

"Oh, sweetie," Evilyn responded, placing one hand on Sofia's shoulder to comfort her. "You two have worked so hard to get the Casbah open. We owe you so much, Sofia. I know how much Frankie relies on you, and we're so glad you're back. Now let's see if we can get this one to take a week off and take us somewhere for vacation."

Relief, if only momentary, swept over Frankie. He realized the gravity of his situation and Sofia's hold over him and his future. His triumph over the secrets they shared was just a shattered illusion. Sofia was escorted out of Carmine's that night, kicking and screaming, but she had not gone quietly into the night. She was back, as calm and as in control as ever.

"I'll walk you out," Frankie said. "Need to fill you in on a few things before you come in tomorrow."

Sofia exchanged pleasantries again with Evilyn before saying goodbye to the children playing in the front room. Once outside, the setting sun had already allowed the desert air to cool while casting deep shadows across the cement driveway. Only then did Frankie notice Sofia's car parked down the street.

"What the fuck are you doing here?" Frankie questioned. "Who the hell do you think you are coming to my home and—"

"Frankie," she interjected calmly and matter-of-factly. "There's something you need to know."

"No, you need to know something," he refuted, growing frustrated and angry while trying to keep a calm and cordial demeanor out in the openness of his driveway, exposed to his neighbors around him and his family inside to witness.

Before Frankie could say another word, however, Sofia spoke. "I didn't come here to cause trouble, Frankie. I came because," she paused, "because there's something important I've been holding onto for a long time."

Frankie's eyes narrowed, his patience wearing thin. "Spit it out, then. What could possibly be so important?"

She hesitated, her gaze dropping to the ground. "I wanted to tell you... I've wanted to tell you for a long time that..." She paused again, taking a deep breath. "That I wish things had turned out differently for us. But that's not why I'm here now."

Frankie's brow furrowed in confusion and suspicion. "Then why are you here, damnit?"

Sofia looked up, her eyes meeting his with sadness and determination. "Because I needed to see you, to remind myself of what we had, and to let you know I'll be at the office in the morning. We have some business to discuss."

Frankie's anger wavered, replaced by a sense of unease. "Business? What kind of business?"

"You'll see," Sofia replied, her voice steady. "Just be ready for an important conversation."

With that, she turned and walked towards her car, leaving

Frankie to stand in his driveway, a storm of emotions churning within him. He watched her drive away, a sense of foreboding settling in as the last rays of sunlight disappeared behind the hills surrounding Paradise Palms.

Frankie let out a heavy sigh as he watched Sofia's car disappear from view. She was back, and the weight of another impending conversation pressed down on him. He turned back towards his house, glancing at the windows behind which his family prepared for dinner. They were blissfully unaware of the secrets and conflicts brewing outside their door.

COME-OUT ROLL

(Present)

J ack watched his wife angrily walk away from him with determination in her stride, almost colliding with the bellman, who was remorsefully walking toward him. Emily knew she had to get away from Jack and the entrance to the concert venue; both were too disappointing for her to bear. Jack knew better than to run after Emily while she was so upset. The bellman, who had observed their confrontation from afar, knew he needed to approach cautiously. He did not want to be intrusive. The bellman's code, after all, calls for respect to privacy and anticipating needs while being mindful not to impose help when not desired.

"Mr. Harper. My deepest apologies, Sir."

"Where the hell were you?"

"Momentarily delayed, Mr. Harper. When I arrived at your table, you and Mrs. Harper had just left."

Jack reached for the black felt box offered to him in the bellman's open palm. "This is all your fault, you know."

"But of course, Sir."

Jack stood there with the gift clutched in his left hand while he ran his fingers through his hair with his right, staring at the flooring sprawled beneath his feet. The carpet was a luxurious shade of midnight blue with hints of gold and silver, an elaborate tapestry of geometric shapes and ornate flourishes, mirroring the surrounding atmosphere, pulsing with the same vibrant energy as the uncertainty pulsing through his mind. Jack rubbed his jawline and then the back of his neck while he tilted his head from side to side, trying to crack his neck joints as if trying to crack the code of options available.

"Sir, perhaps I could deliver the gift for you to Mrs. Harper up in your suite?"

"Absolutely not," Jack commanded. "I'm not letting these out of my sight." His gaze drifted downward again, drawn to the hypnotic allure of the carpet beneath him, searching for answers hidden within its elaborate motifs. Lost in concentration, Jack weighed his tumultuous options as they churned within him. Should he chase Emily to the room and try to figure out what happened with the tickets? Would it be better to give her the space and time to calm down first, letting cooler heads prevail? When should he give her the beautiful and thoughtful gift he selected for her, or has the moment passed? Jack wondered if he should stay, for now, and try his luck at the tables or heed the voice of warning whispering in his ear.

Jack sighed impatiently as the bellman patiently stood by his side and observed the bellman's code not to impose his help when not desired. Straightening his posture, Jack slipped the black felt box into the pocket of his sports coat and retrieved his chip from his slacks, holding the lucky charm firmly within his grasp, securely hidden from the view of others. Jack surveyed his surroundings as a sense of calm swept over him. His sensory faculties returned. His focus on the people and things around him sharpened. He could once again hear activity and opportunity. Jack could feel the ridges of his lucky chip, rubbing his thumb in circular motions around its edge.

Jack looked the bellman in the eyes before dropping his gaze down, past his black bowtie and white shirt, until landing on his black vest and jacket pocket. 'Benjamin,' it read in black letters engraved into the gold lacquered nametag, noting how the name represented the president on the hundred-dollar bill. Jack dismissed the bellman without words or gestures but with contempt, turning in silence and walking away.

Jack wasn't always this way. He had a somewhat typical childhood, raised in a middle-class family in a suburban neighborhood outside San Fransico. Jack's parents provided for him and his older siblings, but the household had underlying tensions. His father struggled with alcoholism, and his mother worked long hours to make ends meet, leaving little time for emotional support. Overshadowed by his more academically successful siblings, Jack learned to fend for himself as they left the household. The void left Jack feeling neglected, and he sought validation wherever he could find it. He found solace in escapism, losing himself in video games for hours, and sometimes on weekends, for days on end.

Jack wasn't unintelligent. He wasn't lazy, either. There were many moments of promise, with flashes of creativity and ambition. He dreamed of a future free from the constraints of his upbringing, achieving success on his terms like his siblings had accomplished. However, self-destructive tendencies often overshadowed those ambitions and dreams of success.

Jack's therapist once explained his tendency to prioritize his own needs and desires above all others may have developed as a coping mechanism in response to his feelings of neglect and the lack of support and direction from his parents and siblings during his formative years. But Jack had been anything but selfish in buying the flight, hotel, concert tickets, and earrings for Emily.

His therapist also explained how his impulsivity contributed to his struggles with alcoholism and gambling as he sought immediate satisfaction without regard for the long-term effects on himself and his wife. Seeking immediate gratification was also rooted in his relationship with his estranged parents and siblings, none of whom he had any contact with for a decade and a half. That's why Jack's relationship with Emily was so meaningful to him and why he vowed to do anything to preserve it.

While in rehab, the counselors instructed Jack to reject excuses and blame. He tended to make excuses when faced with setbacks or failures rather than take responsibility for his actions. He blamed external factors or circumstances for his mistakes, refusing to acknowledge his role in his struggles. But weren't the early family dysfunctions to blame for the recent issues?

Still, Jack was out of recovery and fully rehabilitated, which was all that mattered. He had worked hard to wrap his inner vulnerability in a tough exterior of bravado and self-assuredness. Jack had defeated his feelings of inadequacy and insecurity by wooing and marrying someone like Emily, who was anything but. Marrying her took courage and patience, proving his success in filling the void of his troubled past. His marriage to Emily validated that.

As Jack clutched his lucky chip and walked around the casino floor thinking about her, Emily cried in their hotel room. She had run up there, shocked and angry. She left a message for Dr. Norman, anxious and concerned. Emily now waited for Jack to come to her, confused and bitter. When he didn't, she grew sick and resentful.

***

Jack sauntered through the cacophony of the casino floor, a disharmonic symphony of bells, chatter, and raucousness. He approached the craps table, bustling with excitement where cheers and groans blended in the air like the familiar emotions mixing inside himself: failure by the tickets, abandonment by Emily, and neglect by Benjamin. Bright overhead light cast a glittering sheen on the green felt table as he walked by and glanced at the maze of numbers and betting spaces.

"Hey, it's Jack with all the Jacks," Mike called out.

"Good, we need some help here," Sarah added, her raspy voice sounding even gruffer than before.

Stopping to acknowledge his new friends from earlier in the afternoon, Jack asked where Tom was, sliding his hand and lucky chip back into his pants pocket.

"That old fart is up in the room, probably asleep with the television running. Come play."

"Nah," Jack replied. "Not a craps player, but I'll watch."

"Suit yourself, good-looking, but stand here and rub some of that good luck off on Momma."

Jack smiled and stood beside Sarah while Mike picked up the dice from the green field of battle. "You're going to have to tell me how this works," Jack whispered to her.

"Don't you worry, baby, Momma's got ya." She slid a few of her five-dollar chips Jack's way.

"New shooter," the Dealer announced to the table.

Mike took a deep breath and rolled his shoulders to shake off the weight and stress of the moment. The other players leaned in, holding their collective breath in anticipation. "Come on, Mike, seven or eleven!" someone yelled. Mike's eyes locked onto the end

112

of the table, his focus intense.

"Seven or eleven wins on the come-out roll if you have chips on the pass line," explained Sarah.

Mike finally released the dice with a flick of his wrist. They tumbled down the table before clattering against the back wall and each other before coming to rest: six and a four. Players erupted in a mix of exclamations, the suspense breaking into a wave of cheers and disappointment. *Every roll in life has both winners and losers,* Jack thought.

"Okay, so that's not a win, but it's not a loss either," Sarah clarified. "Ten is the new point number. Mike's gotta roll another ten before he rolls a seven. We crap out if he rolls a seven."

Jack leaned toward the old lady with the raspy voice to hear her explanation of the game, but his curiosity and focus were on the dealers. Their practiced movements were swift and precise, managing bets and payouts with seamless efficiency. Various colored chips stacked high covered the table, but the purple $500 chips caught Jack's eye with their subdued and regal mix of blue and red tones. By contrast, the chip in Jack's pocket was a more profound, darker shade of red. It had an almost maroon hue, like aged red wine or dried deoxygenated blood.

"You gonna stand there all night, or you gonna play?"

Jack looked at Sarah, smiled, and slid the three five-dollar chips she had given him back toward her. "I'll just watch a few more, thanks." He ignored the phone's text message buzzing in his back pocket, the third within the last minute.

Mike's next dice toss landed a four and a three, immediately followed by a chorus of disappointed groans and sighs.

"Ah, crap!" Sarah tilted her head in Jack's direction to add in her graveled voice and slightly irked tone, "Nice roll, asshole."

"Everyone loves you until you crap out on them," Jack whispered to Sarah. Nearly two hours passed, and there was plenty of time to check his phone messages, but he didn't. He thought they were undoubtedly from Emily, but then he considered they could be from the vet, too. Neither were messages Jack wanted to read. Neither would likely be positive or make him feel good about himself.

Sarah playfully elbowed Jack in his side. "You got that right," chuckling at his comment before breaking into a guttural smoker's cough lasting longer than a cough should and was painful to listen to.

Having rolled a seven, Mike backed away from his spot as the shooter and encouraged Jack to take his place. The table's stickman offered the dice to Jack after retrieving them from the end of the table with his long hooked stick. Jack gestured his desire to pass on the opportunity.

"Oh, come on," Sarah encouraged. "Take a throw. We need some of that Jack-luck."

Jack smiled at Sarah, his fingers drumming restlessly on the smooth green felt as the casino noise enveloped him, a constant buzz of excitement and desperation. Jack had not yet gambled this evening despite the encouragement. The temptation was strong, however. The impulse was almost a physical ache. He had stayed on the casino floor to clear his head after the fight with Emily, which now seemed like a mistake.

He glanced around the room, watching the players clutching their chips, their eyes gleaming with hope and fear. He thought them sad and pathetic for being subject to the dice roll, the wheel's spin, and the cards' randomness. He knew the feeling well but still held contempt for their weakness. A fellow player at the table gave him a nod, mistaking Jack's delay and presence for interest, so as the stickman offered him the dice, Jack shook his head and stepped back.

"Not tonight," he muttered, more to himself than anyone else. The urge to stay, to give in and let his lucky chip guide him to success, gnawed at him. But Jack knew if he stayed, he would gamble, and he couldn't afford that. Not tonight, not with everything happening: the earrings not arriving, the counterfeit concert tickets, and the fight with Emily. They all replayed in his mind, her words cutting through the haze of his thoughts. *'You promised, Jack. You promised you wouldn't do this again.'*

Taking a deep breath, Jack turned away from Sarah, Mike, the other players, the stickman, and the table. He could feel the weight of the decision pressing down on him, each step a struggle against the lure of the games and the camaraderie of the players he held so little regard for. They all beckoned him in a way Emily and his current life did not. Still, he kept moving, forcing himself to walk away, his phone buzzing twice again in his back pocket.

Making his way through the crowded casino floor, Jack again looked around at the faces of the gamblers. Some celebrated small victories, while others sank deeper into despair, reflections of his past—moments of fleeting triumph overshadowed by long stretches of loss and regret. Each step brought a pounding in his chest, a mix of anxiety and determination. Jack needed to get back to his room, back to Emily. He had let her cool off for a few hours, but he knew it was time to face her, to try to make things right. But with determination also came light-headedness, shortness of breath, and the sensation of his body flooding with warmth. Jack's fingers ached with the desire to touch his wife as those same fingers reached out to touch the roulette table as he walked up to it. Hypersensitivity to the smooth texture of its lacquered woodgrain rail overtook him, and he was aware of the hair rising on his arms and the nape of his neck as it did. Jack's pace slowed until he paused altogether, his anxiety replaced by a pleasurable shiver and sense of belonging.

Jack just needed a moment. He focused on the table and the small ball revolving in a circular motion in the ball track, opposite the wheel head's spin direction. As the ball moved in the track hanging onto the metal deflector, its speed slowed with each rotation until eventually succumbing to gravity and bouncing off a series of frets or raised ridges separating one numbered pocket from another. It looked and sounded violent and erratic until the ball finally fell into a single red or black pocket, the wheel continuing to turn but slowing on its spindle. Jack wasn't sure of the color but knew it was blood red or midnight black. Once nestled in its numbered pocket, the ball's direction reversed, yielding to the direction of the larger and more powerful wheel. The small ball always yielded to the larger wheel. That was the nature of the game.

Jack held his lucky chip tightly, pressed between his fingers and palm, secure and concealed. The connection was real—a relationship between the ball, the wheel, the chip, and the past. Jack knew the wheel was life; he was the small ball, trapped, traveling in opposite directions—a perpetual state of revolutions in the same groove with violent collisions and eventual falls.

With each wheel spin, the kaleidoscopic blur of the red and black pockets spinning in one direction and the ivory ball spinning in the other mesmerized Jack. He was entranced. Jack watched as the ball fell in the same grooves time after time: one, nine, six, and three. The red one, the red nine, the black six, and the red three repeated themselves in a series, one after another. He stood there and watched, spin after spin, as the outcome never varied. One. Nine. Six. Three.

A different viciousness echoed from those violent collisions of the rotating wheel's frets and the ivory ball. Jack could hear it. He could see it, too, centered within the wheel's spinning outer ring of blurred red and black grooves. Jack listened to the gunshots with each of the ball's collisions. He saw the prominent figure slowly fall to the ground. Jack saw the blood-redness ooze from the victim's limp body out onto the midnight blackness of the dark pavement. With each spin and every gunshot, Jack felt the heat of his lucky chip intensify. The chip felt like the heat of a bullet entering a man's body, piercing his heart, and bringing him down to the ground. For a moment, Jack was sure he was the one shot. The sensation was so powerful it jolted Jack out of his dazed visions. Clear-headed and aware of his surroundings, Jack realized he had only been bumped by someone passing behind him on the crowded casino floor.

MARY'S CAFÉ

(1963)

Frankie pushed the diner's door open as a bell chimed softly above him to announce another customer's entry. The overhead pendant lights radiated a cozy, inviting glow against the early morning desert chill and the bustle of Fremont Street outside. Mary's Café was just two blocks from the Casbah and a favorite of Frankie's for breakfast whenever he did not eat his morning meal at home with Evilyn and the children.

"Good morning, Mr. Grant. And congratulations on the opening."

"Oh, thank you, Suzie," he replied, looking above and around the young waitress to assess how busy the diner was and who was there.

"Ms. Ferranero is already seated, sir. Right this way."

Mary's was a slice of classic Americana. The business owners, politicians, and Vegas elite who called Carmine's their own in the evening didn't frequent Mary's, opting instead to eat breakfast prepared by their wives and house staff at home. No, Mary's was for the working class and the downtown crowd. Few tourists wandered in either, preferring breakfast at the free, all-you-can-eat bars the hotels and casinos provided. Because of that, Mary's Café sometimes felt out of place with less power and greed and more hometown honesty and charm. Shiny chrome bar stools, their red vinyl seats gleaming under the lights, lined the long counter of polished formica patterned with flecks of silver and black. Neatly organized rows of sugar dispensers, napkin holders, and glass jars filled with colorful twirling straws adorned the top of the counter. Frankie often considered bringing Richard in for an ice cream sundae or chocolate malt after school one afternoon or after going to the park on the weekend. The outing would make for a good father-son moment, a treat for Richard, but Frankie was too busy and never followed through on those thoughts.

Frankie followed Suzie, dressed in her crisp white uniform, gliding between the tables and the counter in the cafe's front toward the booths in the back. High-backed dividers separated each booth to provide a sense of privacy and intimacy. Frankie continued scanning the room. To his left was the side wall adorned with black-and-white photographs of Las Vegas landmarks and famous entertainers, as well as framed memorabilia tracing the history of Fremont Street. He wanted to pause and check the wall for newly hung pictures of him at the Casbah's opening. Now was not the time, though. To his right, the open kitchen behind the open pass-through with its comforting aromas of sizzling bacon, brewing coffee, and freshly toasted bread. In the background, he heard the soft clatter of dishes and the muted conversations between table bussers, cooks, dishwashers, and diner patrons. Ahead, Frankie's eyes settled on the secluded booth at the back where Suzie was leading him, away from the occasional glances of other early risers and attentive waitstaff.

"Thank you," Frankie told Suzie as she handed him the menu. "Just coffee for now, thanks."

Sofia was already seated on the opposite side of the booth with her back to the wall facing the cafe's front entrance. She knew of Frankie's preference to face the door in any dining establishment, so she denied him his preference when selecting her seat earlier. He could sit beside her if he had to observe the comings and goings of people, but the odds of him doing that were low.

Sofia looked up from her steaming cup of coffee while Frankie stood silently. She was impeccably dressed despite the early morning hour, and her appearance was as meticulous as yesterday afternoon when Frankie came home early to find her cozily chatting with Evilyn at the dinette table in his home. The tension between them now was palpable, yet there was an undeniable familiarity and vulnerability in both their gazes.

"You could have at least told your goons to let me in the casino this morning," Sofia said, the first to break the silence between them.

"I got the message to meet you here," he replied. "What do you want, Sofia?" Still deciding whether to sit, Frankie asked the question, though he preferred not to hear any answer she might offer him.

"Please, Frankie, sit." Sofia motioned toward the empty bench of the booth opposite her. "I'm not going to bite you." The faint scent of Sofia's sweet perfume mixed with the homely smell of eggs frying and sweet maple syrup poured over freshly griddled and buttered pancakes.

"Here's your coffee, Mr. Grant." As Suzie placed the cup and saucer on the table, Frankie reluctantly slid into the booth facing the wall and his former assistant and mistress. His face was a mask of composure while his heart raced with anticipation and dread. Frankie waited for the waitress to leave, turning his head and shoulders around to ensure no one else was near their booth. When he turned to face Sofia, her eyes locked with his.

"What the hell was that stunt yesterday at the house? Are you crazy for showing up there?"

"I'm not crazy," she replied. "I needed to see you." Her voice was a soft murmur against the background hum of the diner. Sofia had indeed wanted to speak to Frankie, something he had not allowed since their altercation at Carmine's. But her visit with Evilyn was also meant to show her determination and ability to control his actions with the threat of her unspoken secrets. Like the nuclear deterrence of bomb testing outside their city in the Nevada desert, Sofia did not need to use the secret to help Frankie understand its destructive force.

"Well, I'm here now. What's so important?" Frankie's tone was calm, his gaze wary as he scanned her face for clues.

Sofia hesitated while her fingers caressed the handle of her coffee cup. Her hand trembled slightly during her pause, something Frankie had never witnessed in the woman who represented strength and determination. "It's about us, our past, something you don't know. Something significant."

Both Frankie and Sofia wanted to remain calm and controlled. Neither desired a repeat of the scene at Carmine's two weeks prior. Both looked past their anger over one another's recent actions. Instead, they focused on what each needed now. For the moment, an undeclared truce hung in the air, a mutual recognition of each other's strengths and an evaluation of one another's limitations. They both understood a full-out battle against each other would likely lead to mutual destruction.

"What about our past?"

Sofia took a deep breath, her following words spilling out in a rush. "You have a son, Frankie. An older son. *We* have a son."

Her words hit Frankie like a physical blow to the face.

Surprised, he recoiled back into his side of the booth. Frankie burst into laughter, temporarily forgetting his desire to keep their meeting brief and clandestine.

"A son? Why should I believe something like that, Sofia?"

Sofia reached across the table, her hand searching his, but he pulled back and denied her the touch. Frankie's laughter shifted to disbelief over such a rational and efficient business person as herself, the former assistant and mistress he knew so well, could make such a nonsensical and desperate claim. "You *are* crazy," he added.

"He's eighteen now. He's out there somewhere, but he's ours."

"You're not making any sense." Frankie shook his head, a bitter chuckle escaping his lips. "Let's cut the crap, Sofia. What do you want? Money? Your old job back?"

Frankie knew what he wanted. He wanted to get up and leave. Frankie wanted this to be the last time they spoke, the last time he had to deal with her. As valuable as she had been in the past, as much as he needed her services now, and as much as he once thought she was the fire and inspiration in his belly fueling him to the next level of success, dealing with Sofia had become untenable. At first, Sofia wanted a partnership in his business. Then, she wanted him to leave the comfort and security of his wife and children, exploding the world he knew and the reputation he enjoyed, all to be with her. She wanted him to become the cliché of the businessman in a mid-life crisis, leaving his wife and family for the secretary at the office. And now this. An insane fictional story about what, shared parenthood?

"No, it's not about money or the job. It's about our son knowing his father. It's about us maybe being a family." Sofia remained calm, almost as if she were Evilyn conversing with Frankie about what to have for dinner tomorrow. A sensitive and rational woman was sitting across from him now, not the impervious and fiery Italian he knew as Sofia.

"A family?" Frankie's voice is incredulous, his eyes flashing with anger and fear. "I have a family, Sofia. A wife and two kids who know me. What are you trying to do, ruin me with wild accusations?"

Frankie placed the palms of his hands on the red upholstered seat, readying himself to slide out of the booth. He had no time for this. There was too much to do at the casino, and he had already wasted too much time here. Still, Frankie knew Sofia ran on grit and determination. This morning was simply another technique and different approach to achieving her goals. Frankie also knew the resolve and fortitude she was capable of. Sofia's boldness in showing up at his house to sit calmly and chat over afternoon tea with Evilyn yesterday was proof of her resourcefulness. She could have told Evilyn anything, whether lies or the truth, and remained a threat not to be taken lightly. So Frankie placed his hands back on the table, grasping the saucer and cup handle and taking a long and slow sip of hot coffee while refueling with some patience and endurance of his own. When he sat the cup back down, he looked directly into Sofia's eyes and saw they were filling with tears.

"I thought you had a right to know. I thought..." Her words trailed off as she opened her purse to retrieve a tissue, blotting the underside of her eyes dry.

Frankie waited. The clatter of dishes and the murmur of conversation faded into the distance, replaced by The Miracles' "You've Really Got a Hold on Me" playing over the cafe's speakers.

"Where is this supposed son now?" Frankie finally asked.

"I don't know, but we can find him."

"What do you mean you don't know?"

"I don't know because…" Sofia paused again. "I don't know because I had to give him up for adoption." She again patted dry the small amount of wetness from beneath her eyes.

Frankie intended to cross-examine the witness and pick apart Sofia's story with calm logic and questions of surgical precision. The procedure would not take long, he thought.

"And where is the proof?"

Sofia reached into her purse again and placed the envelope on the table. "This is all I have so far. It was a closed adoption. Private. Secret. But he exists. He's your son."

"And how could this be true when we've only known each other for, what, five or six years now?" Though he did not want to be there, Frankie was settling into the line of questioning, almost enjoying the state of her vulnerability. He had never seen Sofia so exposed nor felt so confident he could outmaneuver her.

When Suzie approached with the pot of coffee to top off their cups, Frankie swiftly waved her off politely but intensely, the way individuals engaged in the most private of conversations do.

"It was in Palermo, Frankie. Almost twenty years ago." Sofia did not need to say more.

Frankie leaned back once more, creating as much distance between himself and the memories of his youth sitting across the table from him. He removed his hands from the table and placed them, palm down, upon the red upholstered vinyl again as if preparing to either bolt up and fight or bolt up to exit the booth to take flight. His confidence now felt like exposure. He looked at her and watched as her posture straightened and one eyebrow arched, a look of assuredness gradually surpassing sadness and desperation in her expression. Sofia was now the one who watched and waited for Frankie to speak.

Frankie Grant had been in Palermo nineteen years ago as a young seaman aboard the USS Franklin D. Roosevelt. Palermo was their first port during their long acceptance trials and shakedown voyage at sea. The crew had been given one night's shore leave, on a rotating basis, during their week there. At first, Frankie wasn't going to go ashore. His crewmates relentlessly teased him about staying aboard to write letters to his new wife back in the States. Eventually, the naïve Midwestern teen gave in and joined them. As Frankie searched those distant memories, he remembered the inexperienced teen who had never been away from home and had never drunk alcohol before. The details of that night ashore in Palermo were hazy. Many of them were uncertain. A few of them were unknown.

Sofia watched and waited, absorbing Frankie's indecision as he wrestled with his partial recollections and the believable truths from so long ago churning inside him. The early morning light filtering through the slats of the blinds in the cafe's windows cast striped shadows across the red and black tiled floor, finally reaching the booth in the back where they both sat. To Sofia, its warmth felt like the light of truth.

"And you drop this on me now? After all these years?" A part of Frankie wanted to believe it, to have a firstborn son. His pride tried to believe it, the story of a young American boy, a strong high school athlete, a man in the mighty United States Navy traveling the globe after his country wins a world war; his part in conquering a country and overpowering its people while triumphing over his sexual inexperience. But Frankie already had a firstborn son. He already had a good wife, a daughter, and a successful business. Frankie already had the American dream.

Frankie bolted up and out of the booth, hitting his legs on the table and causing the cups of coffee to splash and spill as he did.

"I don't believe you," he yelled. Gone was any patience and endurance he had before. "Whatever game you're playing, it ends now. Stay away from me, my family, and my business. You hear me, Sofia? Stay the hell away!"

With that, Frankie grabbed the envelope and stormed out of the diner, leaving Sofia alone in the booth in the back of the cafe as the jukebox played softly in the background. He considered ripping the envelope and its contents to shreds and dropping the pieces of paper on the cafe floor but thought better of it. Frankie wanted no evidence of her ridiculous claim left, deciding he would burn the unopened claim at his office instead.

Frankie had arguably won the battle two weeks ago at Carmine's, with Sofia forcibly removed in front of a stunned crowd. Last night, Sofia left Frankie's driveway on her own accord, leaving him exposed and vulnerable with her access to Evilyn and his children and what she might say to them. This morning, however, was a whole new level of stakes and determination for them both.

THE SPLIT

(Present)

Jolted back to reality, Jack stood at the roulette table, unsure of
how long he had been there. No more than a few minutes; he
was sure of it. But he was also sure of what he saw and heard
as the wheel spun and the hard ivory ball bounced off its swirling
frets. Jack's ears rang from the sound of the gunshots. He could
almost smell the gunpowder residue and smoke, the vision of the
figure falling to the ground vivid and fresh in his mind. But when
Jack looked at his watch, the time was 2:14 a.m.—over four hours
since leaving Mike and Sarah at the craps table. He checked his
phone. It, too, read 2:14 a.m.—over four hours since his last text
from Emily upstairs, and that's when a sudden panic surged
through him.

***

She tried to sleep, to put the disappointment behind her, but
all Emily could do was toss and turn. Alone in the room, she had
only her hurt and anger to comfort her. The memories were like
a high-speed train rushing past her as she stood on a subway
platform, a blur and gush of wind hitting her without control and
drowning out any desire to scream in frustration. What good
would screaming do, anyway? The thought of contempt

127

continued, and Emily pleaded with it, begging it to stop. She tried to bargain with it, offering logical consideration in the morning in exchange for a few hours of negotiated calm and serenity now. But she would strike no such agreement this time.

Emily closed her eyes and took deep breaths. Still, the scenes repeatedly replayed in her mind, and she obsessed with every detail—her initial excitement over the surprise trip from Jack followed by her trepidation on the plane. Emily thought about the pool's leisure that morning, the relaxation of the spa's massage in the afternoon, and the sensual embrace of Jack's arms between the two events. She surrendered to his embrace and persuasiveness, as she had done many times before. In the past, whenever Emily thought about leaving Jack, he always found a way to ease her concerns, convincing her he loved her. Each time she wanted to leave him, she fell for him all over again. It is what wives do, her mother would tell her.

Emily thought Jack was perfect for her when they first met. He stopped to rescue her as she stood beside her flat tire that first year in college. Neither had tools nor materials to fix the flat, so Jack traded bicycles with her as the rain fell harder. Emily fell for Jack when he returned her repaired bicycle the next day. She didn't need a man's protection or success. She had that for herself. Emily was instead attracted to Jack's strength and thoughtfulness. His moral compass. His selflessness. Now Emily wondered if Jack was ever who she thought he was.

As the evening's events continued to replay in Emily's unsettled mind, her appreciation of dinner at the Elysian and her excitement and anticipation while walking to the concert quickly melted into surprise and shock at the Colosseum's entrance. Tickets of joy became worthless vouchers of despair. Jack's insistence on their validity was reminiscent of his countless deceptions and dishonesty during his dark years of substance abuse. And then there was the concealment of Casey's illness, the lie about having seen her happily playing with other dogs on their website. *How could he have done that?* Emily reached out to touch and softly stroked the pillow next to her, just as she did each night, to Casey's soft fur as her faithful companion lay between her and Jack on their bed each night. She wanted to reach through the miles and comfort Casey now, to pet away any pain or loneliness she likely felt. Emily wanted Casey to know they were not alone in this dark night of their souls. A single tear flowed down her nose and across her lips into the pillow just as she thought no tears were left to shed.

Emily sat up and took a deep, cleansing breath. Her eyes brightened, adjusting to the dark stillness of the room each time she wiped the wetness and blur from them. Emily no longer questioned whether she should give up on Jack or continue to try to make the relationship work. She would no longer throw good optimism after bad. Emily knew she was in a one-sided relationship and finally accepted it was time to let go. Things were not going to change with Jack. Emily had nothing left; she knew there was nothing left. With this clear-headedness came a renewed determination.

Jumping out of bed, Emily turned on every light in the room and double-checked the swing-bar latch on the door to prevent entry. She then took a shower to wash away any remaining disillusionment and doubt. When done, she wrapped a towel around her wet hair and put her earbuds in, queuing up her favorite Adele playlist. The whole thing was a liberating relief as Emily went to work packing.

***

Emily didn't notice the security bar snap into place when Jack first tried to enter the hotel room. When his second attempt was no more successful, he knocked loudly on the door and tried to peek into the brightly lit room through the small gap allowed by the latch. He knocked again, this time louder and more rapidly.

"Emily? Are you in there?" Jack knocked again. "Let me in, Sweetheart."

A few seconds later, Jack saw a shadow move across the room. He withdrew his face from the space just in time, narrowly missing being hit in the head as Emily slammed the door shut to unlatch the security bar. She did not bother reopening the door, but walked back through the room to continue packing.

As he entered, Jack surveyed the room. "Em, what are you doing?"

"I'm leaving, Jack."

"It's the middle of the night? Where are you going?"

"I'm going home."

"Why are you leaving now? I'm not ready to go yet, Em."

Emily thought about the ridiculousness of the statement, staring at him emotionlessly. Her pause was uncomfortably long before lifting her hands loosely, palms up, in a who cares gesture. "I'm not asking you to come, Jack. I'm on the first flight in the morning."

"But I'm here now, Sweetheart. There's no reason to leave."

Emily cringed at his use of that term of endearment. "That's exactly why I'm leaving now," she answered.

"Come on, Emily. Don't be like that. I'm sorry about the show. That wasn't my fault."

"Whose fault is it, then?" she asked. "Who dragged me out here and then screwed up the tickets, Jack? Who lied to me about Casey being sick?" Emily's eyes watered as she held back years of frustration and exhaustion. "Whose fault was it you lost your job two years ago? Who's to blame for your alcoholism? Who's responsible for your lying around the house all day, gambling online, hiding it from me until we were so far in debt I had to ask my parents for help? My parents, for fuck's sake. Who's to blame, Jack? Am I to blame?"

"No, of course you're not to blame, Em." Thoughts raced through Jack's mind as he struggled to find the right words to regain control of the situation. He could feel his eyes rapidly blink as she stood and watched him with indifference, waiting for his response and refusing to abandon her resolve. Then Jack bent down on one knee and reached into the pocket of his sports coat. "I love you, Em. Look what I've got for you."

Emily watched and thought he looked ridiculous, patting his jacket pockets like a nervous man about to propose. She crossed her arms, forcing herself to remain in the presence of the annoyance, waiting to see what reason or excuse or diversion he would produce next. All Emily wanted to do was continue packing. Why couldn't Jack give her that one small courtesy? How long would she have to fake her interest and hold her impatience at bay?

Jack stood, opened his jacket front, and carefully searched the inner pockets, looking into each one despite his frantic pat down not having produced anything. He clumsily rechecked the outer pockets, looking into them too, hyper-focused on finding the felt box with his trembling fingertips. Emily could hear Jack's hard, visible swallow and nervous voice warbling as he mumbled, "Dammit, where are they?"

"What do you have for me, Jack?" Her tone was short of sarcastic, yet fully incredulous. "Where are *they*?"

Jack shifted from foot to foot and looked down at the carpet.

He retraced his path to the door as if the felt box would magically appear, having somehow fallen from his jacket pocket onto the floor. "Earrings, Em. My anniversary gift for you. They were right here in my..." Jack's words trailed off into the abyss of vulnerability and self-doubt. "I just... You just caught me off guard when I walked in, that's all." Jack awkwardly patted his pockets again, glancing around the room, searching for a rescue or deflection. His thoughts were as scattered and hastily constructed as his stumbling over what to say. His jerky movements searched in vain for the gift not there.

That's when Jack reached into his pocket and pulled out his lucky chip. "Look, I've been on a winning streak all day." He held the chip up for her to see. "It's the chip, Em. I can't lose with the chip."

Emily's mouth slackened, and her eyes widened as disbelief swept over her.

"You still have that stupid poker chip? You told me you turned the envelop in at the front desk. So you lied about that too, Jack?" Emily could hear the pulse of her own beating heart in her ears and could feel her chest tighten, filling with anger. "You've been gambling all day? You've been down there all night gambling while I've been up here sick to my stomach, thinking you were down there somewhere ashamed or sulking about what happened tonight. It's our anniversary, you prick. Instead of spending the time with me, you've been gambling and probably drinking, too."

Any empathy for her husband's past troubles was gone now. Any lingering desire for Jack was now desert dust in the dry, hot wind. Any chance of reconciliation was simply a whisper into the breeze on a cold winter's day.

"No, Em, it's not like that," Jack refuted. "I'm just tired of being a loser, that's all. I'm winning now, see?" Jack unfolded the paper vouchers for his cash-outs and placed them on the bed, separating them. "It's the chip, Em, it's special."

"No, Jack," she snapped back. "What you *had* was special. I am special. My care for you was special." Emily returned to transferring her folded clothes from the dresser drawer to her suitcase. "Ever since we got here, and you found that chip, everything has gone to shit. You're drinking, you're gambling, you're lying. The vet told you Casey is sick. You didn't bother to tell me? She's my dog, damnit! Are you so blind and selfish you can't see what's happening? Can't you see what that damn chip has cost you?"

Emily slammed her suitcase shut and zipped it. Jack reached out his arms to offer comfort as she walked past him, but he had nothing left she wanted.

"Go fuck yourself, Jack." Emily barreled through his outreached arms, her eyes trained on the exit. When the door shut behind her, Jack and his lucky chip clutched in his hand were finally alone.

THE SHOTS

(1963)

Frankie hastily walked the two blocks between Mary's Café and the Casbah, swinging the front doors open before the door attendants could reach the handles to open them for him. Frankie, like all the casino's employees, used the guarded staff entrance on the side of the building. This morning, however, Frankie took the most direct path to his office after his conversation with Sofia at the diner. The jaunt up the stairs to the Eye was swift, and Frankie wasted no time with shortness of breath ascending the steps two at a time.

"Get me Sam Giancarlo on the phone," he demanded, walking over to the large plate glass viewing window. Frankie placed one hand on the window frame and leaned against it, labored to slow his breathing, the effort of his haste now catching up to him. He watched the staff below as they finished their morning sprucing of the gambling floor, vacuuming carpets, carrying boxes of liquor to restock the bars, cleaning the armrests of gaming tables, and polishing the chrome and gold finishes of stool bases and handrails. Flashbacks of his time aboard the Roosevelt, down on the hanger deck abuzz with activity, appeared as he watched the employees below. His crewmates, the importance and seriousness of their duties, and the fun and triviality of the rare times they were granted shore leave. As Frankie's heart rate slowed and fresh supplies of oxygenated blood flowed to his brain, the memories should have become more precise. Some, however, were lost or just too ill-formed to recall.

"Mr. Grant. Mr. Giancarlo is on the line for you."

"I'll take it in my office," he replied to his temporary assistant. She was young but polite. From the Midwest and new to Vegas, she was a waitress hired by Max for the opening. Max sent her to the Eye to help answer the phones and perform small clerical tasks in Sofia's absence.

"Mr. Giancarlo, good morning. It's Frankie. How are you?"

"I'm good. A pleasant surprise, your call. I was just on my way out for a round. How's my favorite new casino?"

"We're good. It's busy. Greed is booming," Frankie nervously chuckled. "I won't keep you long, then."

Sam returned Frankie's chuckle. Greed, indeed, was always booming in Las Vegas. "It's the heartbeat of our world, my boy, and Vegas is its capital."

"Listen, Mr. Giancarlo," Frankie continued, getting right to the point. "I may have a problem with Sofia." He prepared himself for some 'I told you that woman was trouble' reminder from Sam. He had been warned, albeit too late and much after the fact.

"I heard about the nasty incident at Carmine's. On the night of your opening, too," Sam replied. "I understand she left town. They should have locked her up." Naturally, Sam knew about the incident at Carmine's. His knowing Sofia had left town was a bit of a surprise, but Frankie did not have time now to consider how Sam knew. He smirked inwardly over Sam's comment regarding locking her up.

"Yes, well, I saw her this morning. We met at Mary's. She was at my house yesterday. Just popped in for tea and a chat with Evilyn."

"Worlds colliding, Frankie. I told you, family first, business second. There's no room for affairs, especially with a smart-mouthed broad like that. Affairs are messy and bad for business." Frankie had anticipated hearing Sam's opinions when he initiated the call. He was still unclear, however, as to why Sam had taken such a disapproving position against Sofia, someone he was barely acquainted with. "So what did the smart-mouth have to say to your wife?" Sam asked.

"Nothing, yet," Frankie answered. "But she threatened to. There was a bit of a scene in the cafe this morning, too."

"Frankie, listen to me," Sam asserted. "These public spectacles need to stop."

"That's why I'm calling." Frankie chose his following words carefully. "I agree. It needs to stop."

"Say no more, Frankie. Meet me at 190 Hoover Street tonight at ten."

"Oh, tonight? No, I'm sorry, tonight I—"

"Be there and come alone," Sam interjected. "I have something to give you."

The abrupt dial tone cut short anything else Frankie had to say. He momentarily held the phone's black handset to his temple, his new plans for the evening soaking into his brain while contemplating his former plans and how best to change them. Frankie wasn't even sure if there was anything else to say. *Ten o'clock tonight*, he thought. *What could Sam have to give me?*

Frankie had only called Sam to ask for his advice. Or had he called Sam for his help? Frankie wasn't sure now. Perhaps he should have waited to calm down after meeting Sofia instead of hastily calling Sam. Frankie should have allowed Sofia's claim to sink in first, allowing himself time to analyze it, determine its validity, and extract its worth. That was Frankie's problem sometimes: too quick to pull the trigger and too slow to take aim.

Frankie finally lowered the handset and placed it in the phone's cradle. His fingers held the handset a moment longer, though, as he pondered calling Sam back. But to say what, and would anything he said matter? Sam said he was leaving to play golf and was likely gone by now. Releasing the phone's handset, he walked around his desk and sat, tossing the envelope from Sofia into his desk drawer. Reclining in his executive office chair, Frankie crossed his legs and rested his chin on his hands, palms together and fingers interlocked. He sank into deep concentration. Sitting in the chair had been a rare luxury since the Casbah's opening. He had been too busy, but now there was much more than the casino's operation for him to consider.

When Evilyn stopped by the Casbah a few hours later, her visit surprised Frankie. Given his busy schedule, she did not like interrupting her husband at work. Evilyn didn't wholly approve of gambling but understood the casino was a business, and her husband was a businessman. She consciously focused on the hotel and restaurant services of the company over the gambling, helping her reconcile how her husband earned his income and how they fed, clothed, and housed their children. Frankie was still in his office when they announced her arrival. After speaking to Sam, he dismissed every other call and interruption. Evilyn, of course, took priority over his deep focus and would get his full attention.

"Please ask her to meet me in the Oasis Grill," Frankie told his temporary assistant. "I'll be right down."

As they were seated, Evilyn explained she had some errands to run nearby and thought she would surprise him for lunch. "I haven't been here since the opening," she said, ordering an iced tea while Frankie followed with the same. "It certainly has calmed down."

"It was an exciting day," Frankie agreed. His mind went to the worst possible scenario for Evilyn being there. Had Sofia gotten to her already? That was unlikely. Evilyn's style would not be to drop by work for lunch and casually discuss extramarital affairs. No, Evilyn would cook her cheating husband his favorite dinner, clean the kitchen, tuck the kids into bed, pour Frankie a bourbon, and calmly ask him whether the rumors or her intuitions were valid. She would be kind and respectful. A public scene would not be Evilyn's style. Infidelity would be a private family matter to discuss and resolve for the mutual benefit of all family members and public reputations. Evilyn was very much like Sam in that regard.

"Frankie?" Evilyn repeated.

"Oh, sorry," Frankie responded, shaken from his reverie. "What was that, Evie?"

"I was just asking what you were thinking for lunch."

"Yeah, a Caesar salad sounds good."

"Everything alright, dear?" she asked.

"Yes, just lost in work, that's all. Not enough coffee this morning, I guess." Frankie smiled and reached for Evilyn's hand, grasping and holding it above the tabletop, giving her hand a little squeeze to show his appreciation for her concern.

Throughout their pleasant lunch in the relaxing retreat of the Oasis Grill, Frankie wanted to tell Evilyn about Sofia. He wanted to come clean about the affair. Frankie considered informing her of the incident at Carmine's. He was surprised gossip had not already informed her of the ugly event. Frankie wanted to tell his wife firing Sofia was the reason for her absence, not a family visit somewhere in another state. He needed to warn Evilyn about Sofia's new accusations and the threat she posed to his business and their family. He needed to inform her a friendly visit for tea in their home was a clandestine mission to infiltrate their family structure, a coercive attack from within.

Finished with their salads and the plates cleared, Evilyn searched her pocketbook to retrieve something. Frankie watched her maneuver the mirrored compact to reapply her lipstick, puckering her lips and carefully smoothing the vibrant yet classy color. Evilyn snapped the compact shut, looked up, and fixed her gaze on him with a knowing smile as if she had just completed a well-rehearsed performance.

"Evie," he said, taking a deep, pained breath and closing his eyes to shield himself from her stare. Frankie wished he could go back and change what had happened. He wanted to confess and cleared his throat. "Evie, I'm sorry, but…"

"What is it, dear?"

"Evie, I love you, and …"

"Aww, I love you, too."

"Evie," he continued, "I'm sorry, but I've got to work tonight. There's a meeting at ten, and—"

"Oh, Frankie. Really? So late? Do you have to?"

"I'm afraid, yes. It's important."

Evilyn glanced down momentarily, putting her compact and lipstick back into her purse before looking back into her husband's eyes. She smiled again and patted his large hands with reassurance and understanding. "I'll wait up for you, dear."

Hoover Street was a depressed stretch of old Vegas, lined with rows of aging warehouses leaning into the darkness that cast long, eerie shadows. At night, the street transformed into a menacing labyrinth of narrow, winding alleys where the air smelled of filth and decay. Flickering streetlights, more often than not shrouded in the mist from the nearby industrial district, barely penetrated the oppressive gloom.

It hadn't always been this way. In its heyday, Hoover Street was the beating heart of Las Vegas's industrial and commercial efforts. Constructed in the 1940s and 1950s, the streets and buildings of the area were integral to the city's supply chain, storing everything from construction materials for the expanding strip to goods and provisions for the local businesses and casinos beginning to dot the landscape. Now, Hoover Street at night was where the city's underbelly came to life, a deserted and dangerous no-man's-land where a wrong turn could mean the difference between life and death.

With their chipped and crumbling brick exteriors and broken windows, the warehouses stood as silent sentinels to the illicit activities within their walls. Graffiti and faded, peeling posters clung to the brick walls, remnants of a forgotten past. The occasional distant siren or the muffled roar of an engine as a car sped down the street punctuated the silence of the area in the after-hours. Frankie thought the location was an odd and uncomfortable place for Sam to want to rendezvous at any hour of the day. Their meeting place must be the secret storage location of whatever Sam wanted to give Frankie.

Dark alleys crisscrossed the area, leading to dead ends, shadowy doorways, and rooms where unsavory deals were commonplace, the deals forever altering the lives they entangled. Crates and barrels, haphazardly stacked, created the perfect cover for anyone seeking to remain unseen.

Frankie parked his car on the other side of Hoover Street, across from the address Sam gave him, under one of the few dimly lit working street lamps. He exited his car and looked in both directions, then up toward rooflines and broken glass windows. Frankie crossed the street to enter the dark entrance before finding the lit room and two gentlemen waiting for him. After shaking hands and exchanging pleasantries, Sam's driver motioned for Frankie to sit. Sam was already sitting on the other side of the small table. The makeshift arrangement of a table and two chairs was purposeful amongst the decay of the expanded space with its exposed beams and half-removed walls.

Being anywhere near 190 Hoover Street at that time of night was dangerous. Their discussion was to be private, but following Frankie there had been easy. Still, the uninvited figure hiding in the shadows could not help but inch forward to better look at the two men and hear their conversation. Despite his reluctance to attend, Frankie Grant was there. A business owner like himself in Las Vegas can only decline or delay offers from The Alliance so many times.

"Look, Frankie, I understand," Sam spoke empathetically as he leaned forward, calm and confident. "We all want to be kings of our castles. But even kings need allies. It's like treaties between countries. Agreements and accords. No king stands alone. We all need partnerships. You know, people we can trust for help when enemies attack. We gotta all stand together here, Frankie. Like a family, you know?"

"Mr. Giancarlo, I appreciate—"

"Please, Frankie, it's Sam," he interrupted, smiling and leaning back in his chair. Sam brought his palms into his chest as if he would caress his own heart before sharing a piece of it. "You're a success now, Frankie. The Casbah is open. We're family, so talk to me like a brother." He leaned back into the intimate yet intimidating conversation, his eyes fixed and focused on Frankie's apprehension.

The fat envelope lay in the middle of the table between the two men as they debated the concepts and merits of independence and interdependence, autonomy, and business interactions. Each had their own agendas and goals. Each also had their own instructions. They were playing a high-stakes game, and only one could emerge the winner this time. Frankie had already had one too many pushes, and neither the dealer nor the player had won.

Cigar smoke filled the stale air of the dim room as Frankie hesitated. He finally reached for the envelope with his left hand and rose to shake Sam's hand with his right. Frankie was both relieved and frightened as he did. Sam's investment in the just-opened Casbah Hotel and Casino was now secure—their arrangement and partnership sealed. There were no contracts to sign or lawyers to review terms. The handshake was binding and the only thing required. The handshake was as good as a blood oath. Sam had dealt Frankie a hand he did not want, and although Frankie was holding the cash, Sam and The Alliance won the game. As they shook and exchanged salutations before exiting through separate doors, the slender figure in the darkness slowly backed away from the silent vantage point in the shadows so as not to be discovered.

After Sam exited the room, Frankie returned the envelope to the center of the table and sat down again. He savored the remainder of his cigar like a convicted man, relishing the last few minutes of his freedom. Frankie contemplated the weight of his action for twenty minutes. All circumstances have options, and all decisions have costs. Some people benefit while some people pay. Frankie was trying to decide on which side of the coin the people he cared for would land.

Frankie pondered the weight of his decision. There was more at stake than personal gain or loss or business success or failure. His choice was a ripple that would touch the lives of those he cared for. Sofia deemed the partnership necessary, and without Sam's intervention and The Alliance, the Casbah would not have received a gaming license or now be open. But what Sofia believed did not matter now. Evilyn would have been vehemently against the deal had she known. And what of Richard and Lucy? How their father's association with members of organized crime would impact them in the future could not be anticipated or known.

The irony of power and control struck Frankie. How often they are but illusions in the face of inevitable outcomes. As the ash from his cigar fell, so did his certainty he had made the right decision.

Frankie exited through the front door of the abandoned building and walked toward his car, cutting through the chilly desert air befalling the City of Sin at night. The time was nearly eleven o'clock, and as he pressed the door handle's button to open the driver's door, he realized how hungry he was. Frankie knew his children would be safely in bed by now and wondered if Evilyn had saved him some warm dinner in the oven. She had, of course. She always did.

"Grant!" the voice shouted out from behind.

As he turned, the first shot cut through the clear night air and hit Frankie in the stomach. The second and third shots cut through his jacket and shirt to hit him squarely in the chest. As the bullets drove him backward, he tried to brace himself against the car door's interior handle with his right hand, but his shoulder slid against the door panel on his way down. The fourth shot pierced his arm as his assailant walked closer to him. Frankie was a big man, the kind of man who goes down to the ground slowly, unwillingly. He murmured something, struggling to reach into his vest pocket for something precious. But his struggle ceased when the fifth, and then final sixth shot, struck Frankie. His head slowly fell to rest in the pool of dark blood forming under his large frame on the pavement, illuminated only by the dimly lit streetlamp above where he lay.

After removing the precious something from Frankie's vest pocket, the dark figure strode into the still-darker shadows of the adjacent buildings and the lights and glamor of the Vegas strip in the distance.

THE NEWS

The wail of sirens pierced the early morning calm as the ambulance sped through the streets of Las Vegas. The first rays of sunlight also pierced the dawn tranquility as the first beams of daybreak shone through the Sunrise Mountain range east of the city, gradually illuminating the town and surrounding desert.

Inside, two ambulance attendants worked frantically over Frankie, strapped to the gurney with gunshot wounds marring his body. From what they could tell, the attack had occurred hours before, and now, in the early hours of dawn, he was clinging to life as they approached Southern Nevada Memorial Hospital.

The ambulance screeched to a halt at the emergency room entrance. The back doors flew open, and the attendants swiftly pulled the gurney out, shouting urgent medical jargon to the night shift doctors and nurses, who had already been alerted by the radio call and rushed to meet them.

"Gunshot victim! Six wounds from what we can tell," one of them yelled as they wheeled Frankie inside, the hospital's fluorescent lights glaring down on the grim scene.

Dr. Moore, the on-duty trauma surgeon, took immediate charge. "Get him to ICU! Let's move, people!"

Frankie's face was pale, a stark contrast to the dark patches of blood soaking through the makeshift bandages. His breathing was shallow and his pulse weak. The ambulance attendants rattled off his vitals as the team maneuvered the gurney through the swinging doors and into the emergency room, where stainless steel instruments and special equipment lay ready for serious trauma arrivals.

"BP is dropping, 70 over 40! We've got a pneumothorax on the right side and severe bleeding from the abdomen," a nurse reported, her voice steady despite the chaos.

Dr. Moore quickly assessed the situation, his eyes scanning Frankie's wounds. "We need to stabilize him. Prep for a chest tube and get the O-negative blood ready. Let's intubate him now."

The room buzzed with controlled urgency. Nurses and assistants moved with practiced precision, hooking Frankie up to monitors, inserting IV lines, and prepping surgical equipment. The flurry of medical activity and the rhythmic scratching and printing of EKG readings filled the air.

Frankie's consciousness wavered, a dim awareness of the flurry around him as he fought against the encroaching darkness. Images of his life flickered in his mind—the bright lights of his casino, the faces of his loved ones, the sharp crack of gunfire echoing in the streets.

"Stay with us, Mr. Grant," Dr. Moore stated as he inserted the chest tube, releasing the trapped air in his chest with a hiss.

A nurse held up a clear bag of plasma and swiftly connected it to the IV. "Transfusion started," she announced.

Dr. Moore's hands moved deftly, his focus unbroken. "We need to locate the internal bleeding. Get me a portable X-ray now."

The room's intensity was palpable, every second crucial. Outside, a police officer entered, seeking information from the hospital staff and the ambulance attendants. "Do we know what happened?" he asked.

One of the ambulance attendants shook his head. "We found him lying in the street. It was called in, but no one was there when we arrived. No witnesses."

Inside the ICU room, the battle for Frankie's life continued. "Heart rate is stabilizing, but we're not out of the woods yet," Dr. Moore said, his voice a blend of focus and determination.

As the minutes ticked by, the hospital team's relentless efforts showed signs of hope. Frankie's vitals steadied. The transfusion took effect, and the immediate threat of pneumothorax was mitigated. But the underlying danger remained, with bullets still lodged inside and internal damage yet to be fully addressed.

"We need to get him to the OR, STAT people," Dr. Moore instructed. "Notify the surgical team. We're running out of time."

The gurney moved again, wheeled swiftly towards the operating room, where a longer and more intricate fight awaited. The hospital's corridors echoed their mission's urgency, a relentless race against death.

As they prepped Frankie for surgery, the mystery of his shooter lingered.

***

Evilyn raced toward the hospital's emergency entrance; Lucy cradled in one arm while her fingers tightened around Richard's hand. Urgency fueled her every step as she ushered them through the sliding glass doors, her heart hammering in her chest. The harsh glare of overhead fluorescents bathed the sterile environment in stark light, revealing the intense pace of medical staff and the muted concern of patients and visitors already there.

As Evilyn approached the front desk and put Lucy down, a wave of anxiety washed over her. She told Richard to take his little sister and sit down, instructing them to be still until she could join them. Evilyn clutched her purse tightly to her chest, her fingers trembling with fear and uncertainty, as she turned to the nurse behind the check-in desk. "I need to see my husband, Frankie Grant. He was brought in," she stammered, her voice polite but barely above a whisper. "He's been shot."

The nurse looked up and saw Evilyn's distraught expression. "Of course, ma'am. Let me check for you," she said, her fingers flying over the clipboards as she searched for information.

"Mommy, is Daddy going to be okay?" Richard's voice trembled with fear, his eyes wide with concern.

"Do as I asked and take Lucy over there to sit down, please."

Moments stretched into eternity as Evilyn waited, her heart racing with every passing second. Finally, after two phone calls, the receptionist looked up, her expression grave. "Mrs. Grant, your husband has been taken to the intensive care unit. He's in surgery now. Follow me, and I'll take you to the ICU waiting area," she said, her voice filled with sympathy.

Evilyn gathered her children close, wrapping them in a comforting embrace. "The doctors are helping Daddy now," she reassured them, her voice tinged with uncertainty.

With a nod of gratitude, Evilyn followed the nurse through the maze of corridors, her footsteps echoing against the linoleum floors. The journey felt endless, despite each step bringing her closer to the moment she could see her husband and speak to the doctors.

As they reached the ICU waiting area, Evilyn's heart leaped

into her throat at the sight of the swinging doors leading to the treatment rooms beyond. Frankie was likely in one of those rooms before surgery and would likely return to one after. With a deep breath to steady her nerves, Evilyn tried to view what was behind those doors in search of her husband.

"If you would like to have a seat, Mrs. Grant," the nurse instructed. "We'll let the doctors know you're here now."

Sitting and waiting was all Evilyn had done all night. She became concerned when Frankie failed to call to let her know he was on the way home. She would usually ask him if he had eaten and if she should heat some leftovers. Frankie would answer her and give her an estimate of when he would get home. Evilyn would have some dinner heated anyway, just in case he had changed his mind. That's the way they worked together as husband and wife.

Evilyn's concern escalated to worry when midnight arrived. She called the casino at 1:00 a.m. to see if he was there. When he wasn't, she waited until 2:00 a.m. to phone Carmine's, whose bar stayed open as late as its clientele required. When Frankie was not there either, Evilyn waited until 3:00 a.m. before deciding to get dressed, 'just in case.' Her kitchen phone rang at 5:30 a.m. as she sipped a freshly brewed coffee. At the time, she debated whether to greet Frankie with relief or resentment when he walked through the side door from the driveway. The call changed everything. Within minutes, Evilyn had the children awakened, dressed, and rushing to the hospital.

Lucy's lower lip quivered, her eyes brimming with tears. "I want Daddy to be alright," she whimpered, her small hands clutching Evilyn's tightly.

A sympathetic smile touched Evilyn's lips as she brushed a gentle hand over Lucy's hair. "I know, darling. We all want Daddy to be alright," she murmured, her heart aching with their shared worry.

Just then, a familiar face appeared in the doorway—Evilyn's best friend and kind-hearted neighbor, Jean Jenkins, who lived down the street in Paradise Palms. Evilyn breathed a sigh of relief at the sight of her, grateful for the support she offered. "Jean, thank you for coming," Evilyn greeted her with a weary smile, her voice tinged with gratitude.

Mrs. Jenkins nodded, her expression filled with concern. "Of course, dear. I'll take the children home with me while you sort things out here," she offered kindly, her warm presence a comfort amidst the chaos of the hospital. "I assume no school today? I can get them ready and take them if you like?"

Evilyn nodded in appreciation, her heart swelling with gratitude for her friend's generosity. "No. Let's keep them home today. They've already had a traumatic morning." Evilyn's voice quivered as she added, "But would you call the school for me? I don't know what I would do without you."

"Of course, dear. You call me when you know something."

Evilyn kissed and hugged Richard and Lucy before Mrs. Jenkins ushered them out of the waiting room. She watched them go, a bittersweet mix of relief and sadness washing over her. With her children safely in Mrs. Jenkins' care, she could focus all her attention on Frankie and the uncertainty ahead.

The hours passed as Evilyn waited in the sparsely occupied room, the quiet hum of the air conditioner punctuating the silence. She clasped her hands tightly in her lap, her knuckles white, as she stared at the clock on the wall. The clock's second hand slowly and methodically ticked away the time as Evilyn's mind drifted back to the early days of her relationship with Frankie. They had met at a high school dance, introduced formally by a mutual friend, and spent the rest of the night talking and dancing. Frankie seemed so charming and confident, his laughter infectious, his eyes filled with a mischievous glint, drawing her in instantly. He was a farm boy who dreamed of adventure and something bigger. She was the daughter of a wealthy businessman and a devoted wife and mother, focused on maintaining the highest standards for her family. Frankie and Evilyn were instantly attracted to one another, longing to taste and touch the worlds from which each other came.

Their marriage was quick, just after graduating high school and before Frankie enlisted in the Navy. College and starting a family would have to wait, so they did. The remaining years were mostly filled with happiness, a rich tapestry of joyful moments and shared challenges. Frankie's ambition had taken them from modest beginnings to the bustling world of casinos and high stakes. Throughout their marriage, Evilyn remained his steadfast support. She had seen him at his best and his worst. She celebrated his victories and consoled him in defeat. Evilyn's devotion to Frankie and their children had never wavered, a constant in their fast-paced and ever-challenging lives.

But now, as she sat alone in the cold, impersonal waiting room, fear gnawed at the edges of her mind. What would happen to her and the children if Frankie didn't survive the surgery? Richard was at the cusp of adolescence while Lucy clung to her innocence. They both adored their father, and the thought of them growing up without him was unbearable.

Evilyn tried to push the dark thoughts aside, but they continued to creep in, one after another. What would she do with a business she was never comfortable with, at least not sincerely or totally? How would she support the family? She had always been the rock of stability, the one who kept everything together. Still, without Frankie, she felt the foundations of her world trembling. Evilyn couldn't imagine life without his presence, laughter, and strength.

When the door to the ICU swung open, Evilyn's breath caught in her throat. A doctor in scrubs approached—his expression drawn with fatigue but carrying an air of professional composure. She stood up; her legs were shaky as she braced herself for the news that would either shatter her world or give her a glimmer of hope.

"Mrs. Grant? Hello, I'm Dr. Moore." He extended his hand to her, but his face was unreadable.

"Doctor, how is he? Is he going to be okay?" Evilyn's voice trembled with worry.

Dr. Moore smiled sympathetically, relinquishing the handshake and motioning her to sit. "He's alive, Mrs. Grant. We've stabilized his condition, but he's still critical. They're wrapping up the surgery, and we're doing everything possible."

Relief washed over Evilyn, albeit tempered by the gravity of the situation. She nodded, grateful for his presence and update. "What happened, Doctor?"

"I can only say, Mrs. Grant, your husband suffered multiple gunshot wounds."

Evilyn wanted to interrupt as the questions flooded her brain. *But why? By whom? Where?* Instead, she listened and tried to keep her emotions at bay.

"Some of the wounds to the chest cavity are very serious," he continued. "In this instance, there is some benefit that your husband carried extra weight on him, and the projectiles were of a smaller caliber."

"Can I see him now?" she asked.

"I'm afraid not, Mrs. Grant, not yet. He's still in surgery. We'll move him to an ICU recovery room for monitoring and then a regular ICU room. Your husband's going to be unconscious for some time while we work to stabilize him."

With each piece of information, Evilyn shook her head to acknowledge Dr. Moore's words. However, questions continued to surge within her heart and mind. *Is he going to be alright? Will there be any permanent damage? How long will he need to stay here? What am I going to tell my children?* She was still clutching her purse close to her chest. She had picked her purse up when Dr. Moore first approached her, gripping it to shield herself from any bad news that might slip from the doctor's mouth.

"Perhaps you should go home and rest while we're at this stage. We can call you if there's any—"

"No," she quickly interjected. "Thank you, Doctor," she continued in a quieter, calmer tone, "but I'll stay here if you don't mind."

"Of course, Mrs. Grant. Perhaps there's someone you can call to wait with you, then?"

"Thank you, Doctor." Evilyn nodded in appreciation and again lowered her purse to the floor beside her chair.

Dr. Moore returned the response and turned to walk back through the swinging doors while Evilyn sank into the waiting room chair, her mind swirling with fear and uncertainty. She barely had a moment to collect her thoughts before a uniformed police officer approached her, his expression grave.

"Mrs. Grant, I'm Officer Thompson. I need to ask you a few questions about what happened tonight," he said, his tone serious.

"Officer." Evilyn quickly stood, extending her hand as she mentally loaded her list of questions and fired them at the officer.

"Can you tell me what happened, please? What do you know about what happened to my husband? Who shot Frankie? Why? Are you looking for someone yet?"

"All we know, Ma'am, is that Mr. Grant was found in the early morning hours on Hoover Street, lying beside his car."

"Hoover Street? Where's that?"

"It's an industrial area, Ma'am. Not much in the way of open businesses. You don't know why he would be there, do you?"

"Why Frankie was *there*," Evilyn responded. "No, why would he be there?"

"That's what we'd like to know, Mrs. Grant. Can you tell me when you last saw your husband?"

"Yesterday. We had lunch at the casino. Frankie told me he had a meeting at 10:00 p.m., but—"

"That's the Casbah, correct? The new casino."

"Yes, that's right."

"Ten o'clock is rather late in the evening for a meeting, isn't it?"

"No, not always," Evilyn answered. "Not in Las Vegas. Not when you own a casino and hotel. You understand that, right?" Evilyn's mood began to tense; she felt unsettled and slightly dismayed by the officer's questions. Why weren't they out there interviewing witnesses or looking for whoever shot her husband? Why couldn't they tell her what happened?

"If you don't mind, Mrs. Grant, perhaps we could have a seat." The officer proceeded to question Evilyn about the events leading up to Frankie's shooting, probing for any details to shed light on the circumstances surrounding the attack. Evilyn recounted everything she knew, from their lunch at The Oasis to the unexpected phone call early that morning to her frantic rush to the hospital.

As she spoke, Evilyn's thoughts drifted to the unanswered questions lingering in her mind. Who would want to harm Frankie, and why? And what would become of their lives if he didn't pull through? With each question and passing moment, the weight of uncertainty pressed upon Evilyn's shoulders. But amidst the fear and doubt, one thing remained clear. Evilyn would do whatever was necessary to ensure her husband's survival, no matter the cost.

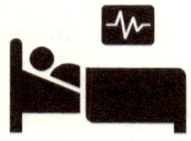

THE PROMISE

F rankie lay motionless in the hospital bed, the slow beep of the heart monitor a stark reminder of his fragile hold on life. He was in critical condition but alive, trapped in a coma that rendered him a silent bystander of the world around him.

The day following his emergency surgery, doctors told Evilyn the anesthesia needed time to wear off, and his unconsciousness was normal. On the second day, they advised her his body needed additional rest from the trauma endured from both the shooting and the surgery. When Frankie remained unconscious into the third evening, Dr. Moore consulted with Evilyn, informing her complications during recovery often emerge. The doctors would run additional tests.

With the help of Mrs. Jenkins and other neighbors and friends, Evilyn spent as much time at Frankie's side as she could. She held his hand, read to him, and talked about where they might go on their next vacation. She updated him on the school projects Richard and Lucy were working on. Evilyn mentioned nothing about the shooting. She relayed no information regarding the police investigation since there was not much to report. The hospital and doctors allowed no general visitors during his time in the ICU, which was okay with Evilyn since she wanted none.

Except for the frequent comings and goings of nurses and doctors for his care, Evilyn spent every minute by Frankie's side, leaving only to go home and check on their children, shower, and change clothes. She ate hospital food when she ate and slept by his side in the room's pale blue recliner pushed up to his bedside.

On the fifth day of Frankie's unconsciousness, Dr. Moore sat Evilyn down to explain what it meant when a person is in a prolonged state of unconsciousness, unresponsive to their environment, and cannot be awakened, even with vigorous stimulation. The fifth day is when Dr. Moore used the word 'coma' for the first time.

It was true. Frankie did not exhibit purposeful movements. There had been no response to any external stimuli. He had not spoken or exhibited any form of non-verbal communication. Frankie's eyes remained closed and had not opened spontaneously since his arrival after the shooting. Though he could not move or speak, Frankie's mind *was* alert. He was processing events around him in the dimly lit and cold hospital room.

After Dr. Moore's prognosis that Frankie might never regain consciousness and, if he did, might remain in a vegetative state, Evilyn brought Richard and Lucy to visit with their father. Clutching their small hands tightly, Evilyn guided them to their father's bedside. Richard tried to be brave for his younger sister, moving forward to grasp his father's large, still hands through the bed's side rails. Lucy clung to her mother, her innocent eyes wide and filled with tears.

"Daddy, please wake up," Lucy whispered, her voice trembling. Following Richard's lead, she reached out to touch Frankie's hand, her tiny fingers barely encircling his. Richard stood silently, his eyes fixed on the floor, unable to look at his father's unnatural state of stillness and defenselessness or the mass of tubes and monitoring wires surrounding him.

Evilyn's heart broke as she watched her children struggle to understand. She kneeled beside them, her voice gentle and reassuring. "Daddy's just resting right now, but he can hear you. Keep talking to him, okay?"

Frankie felt a deep pang of sorrow as he listened to a cloud of his children's voices, sensing their confusion and worry. He wished he could reach out and comfort them, telling them everything would be okay. But Frankie remained still, his thoughts swirling in a tempest of helplessness within.

Hours later, after Evilyn had taken the children home, other shadows of chatter in hushed tones crept into Frankie's consciousness. They felt dark and foreboding and were more difficult to understand or to know if they were real, unlike the certainty he felt when his family was there a few hours earlier. No, these shadows of awareness felt cold and calculating, almost like a storm brewing in the distance. Frankie strained to catch snippets of conversation, fragments of words slipping through the fog of his semiconsciousness.

'...Casbah...'

'...our interests...'

'...Evilyn is weak...'

The sinister undertones sent chills through Frankie's already cold body as he tried to piece together what he was experiencing, the voices he recognized but could not place. His mind, trapped in a state of inescapable paralysis, recoiled at the implications of what he was sensing. Frankie knew these were not the voices of his loved ones but of those seeking to exploit his vulnerability.

Sam's voice, unmistakable and confident, filtered through the haze. *"Our plans for the Casbah need to remain on track. We can't afford any interference, especially from Evilyn."*

Sofia's response was cold and venomous. *"Don't worry, she's too busy hoping for a miracle to interfere. I'll keep her distracted."*

Frankie's heart was desperate to warn Evilyn and protect her and their children. His body betrayed him, however. Frankie was trapped in silence, unable to act or speak. The darkness around him tightened as the cold reality of his helplessness sank in. If he could only move a finger, a slight twitch to let someone know he was in there, aware of what was happening. But he couldn't. Frankie was locked in isolation, with only his memories and regrets. His mind whirled about his childhood, ambitions, wife and children, business, success, and greed. He wanted so much. He had wanted it all. Frankie thought he could have it all, and in many ways, he did—Evilyn's unwavering support, the laughter of his children, the love carrying them through so much. Now, the simplest of movements would be a gift.

Frankie understood the danger looming over his family and his beloved Casbah. He surged with frustration and anger, desperate to warn Evilyn about the threat posed by Sam and Sofia. Frankie wanted to tell Evilyn everything, to admit to his affair with Sofia and the betrayal of his family. He had been close to telling Evilyn everything the day of the shooting at the Oasis Grill. He had chosen not to, though, and now he couldn't. Frankie's body refused to obey, leaving him trapped in his silence.

Evilyn returned to the hospital later that evening. Exhausted, she sat beside his bed and rested her hand on his. Evilyn's eyes watered as she whispered, "Frankie, dear, please wake up." Her voice broke as she remembered their last lunch together the day of the shooting. She had smiled and patted his large hands with reassurance and understanding after he informed her of his late-night meeting. She said she would wait up for him, and she had.

"Frankie," she continued after pausing, "I know I haven't supported you in every way possible. I haven't always been there for you in the way you needed me." Evilyn spoke slowly and with intent, carefully choosing her words while letting her heart say what needed to be said. "Frankie, I promise I'll get involved in running the Casbah. We can do this together. I know how much the casino means to you. I'll do whatever it takes to keep our family and you happy. Just come back to us, dear."

In his coma, Frankie processed the weight of her words, the depth of her commitment. He reflected on their life's challenges and the love sustaining them. Frankie now knew Evilyn was stronger than he had ever given her credit for. He knew now she would find a way to protect their family and the Casbah.

As the next few days passed, Frankie's condition remained unchanged. He continued to absorb the fragments of conversations, the tender moments with his children, and the unspoken fears permeating the room where he lay still and silent. Gradually, he accepted the essence of his life's story—the relentless pursuit of success and recognition, the joyful bonds of family, the perils of unrestrained ambition, and the constant shadow of betrayal. Frankie had gambled away the most precious thing imaginable: gratitude for what he already had.

On the thirteenth day following the shooting, Frankie's mind grew quiet. A profound sense of peace replaced his fear and frustration as he took his last breath. Frankie knew Evilyn would fight for their legacy, and his children would grow up with the strength and resilience he had always admired in others. As Evilyn's sobs echoed through the room, the dawn broke over the desert horizon, casting the warm glow of sunlight over the hospital room and Frankie Grant's lifeless body.

BLACK JACK

(Present)

E mily was gone. Hours after their argument, Jack sat in the room's only chair, alone and despondent in the dimly lit hotel room, the remnants of their last encounter scattered around him. The pillows and bedsheets were in twisted disarray from Emily's tossing and turning while Jack was downstairs on the casino floor. Jack's sports coat lay on the floor where he had tossed it after turning its pockets inside out, looking for his anniversary gift for her. The tickets to the concert she did not attend lay on the coffee table, ripped in half, as useless now as before. The room was empty and cold, the silence deafening, broken only by the faint echo of Emily's words and the stinging realization of their truth.

Jack clutched the lucky chip in his hand, staring at the plastic disk as his mind raced, replaying every moment of the evening and the events that drove Emily away. He stared at the chip as if it could explain what had happened. Jack shifted his gaze toward his nightstand, where he found the yellowed envelope and the old chip just yesterday. How could so much have happened in just one day? Where did this poker chip come from?

Jack strained to remember the handwriting on the old envelope containing the chip before tossing it in a garbage can on the casino floor early that morning while waiting for Emily. Jack recalled the envelope's red letterhead that read 'Casbah Hotel and Casino.' He was sure of that. But his memory of the envelope's handwriting was not as clear. He remembered words: "Sofia," and "Sorry," and "Frank." No, it said "Frankie." Jack remembered Emily telling him, "You're not Frankie," when he opened it after she told him not to. Yes, Jack remembered Emily's exact words: "It says Frankie," she had said. "You are not Frankie, Jack." For the first time since discovering it, Jack had more interest in the envelope than exhilaration over its contents. He wondered about the Casbah Hotel and Casino and who Sofia was. Why was Frankie sorry?

Jack's thoughts drifted back to when he and Emily first met, remembering the flat tire and the rain bringing them together. Emily's eyes—deep, ocean blue—sparkled on even the most overcast day. He used to get lost in those eyes, finding solace and love in their depths. Those early years were filled with love and promise before everything unraveled. How had such a strong bond and bright future spiraled into the slow, insidious creep of his addictions and the fracture of their relationship?

There was a time when Emily's laughter was light and infectious. It could lift Jack's spirits no matter how dark the day. But that was before the addiction, before the late nights that stretched into early mornings, before the lies and the broken promises.

It started innocently enough—occasional drinks with colleagues after a long workday, cocktails during client dinners, harmless bets on sporting events, and monthly poker nights with the guys. Jack told himself it was just a way to unwind, a slight reprieve from the stress. But soon, those drinks became a nightly ritual, and online gambling became a secret escape, a thrill he chased in the quiet hours after Emily had gone to bed. He didn't notice the subtle changes at first—a missed deadline here, a careless mistake there—but they began accumulating, snowballing into late nights, mounting debt, and the suffocating guilt every time he logged in to place another bet. Emily had no idea what he was doing. By the time she found out and confronted Jack, it was too late. His colleagues lost respect for him, clients complained, and his performance plummeted. Eventually, the firm unjustly fired him from the Sales Executive role he once took pride in. That's how Jack saw it, at least.

Jack remembered one night in particular when he came home late with the stench of whiskey on his breath. Emily had been waiting up, her eyes red from crying. "This has to stop, Jack," she'd pleaded, her voice trembling. But he brushed past her, mumbling an apology that neither believed. The walls were closing in, he claimed—the pressure of meeting sales targets, the competition from peers, and the unreasonable demands of an overbearing manager.

Another memory surfaced—Emily standing by the living room window, her shoulders slumped in defeat as she watched him storm out to his car and leave for another long evening drive. Jack said the quiet time helped him clear his head, but those drives only widened the distance between them until all that was left was a hollow shell of what they had meant to one another.

Jack shook his head, trying to push the negative memories away, but they clung to him, a constant reminder of what he had lost and what he still stood to lose. He knew he had hurt Emily in ways that would not be easily repaired, and no matter how much time had passed, the guilt was always there, lurking just beneath the surface.

As he sat there, the weight of his actions pressed heavily on his chest. Jack saw the pattern of his behavior—the endless search for validation, the lies, and the selfishness. He had inherited his father's alcoholism and absorbed his mother's emotional distancing. What began as adolescent escapism into video games had matured into far more dangerous diversions. Jack began to understand how his obsession with success and the chip had driven a wedge between him and everything he loved.

Jack could almost hear Emily's voice, her final words echoing in the quiet room. "I am special. My care for you was special." He realized how right she was. He had taken her love and trust for granted, believing everything else would fall into place as long as he kept winning. Jack's actions were aimed at conquering his past demons, not at caring for the woman who was his present.

The once inviting hotel room now felt like a prison, its dim light highlighting Jack's isolation and reflecting the dark state of his mind. The lucky chip in his hand felt heavier than ever. It was cold, a tangible reminder of everything he had lost.

Jack finally accepted that his obsession with the chip and his lying cost him the most valuable thing in his life. Emily's departure was not just about the concert, the earrings, his gambling, or the chip. Her leaving was about his broken promises, lies, deception, and selfishness. The lucky chip was not so lucky after all.

A new wave of determination washed over Jack as he stood up. He knew he had to change, not just for Emily, but for himself. He could no longer be the man who allowed his desires and self-destructive tendencies to overshadow what was good in his life. He denounced the idea of a 'lucky' poker chip and everything it represented: gambling, greed, false security. Jack realized true success was measured by love and trust, not money or winnings. He gathered the evidence of his gambling—the lucky chip, a few other poker chips, and the vouchers from his winnings, everything tying him to his destructive weekend—and placed them on the tabletop. He was determined to leave that life behind for good.

Jack's heart now pounded with a newfound urgency. Emily was on her way to the airport, and he needed to catch her before it was too late. Jack needed to show Emily he had genuinely changed and was ready to put her and their relationship first. He needed to convince her that his readiness to change was sincere this time.

Jack grabbed his phone and logged in to his airline account. As he did, he noticed that the remaining battery power level in the status bar was fifteen percent. Instinctively, he moved toward the nightstand before realizing Emily had taken her charger. *Of course*, Jack thought, feeling foolish to have even reached for it. *That's fine. Stay focused*, he told himself. His Skymiles account verified what Emily said she did. Sunday evening's return flight indicated the seat next to Jack was now available. Emily had indeed rebooked her flight, or at least was no longer occupying the seat next to him. After a call to the airline, a few identity verification questions, and a convincing story about why he didn't know what flight his wife had rebooked to, Jack knew Emily's new flight number and purchased its last seat available. Flight 3808 would depart Las Vegas at 6:05 a.m., arriving in Kansas City at 10:50 a.m., the very first flight out and first to land in their hometown. The call cost him a flight change fee and another four percent battery power. Still, he felt fortunate to have secured the last seat and possibly a chance to save his marriage.

[Em, you were right about everything] Jack texted his wife. The whooshing sound of his message's successful dispatch comforted him. Still, the comfort soon turned to anxiety when there was no immediate reply. He worried about the extent of his mistakes this time and their impact on their relationship.

[I changed my flight to yours] he texted next. Jack stared at his phone and waited for a response but got none. Anticipation grew with each second passing.

[Seat 34B. Headed out soon. See you there] he texted again,

hoping for acknowledgment and wanting a resolution. Jack waited a few minutes for a response that did not come. He considered plausible reasons she wasn't replying. Emily could be catching a short nap in the Sky Rewards lounge and had not seen his messages yet. Perhaps his messages were not going through for some technical reason. In a worst-case scenario, Emily was ignoring him.

[I'm sorry, Em] his next text stated. [I love you]. Each moment of silence felt exceedingly prolonged, exacerbating his anxiety. Jack's messages were increasingly urgent as he tried to convey his remorse and seek forgiveness. Each period of silence between text messages gave Jack time to reflect on his actions. He felt guilt and frustration as his mind replayed the trip's events, wishing he could undo the weekend's mistakes.

The subsequent text was a string of red heart emojis, sent hoping persistence would eventually lead to a response. Jack's only response was restlessness, the disquieting turmoil that comes from wishing, waiting, anticipating, and knowing.

Jack could have called Emily instead of enduring the silence of waiting for a text reply. He considered it, but texting was less intimidating. Jack told himself a call might wake her if she had caught a few hours of sleep before their flight. He did not want to be intrusive or demanding. But Jack knew his truth. He texted not out of respect but out of fear of direct rejection, an immediate, unambiguous rejection.

As Jack began packing his carry-on, his phone sat on the bed next to his leather duffel, the screen black with emptiness.

NEW OWNERSHIP

(1963)

Overcast skies and a slight drizzle added to the somber atmosphere at Frankie's funeral service. The weather was uncharacteristically gloomy for Las Vegas. Still, the weather did not detract from the crowds of family, friends, and colleagues coming to pay their respects. The press was there, along with police officers and the detective investigating the shooting. Frankie's commemorative poker chip, his lucky chip given to him by Sofia on the Casbah's opening day, was also somewhere in the crowd.

First United Methodist Church, with its stained glass windows and high ceiling, created an atmosphere of reverence and reflection for all in attendance. Organ music filled the space with somber melodies as Evilyn, Richard, and Lucy sat in the first row of wooden pews, awaiting the start of the service. In front of them lay Frankie, his elegant casket flanked with large floral arrangements of white lilies and roses and his portrait placed on top of it.

After welcoming the attendees, Reverend Maynard offered an opening prayer to begin the services. He then read selected passages from the Bible to provide solace to all those grieving.

"Fear thou not; for I *am* with thee: be not dismayed; for I *am* thy God: I will strengthen thee; yea, I will help thee; yea, I will uphold thee with the right hand of my righteousness. Isaiah chapter 41, verse 10." Still, Evilyn saw no righteousness in what had happened to her husband.

After Reverend Maynard's readings and reflections, Mayor Gragson stepped up to the podium to deliver the eulogy. His voice was steady, as most city leader's voices were in times of tragedy, though his eyes reflected deep sadness.

"Ladies and gentlemen, friends and family of Frankie Grant, I stand before you today not only as your mayor but as a member of this grieving community. Frankie's tragic and untimely death has left an indelible mark on all of us, and we share in the deep sorrow felt by his wife, Evilyn, and their children, Richard and Lucy."

"In these moments of profound loss," he continued, "we turn to each other and our faith for strength and solace. The words of Isaiah 41:10 remind us of God's promise to uphold us with His right hand of righteousness. As we draw comfort from this divine assurance, let me also commit that justice will be served."

Just two rows behind the grieving Grant family sat Sofia. She sat directly behind Evilyn and watched how a mother comforts her children when their world is shattered without warning, and all seems lost. Dressed in one of her finest black dresses and wearing the Trinacria necklace, Sofia pondered if her justice would be served as the mayor spoke.

Mayor Gragson continued. "I promise you this: we will leave no stone unturned in investigating this heinous crime. Our law enforcement agencies are working tirelessly, and we will bring Frankie Grant's killer to justice. This community will not rest until those responsible are held accountable."

Sam Giancarlo and a few of his lieutenants sat near the rear of the crowded church. One of Sam's loyal men stifled a laugh when he heard the mayor's words. "Can you believe this guy?" he muttered mockingly to his boss. Sam jabbed his elbow into the man's side, silencing him with a stony stare before returning his attention to the podium.

"We owe it to Frankie's memory, his family, and each other to ensure our city remains a place of safety and justice. Together, we will prevail, and together, we will honor Frankie's legacy by upholding the values he stood for. Thank you."

When the mayor stepped down, Evilyn approached the podium, holding Richard's hand. At the same time, Mrs. Jenkins sat with Lucy, her arm around the girl to comfort her. Evilyn and Richard touched the casket and kissed it before turning to address all those who gathered to honor Frankie. Evilyn wore a simple black dress and veil, her voice quivering with emotion as she read from a short prepared statement.

"My husband was my rock, my love, and my partner in everything. Our children meant the world to him. We will miss him more than words can say, but we will carry his love with us forever."

"Frankie was not just my husband; he was my confidant and best friend. His unwavering support and love sustained me through every joy and challenge. He cherished Richard and Lucy with all his heart. He was their protector and their biggest fan. He taught them the values of kindness, resilience, and laughter. Richard and Lucy were his pride and joy; he will live on in their hearts forever."

Sofia stared at Richard intently from her third-row pew as Evilyn's words echoed in her ears.

"While our hearts are heavy with grief, we find comfort in the

169

memories we shared and the love surrounding us. Frankie's legacy of love and generosity will continue to inspire us all. Let us honor his life by carrying forward his spirit of compassion and strength."

Sofia's eyes teared, and she wanted to scream out her truth. What about her grief and their love shared and lost? 'Compassion and strength?' Evilyn's words stoked the fire in her heart and hatred in her soul. Sofia could feel her body temperature rise and her heartbeat quicken as if the head of Medusa, the symbol of female rage and empowerment in the center of the Trinacria dangling from her necklace, was searing a hole into her chest. Still, Sofia kept her composure, her facial expression conveying a deep empathy and shared grief as Evilyn addressed the congregation and made eye contact with her.

"Thank you to everyone who has supported our family during this difficult time," Evilyn continued. "Your kindness and presence mean the world to us. May we find comfort in each other as we remember and celebrate my husband's life."

Standing bravely beside his mother, Richard then read a short note he had written. "Dad, you were the best. I promise to make you proud by taking care of Mom and Lucy. I love you."

Sofia looked intently at the boy but could only imagine her son standing there, wondering what the older boy would say to the deceased father he never knew.

The choir's harmonious voices echoed through the church as they sang "Amazing Grace." When finished, Reverend Maynard concluded the service with closing remarks and a final prayer, sending attendees off with a blessing.

The burial was a blur to Evilyn: the ride in the black limousine with her children following the hearse to Woodlawn Cemetery, the sea of black umbrellas as Reverend Maynard led the final rights in the gentle drizzle, the black casket lowered into the ground. As the service concluded, Evilyn returned to the limousine. The drizzle turned to rain, gently falling and mingling with her tears, each drop echoing the difficult decisions and the enormity of the challenges ahead.

***

Evilyn waited a week after her husband's service before entering the Casbah. Most of that time was spent with Richard and Lucy at home, helping them cope with their grief. While she kept them out of school, Evilyn maintained their other daily routines, like regular schedules for meals and bedtime, to help encourage some sense of stability. They looked at family photo albums, shared stories about their father, and even started a memory book together. Evilyn encouraged the children to express their feelings and ask questions, letting them know it was okay to feel sad, angry, or confused. Reassuring her children of her presence and love was important to Evilyn, although she felt the same sadness, anger, and confusion as they did. Why was Frankie shot? Who would do such a thing? What were they going to do now without him?

As Evilyn sat in the guest chair in front of the desk in Frankie's office, she slowly surveyed the room. She had never actually been to the office up in the Eye before. The farthest into the casino she had ever made was the Oasis Grill, where she and Frankie ate their last meal together the day of the shooting. Displayed on the credenza behind the desk was an old football from a high school game victory, a fumble Frankie recovered to bull his way into the end zone and win the season's championship game for his team. A few framed black and white photographs of Frankie shaking hands with local business leaders adorned the walls. Their last family portrait, framed in a 5x7 frame Evilyn gave him, sat on his desk facing his executive chair. A few cigarettes burned to their smashed filters, and a half-smoked cigar lay in the ashtray beside the desk phone. Evilyn absorbed all the information the office had to tell her. She imagined his workday reviewing reports or talking to the bank or government regulators on the phone. As far as she could guess, everything was where Frankie had left it.

"Mrs. Grant," the new assistant announced, "Mr. Giancarlo is here for his appointment with you."

Sam removed his hat and walked in, his demeanor a mix of sympathy and determination.

Evilyn rose and, with her palms, brushed smooth the simple black dress she wore before offering her hand to greet him. "Mr. Giancarlo," she stated as much a question as a greeting. "Thank you for meeting me here. I wasn't sure what to expect when you sent word and asked if we could meet."

"Mrs. Grant," he replied, "My deepest condolences for your loss. Your husband was a good man and a dear friend. His death is a shock for all of us."

"Thank you, Mr. Giancarlo. How exactly did you know my husband?" Evilyn motioned for Sam to sit in the guest chair opposite where she was sitting.

After unbuttoning his suit jacket, Sam sat and faced Evilyn. "Thank you, and please call me Sam."

Evilyn nodded. Sam looked familiar, but she could not recall being formally introduced. When Sam told Evilyn he and Frankie had been business associates, she thought perhaps they had met briefly at the Casbah's grand opening or some business dinner somewhere. She could have seen him at the funeral service. The day was all a blur to Evilyn now.

"The service was beautiful, Mrs. Grant."

"You were there?"

"Yes," Sam answered. "So, how are you and your children

doing? I know it's only been a short time. Terrible thing, what happened."

Evilyn smiled and politely acknowledged Sam's sympathy and concern. However, she couldn't quite fit the pieces together to see where his sympathy and concern came from. Sam spoke familiarly, as though they knew one another and were good friends, as though he had a genuine interest in their well-being. But they were not friends, and Sam's business association with her late husband was still unclear.

"It's been difficult. I won't lie," Evilyn responded. "The kids are devastated, of course. And the casino," she paused and looked around, "I don't even know where to begin."

Sam leaned forward into the conversation. "That's why I wanted to talk to you, Mrs. Grant. Frankie poured his heart and soul into the Casbah to get it opened. I know. I helped him. He had big plans for this place, but running a casino will be challenging without him, especially with everything else you're dealing with."

Evilyn sighed. "You are correct, Mr. Giancarlo. My husband had big plans for the Casbah. And I fully anticipate running it will be quite a challenge."

"Mrs. Grant," Sam replied, "you aren't thinking of operating a casino yourself, are you?"

"The Casbah was my husband's dream. Anything else feels like betraying him."

Sam wanted to laugh or pat her head like a young girl with dreams of going to prom. The idea of discussing casino management with a homemaker felt undignified to him. Yet Sam remained patient. "It's not a betrayal, Mrs. Grant. It's about securing a stable future for you and your children. Frankie wouldn't want you to carry this burden, especially now."

"What are you suggesting?" Evilyn asked, sensing Sam's motives but wanting to hear them herself. Evilyn was used to sensing men's real motives: her father in his later years, school administrators when dealing with PTA mothers, bankers, and automobile dealerships who still thought wives needed their husband's permission to withdraw money from their joint accounts or to buy a new car.

Sam leaned forward again and lowered his voice as if speaking softly or more slowly would help what he was about to say sound more convincing. "I'm suggesting you consider selling the Casbah to me, Mrs. Grant. I'll make sure it thrives, honoring Frankie's vision. You and the kids will be financially secure, and you can focus on what matters most right now—each other."

And there it was. With the introductions and warm-up finished, it was time for the music and dancing.

"But why you, Mr. Giancarlo? Why are you interested in the Casbah?"

Sam paused to choose his words. "Let's just say I have an interest in seeing this place succeed. Frankie and I had plans, and I want to see them through. But more importantly, I want to ensure you're taken care of. You shouldn't have to shoulder this alone."

Evilyn looked down and straightened the hem of her dress where one of her knees crossed the other as if pausing momentarily to consider his offer of relieving her burden because she shouldn't have to shoulder the burden alone. "There's so much to think about," she replied. "I don't want to make rash decisions, Mr. Giancarlo."

Sam nodded. "Take your time, Mrs. Grant. But do consider my

offer. Remember, this is an opportunity to secure your future without the stress of running a casino, which is difficult under the best of circumstances. I promise to honor Frankie's memory and ensure the Casbah remains successful."

Evilyn stood and extended her hand. "I appreciate that. I'll think about it. Thank you, Mr. Giancarlo." The casino's staff, who had been carefully watching their interaction through the glass walls of Frankie's office, jumped back to their positions when they saw Evilyn rise. Today was her first time in Frankie's office, her first appointment and business interaction, and the staff's first impression of their new boss.

"I'm here to help, Mrs. Grant. I'll be in touch soon."

The door closed softly behind Sam as he left. Evilyn took a deep breath and looked around the office, again noting the location and placement of Frankie's possessions: the pictures, his chair, and the football. She wanted to touch them all, to feel her husband, to know what he knew, and to draw strength from his confidence and experience. In time, she might be able to sit in his chair or open a desk drawer to examine its contents. For now, though, everything remained precisely how he left it.

***

The second week following the funeral, after Evilyn met Sam in Frankie's office, marked a subtle but significant shift for Evilyn. While one might expect the grieving period for the loss of a spouse to last months or even a year, Evilyn did not have that kind of time. She needed her family to return to everyday routines and activities as soon as possible, restoring a sense of security for her children. There were wills and financial paperwork to sort through with bankers and lawyers and, of course, the police's ongoing investigation of the shooting to contend with. Evilyn also needed to decide what to do with Frankie's business, how to navigate the debt he had incurred to get the Casbah built and opened, and what she would do to secure an income for the family moving forward.

Evilyn saved her emotional grieving for late at night. The weeping happened quietly when Richard and Lucy were asleep, often lying in the bed beside her. Sleeping in the large bed together comforted them all, filling the unexpected void left by the absence of her husband and their father. Evilyn often got out of bed in the middle of the night to clean the kitchen, putting away the leftovers she had placed in the oven to keep warm, as she had done so often before. She found the habit hard to break. Throughout Frankie's hospital stay and in the weeks following his death, Evilyn still made dinner for four each night, saving some of the meal for the man who would never come home. It was a habit she was not ready to let go of.

Richard and Lucy returned to school the week after Evilyn and Sam's first meeting. Their return to school allowed Evilyn to resume some of her daily activities with the PTA and local charities. She could not, however, return to her volunteer work at the hospital. It was too soon for that. Evilyn restarted her routine of household chores, grocery shopping, and other daily tasks that had become erratic in the past weeks. These activities, though mundane, offered her a slight sense of control and normalcy.

When her children were in school, and Evilyn finished whatever daily tasks she had to do, she began reading through the sympathy cards arriving daily since the shooting. Each was a mix of solace and sorrow. There was comfort in the cards and letters, as well as their kind words and shared memories of Frankie. As Evilyn read them and sorted them into piles, she began the slow and lengthy process of responding to each with calls or mailed notes of gratitude for their support. Each card read or thank you note written might bring moments of unexpected tears. They could also bring brief periods of calm and reflection. When it was time to pick up the children from school, Evilyn put the cards and notes away to return to them the following day.

Close friends and family members continued to call the house to check in, offering help with the children, a lunch date for diversion, or anything else Evilyn might need. The first week after Frankie died, before the funeral service and burial, Evilyn didn't bother picking up the phone. The week following the funeral, when her son and daughter were home from school and processing their loss together as a family, Evilyn talked with a few of the callers if Richard or Lucy picked up the ringing phone. Evilyn answered a few of the calls herself, instinctively, when the kitchen wall phone rang while she was preparing a meal. During one of those times, on the evening of Sam's office visit, Evilyn answered Sofia's call.

"Evilyn, how are you? How are the kids?" Sofia asked.

"We're getting by, thank you," Evilyn answered. She felt guilty for not yet responding to Sofia's previous outreaches. "Dear, I'm so sorry for not replying to your card. And thank you for the arrangement at the cemetery. The flowers were so beautiful. It's just been so—." There was a pause in Evilyn's voice. "It's been difficult, you know."

"Yes, of course, my friend," Sofia replied. "Don't worry about it another minute. What can I do to help?"

Sofia had been trying to reach Evilyn since the shooting. The hospital did not let Sofia in to see Frankie. Her cards wishing him a speedy recovery went unanswered. Sofia was at the cemetery during the burial, under one of the many black umbrellas close to Evilyn. Because of the rain, however, Sofia missed her chance to console her before Evilyn and the children were whisked away into the waiting limousine. In the weeks following the funeral, Sofia's calls to the house went unanswered until now.

Evilyn thought about Sofia's question for a moment. "I was at the Casbah yesterday, dear. I'm so sorry I didn't see you there."

"Oh?" Sofia replied, surprised by the statement but anxious to hear more about the visit. "I'm sorry I missed you, too. How did it go?"

"I had a meeting with," Evilyn paused to think of the correct relationship term, "a Sam Giancarlo. You must know him. He said he and Frankie had been business associates. I'm not sure exactly how, though."

"Oh, Evilyn," Sofia whispered in a hushed tone. "Do be careful. What did he talk to you about?" Sofia wasn't sure which of them asked for the meeting, but she had a pretty good idea. She thought it unlikely Evilyn would know who Sam was and even less likely she would ask for a meeting with him.

'Careful,' Evilyn mentally repeated to herself, trying to interpret the meaning of Sofia's warning before replying. "He said he wants to buy the Casbah, and that—"

"You can't do business with that man," Sofia interrupted. "We need to talk, Evilyn. Please promise me."

"Yes, of course, dear," Evilyn assured to ease Sofia's concern. "That's why I need you, Sofia. You know so much about the business."

Evilyn again regretted not contacting Sofia sooner regarding how the business was doing. Only a few short weeks had passed, and so many other immediate issues required her attention. Evilyn assumed the casino was operating normally, all things considered, and Sofia had everything under control. She had no way of knowing Frankie had fired and banished Sofia from the Casbah. But now was the time to focus on Frankie's business and make decisions. Evilyn was pleased to have picked up on Sofia's call.

As Richard and Lucy ran around the kitchen and tugged at their mother's dress in need of something, Evilyn continued, "Sofia, I'll come back in tomorrow. Do you have time to chat with me in Frankie's office? What time would be good for you, dear?"

"Let's meet at Mary's Café in the morning after you drop the kids at school," Sofia offered. "That way, we can chat privately over coffee, and I can bring you up to speed before we go in *together.*"

***

Evilyn was the first to arrive and selected a booth by the window in the front half of Mary's. She had not sat to chat in person with Frankie's assistant since Sofia's surprise visit to her home to have tea the afternoon before the shooting. Evilyn wrapped her hands around a mug of coffee and waited, the familiar clatter of dishes and low hum of conversation offering a brief respite from the weight of the decision she faced. She looked up just as Sofia walked in, a reassuring smile on her face.

"It's so good to see you," Evilyn said, extending her hand to Sofia as she approached the booth. "Thanks for meeting me. I so needed to talk."

"Of course. How are you holding up?" Sofia asked, bending down to hug Evilyn before sliding into the bench seat opposite her. She settled in and ordered a cup of coffee for herself.

"It's been a bit overwhelming, to be honest." Evilyn hesitated, her gaze dropping to the cup still cradled in the palms of her hand. "I miss him. Even with as much as there is to do right now."

Sofia reached across the table to embrace Evilyn's hands. "I know. We all miss him. It's going to take time, you know." Sofia squinted as she spoke to keep her own emotions in check. She missed Frankie, too, in a different way. But the game had changed, and Sofia knew she needed to adjust to the new rules. Sofia had a new role to play if she was going to have a chance of getting what she wanted.

"Yes, I know. I need time to adjust. It's just there's so much to think about. So many decisions to make."

Sofia's breathing grew heavier as she wished time would speed up, asserting mental restraint to avoid seeming impatient or insensitive to Evilyn's words.

"The thought of raising the kids and running a big business like that," Evilyn continued. "I have no experience in the hotel or casino business. I don't know the first thing about it, Sofia. Tell me, what do you know about Sam Giancarlo?"

"Evilyn, you don't want to talk to Sam. Frankie didn't like him. Sam's not a good person. Selling to him isn't the best move. Frankie wouldn't want the casino in his hands."

"That's funny," Evilyn replied. "I didn't exactly feel comfortable with him when we met."

Sofia sat back and took a sip of her coffee. "You see, we women have great intuition. We know when something is off. You must follow your intuition, dear." As she spoke, Evilyn looked into Sofia's eyes, a knowing smile slowly forming at the corner of her lips.

"So you think I should not sell the Casbah to Sam?"

"I don't think you should sell it to anyone," Sofia confidently replied. "You should run it yourself."

"But what about the casino business—its reputation? I don't want to be associated with all that. I don't want my kids to grow up as a part of the gambling world."

"It's regulated. There are bankers, lawyers, and other people who can help you. Evilyn," Sofia said, leaning into the space between them to focus her words on the objective. "The casino was Frankie's dream. You have the strength to keep his dream alive. It's about honoring his legacy. You don't have to do it alone. I know the business inside and out. I can help you. No one knows more about the Casbah than I do. We can run it together."

Evilyn looked down at her half-empty cup, its warmth almost wholly cooled now, and then glanced back at Sofia, feeling both relief and uncertainty. "You really think we could do it? I want to honor Frankie, but I'm nervous."

"Absolutely," Sofia shot back. "Together, we can preserve what Frankie built. Don't let Sam take it away. The Casbah is your family's legacy."

Evilyn took a deep breath, contemplating Sofia's words. "So you would help me run it? Your experience is invaluable."

Sofia's smile widened, though a hint of something unspoken lingered in her eyes. "I'd be honored, Evilyn. Let's do this together, for Frankie." She extended her hand across the table as Evilyn took it, shaking to their promised alliance.

Evilyn nodded, a sense of relief and gratitude breaking through her apprehension. "Thank you, Sofia. I don't know what I would do without you."

New Directions

E vilyn stood at the large oak desk in Frankie's office, the room still carrying a slight, lingering scent of his cologne all these weeks since he was last here. She took a deep breath, bracing herself. Today marked the beginning of a new chapter where she would step into her late husband's shoes and run the Casbah. She glanced up as Sofia entered, her presence radiating confidence and intimidation.

"Morning, Sofia. Ready to get started?" Evilyn asked, her voice carrying a hint of apprehension as she sat in the guest chair in front of Frankie's desk. The chair was the same one she sat in when meeting Sam Giancarlo. Sitting in the big chair behind the desk was still an uncomfortable thought for Evilyn. She had not earned that privilege yet and still subconsciously thought she might glance over and see her husband sitting in it, listening and evaluating her decisions and actions.

"Absolutely," Sofia replied, settling into the seat across from her, the same seat Sam had sat in, her expression filled with as much resolve as his was when they met.

"I was thinking about the leadership team," Evilyn said, her hands steadied on the chair's wooden armrests. "I want you to handle day-to-day operations as the General Manager. You'll oversee everything on the casino floor," Evilyn said.

"Of course. I know the business well," Sofia replied.

"As for legal advice, I'll rely on my attorney, Mr. Watkins," Evilyn continued, checking off items and making notes on a stenographer's pad she purchased after her breakfast meeting with Sofia the previous day.

"I'd like to also bring in my banker as our Financial Officer, Lawrence Graham. He's been reliable, and I trust his judgment with our accounts," Evilyn added, thinking of the banker's steady hand during turbulent times in some of Frankie's other business ventures.

Sofia nodded as a seasoned chef might acknowledge a novice cook's ambitious recipe suggestion—patient and polite but slightly amused, fully aware of the likely outcome.

Evilyn hesitated before speaking again. "Regarding regulatory compliance, we should bring Sam Giancarlo on board. In a consulting capacity. Despite my reservations, he knows the regulatory landscape well and can help us avoid trouble."

Sofia's expression darkened, no longer amused by Evilyn's naivety. "Evilyn, that's a bad idea. Sam wants to own the casino, not help you operate it." She chuckled as the words left her mouth.

"I understand, but his knowledge of the casino business is invaluable," Evilyn countered.

"Evilyn, Sam is not one of your PTA mothers with an opposing view you'd like to win over with baked cookies and niceties. Sam is a casino operator and a competitor. He's not going to work for you. Sam expects you to sell this place to him." Sofia spoke with a scoff in her tone. She wanted to tell Evilyn Sam was a gangster, a mob boss, a Capomandamento. Sofia wanted to tell

Evilyn she was beginning to sound like Frankie, but she didn't.

"I just thought," Evilyn said before pausing and leaning back in the guest chair. "Of course, you're right, Sofia. Silly thought."

Evilyn and Sofia discussed the rest of the existing staff: the security director, the human resources manager, the hospitality manager, and the food and beverage manager, agreeing they were all doing a fine job and should remain in place. Then, they returned to the topic of Sam.

"I guess it's time to give Sam an answer." Evilyn gripped her hands tightly as she stared at the phone on Frankie's desk. Next to it, Sam's business card lay like a taunting reminder of the decision she had to make.

"I'll get him on the line for you," Sofia said, calm and reassuring. Both women stood as Sofia dialed the number and waited before speaking. She asked to be connected to Mr. Giancarlo, announcing the call from Evilyn Grant at the Casbah. "Hold for Mrs. Grant, please," she said as she handed the receiver to Evilyn.

"Mr. Giancarlo, it's Evilyn Grant." Despite the dryness in her mouth and the rapid beating of her heart, her voice came out with a surprising firmness as she paced in a small circle before Frankie's desk. "I've reached a decision regarding the Casbah," she began, her tone unwavering.

"Evilyn, good to hear from you. I assume you're calling with good news," Sam replied, his voice brimming with expectation.

"I'm not selling the Casbah, Mr. Giancarlo. We're going to keep it. I appreciate the offer, but—"

"But what, Mrs. Grant?" Sam cut in sharply. "You think you can run a casino? In this town? With no experience or connections? You can't be serious."

Evilyn paused and took a deep breath to steady herself. Despite the tension in her posture, Sofia was surprised at the calm resolve in Evilyn's voice. Even from across the desk, Sofia could hear the rising irritation in Sam's voice through the earpiece.

"Mr. Giancarlo, as I was saying, I appreciate your offer. Perhaps we can partner on some future project, but as far as the Casbah is concerned, I will not sell it." Her words were concise and left no room for doubt.

"You listen here, Mrs. Grant. Your husband and I had an agreement. I gave him one hundred and fifty thousand dollars as an investment and—"

"Thank you, Mr. Giancarlo," Evilyn interjected, her tone final and unyielding. "Have a good day." She firmly pressed the button in the phone's cradle to end the call, lowering the handset to her chest as she disconnected with a sense of finality. Evilyn turned to Sofia, searching her face for a reaction.

Sofia nodded. "Well done, Evilyn." Her voice was a mix of admiration and hidden skepticism.

But as Evilyn looked away, relieved to have crossed this hurdle, Sofia's expression shifted. Her eyes narrowed, and a faint, calculating smile touched her lips, revealing the conflicting emotions beneath her composed exterior. "We'll see how this plays out," she muttered, her thoughts already turning to her next move.

***

Later that evening, Sam and Sofia met in a quiet corner of the Flamingo Hotel's Champagne Room, a popular spot for high-profile guests. Meeting there was Sam's choice, given Carmine had banned Sofia from entering his restaurant. When they met, their expressions were a mix of tension and calculation.

"Never thought I'd be seeing you again," Sam said, his voice dripping with sarcasm. He didn't bother to rise as Sofia approached the table and pulled her chair out to sit.

"Is that the way you greet a lady, Sam?"

Sam exhaled a chuckle as the smoke from his cigar rose and circled above his head, lingering like the complex mix of history, emotion, and unresolved issues characterizing their long-standing grudges and deeply ingrained dynamics. "Is that what we're calling ourselves now? A lady?"

"I didn't come here for petty squabbling, Sam. What do you want?" she asked, waving off the waitress approaching the table to take her drink order. Sofia did not intend to be there long.

"You hooked your wagon to one Grant, and look what happened to him. Now you've managed to get your claws into the other. You're soulless, sister."

"I'm not here to listen to your insults, Sam. I'm here for the Casbah and for Evilyn," Sofia shot back, her eyes narrowing. "What do you want to discuss?"

Sam and Sofia's contempt for one another, steeped in shared history and past conflicts, was a minefield of old wounds and memories never fully healed. Long-term disagreements and conflicts had become part of their on-again, off-again relationship dynamic.

Sam's rise to power had been meteoric and brutal. He was a cunning strategist with an almost preternatural ability to anticipate his rivals' moves. He started as a lowly enforcer within his own family, his ascent marked by a series of ruthless decisions and calculated betrayals. Sam knew when to eliminate a threat and when to form an alliance, often switching allegiances at the perfect moment to gain the upper hand. By his mid-twenties, he had outmaneuvered many older, more experienced men, earning a reputation for being both feared and respected. His rapid climb to the position of Capodecina was a testament to his intelligence and sheer willpower.

"You're here for Evilyn?" Sam asked mockingly, again snickering before leaning in closer. "We both know why we're sitting here. Evilyn is in over her head. If we play this right, we can take the Casbah without complications or ugliness. Let's keep things simple and civil this time."

Sofia studied Sam's expression. Nothing about their ancient grievances and nostalgic tensions had ever been simple or civil. Sam's words were the emotional echoes of rehashed step-sibling rivalry and competition, deeply entrenched, festering since the Giancarlo family took Sofia in after the death of her parents in Allied bombings. She once admired her older stepbrother's ambition and determination. She emulated them. Still, tradition prevailed when she became pregnant out of wedlock, even under the chaotic circumstances of post-war-torn Sicily. As her older brother and a young Capodecina in the Cosa Nostra, Sam was the one charged with arranging Sofia's sequestering in the church, the adoption of her child after its birth, and her exile to the United States. In one way, Sam spared her life, yet in another, he condemned it.

There had been a short time when they were inseparable, allies against the occupiers in Sicily who would sometimes seek to take advantage of their people. Sofia had been Sam's confidant, the only one who knew the softer side of the ruthless enforcer. But when she became pregnant, the family's code demanded Sam make the cold decision to uphold tradition. She was an unwed teen whose child's father she would not reveal. Sam's acts severed their bond, transforming her admiration into a simmering resentment.

"You think I don't know that? That's why I'm working with her, from the inside," Sofia replied, her voice low and dangerous. "I just need you to sit still and be patient. Don't do anything rash like trying to pull our gaming license or messing with our vendors."

Sam took a long draw on his cigar and stared at Sofia. He was unaccustomed to inaction but experienced delegating more unsavory tasks to others. "Agreed. I'll play along for now." Sam held his cigar between his index and middle fingers and pointed it at Sofia. "But the first chance we get, I take over," he said, a sinister smile forming.

Sofia nodded, her eyes cold and calculating. "For now, we keep this to ourselves." She stood and turned, walking out of The Champagne Room with their temporary alliance forged by mutual ambition and deceit.

Their agreement was a fragile truce, a dance on a knife's edge, poised to cut deep at the slightest misstep. As Sofia exited, she couldn't help but glance back at Sam, a man she once saw as her protector but now viewed as a dangerous rival. In the murky world of organized crime, the line between family and foe was perilously thin, and the step-siblings' shared past was a testament to how easily it could be crossed.

ALL OR NOTHING

(Present)

Jack stood in the lobby in front of the bank of elevators, his overnight bag in one hand and pay-out vouchers in the other. He could see the cashier's window straight ahead while the noise of slot machines and the chatter of early morning gamblers from the casino floor filled the air to his left. To Jack's right was the hotel's front desk, where he would soon check out. He glanced at his watch; just enough time to exchange the remaining vouchers for cash and check out before heading to the airport.

Stepping away from the window, Jack folded the bills and put them into his pocket, where he felt his lucky chip. The chip was warm again, beckoning him to try his luck one last time before going home. Jack paused, tightening his grip on the suitcase handle before turning right and walking to the blackjack table where he had been so lucky the evening before.

Jack's heart raced as he walked over. The thrill of the game and the rush of winning were irresistible. He was confident in his skills, and the positive energy radiated from within his pocket. Jack took the same seat at the table where he had sat before and laid the folded bills from his pocket onto the green felt. Exchanged for chips from the dealer, Jack pushed the stack away from him in

189

one last gesture of unwavering confidence in himself—an all-or-nothing wager on fortune.

The dealer dealt two cards to him: a one-eyed Jack of Spades and a Two of Hearts. Twelve. The deal was a hugely positive sign, he thought. One card was a Jack, representing him by name, a perfect omen. The Two of Hearts symbolized him and Emily, married and in love.

Across the table, the dealer had a Six of Spades showing, meaning the odds were the down card was a ten. Sixteen required the dealer to take another hit, potentially a bust. The fact the card was a spade suggested the dealer was digging herself into a hole with the house hand. The signs were clear to Jack, and his confidence soared while the chip in his pocket grew warmer.

Jack felt good about what his hand signified, but twelve is far from twenty-one, and the dealer likely had sixteen already. Jack tapped the table for another card, trusting his intuition and what the Casbah chip told him.

The dealer flipped a Queen of Clubs. Twenty-two. Bust.

Jack's stomach dropped. His remaining winnings and any cash he had in his pocket were gone in an instant. Their value was all meaningless now. The Casbah chip, the cards, the dealer, the table—all had betrayed him. He cursed under his breath, frustration bubbling up. But he didn't have time to wallow in his loss.

Money wasn't what mattered, he told himself. After all, he had been playing with the house's money; his initial one-dollar slot machine bet was all he truthfully lost. Emily truly mattered, and Jack needed to get to his flight. He needed to get to his wife and find a way to win her back.

The early morning sounds of the casino faded as Jack walked

toward the lobby's desk to check out. Faded also were the dreams of his grand gestures: the weekend trip to Vegas, the Adele concert, and the beautiful earrings as an anniversary gift. Jack's vision of winning Emily's trust, confidence, and admiration back seemed an illusion now, too, like the wavering mirages in the desert heat.

THE LEAD

(1963)

Detectives Marshall and Ramirez pulled up to the Casbah's porte-cochère from the street in their unmarked car, the neon lights of the strip at dusk reflecting off the polished hood. They parked just past the doors and stepped out, adjusting their jackets as they walked toward the entrance.

"Valet it for you, sir?" the attendant asked, running up to the driver with his hand outstretched to accept the car keys.

"No, leave it there," Marshall replied. "Won't be long."

Inside, the bustling sounds of slot machines and chatter filled the air. The detectives approached the first uniformed security guard they saw, a burly guard standing watch inside the entrance.

"Good evening, officers. How can I help you?" the guard asked, eyeing the badges waved in front of him.

"We're not officers. We're detectives," Ramirez responded sharply.

"We're here to speak with Sofia Ferranero," Detective Marshall added. "Is she here?"

"I believe so. Just a moment, please." The guard nodded and picked up the phone, dialing an internal extension. After waiting a few minutes, another of the casino's security officers approached them.

"Gentlemen, how may I be of assistance?"

"Sofia Ferranero. Is she here?" Marshall asked once more.

"May I inform Ms. Ferranero what this is regarding?" he asked, closely inspecting their identification.

"You may not," Ramirez retorted. "We have some questions for her."

"Certainly, Gentlemen," the Casbah's Head of Security acknowledged. "Follow me, please." He led them through the casino and several back hallways to a small, quiet office near the cash room, away from the noise of the casino floor. The windowless room was sparsely furnished, with a few chairs and a small table.

Sofia walked in, her expression intentionally guarded, and thanked her Head of Security before excusing him to return to his duties. "Detectives, what can I do for you?"

"Thank you for meeting with us, Miss Ferranero. I'm Detective Marshall, and this is Detective Ramirez," Marshall began, taking a seat. "We're investigating the shooting of Mr. Grant. We have a few questions regarding your interactions with Mr. Grant before his death."

Sofia sat down across from them, her demeanor composed. "Of course. I'll do my best to help."

Following a few basic questions regarding Sofia's employment length and job responsibilities at the Casbah, Marshall flipped open his notebook. "We have reports of an altercation between yourself and Frankie Grant shortly before his death. Is that correct?"

"Two altercations, actually," interrupted Ramirez.

"Yes. Two altercations. Thank you," Marshall said, glancing over at his partner.

"Altercations?" Sofia asked for clarification.

"Yes," Ramirez quickly interjected. "You know, public confrontations, disputes, quarrels. One on the night of the 10th, the day of the Grand Opening, at Carmine's, at or around 10:30 p.m.. The second on the morning of the 27th, at Mary's Café at approximately 9:15 a.m.."

"Yes," she admitted, her voice steady. "We did have a couple of heated arguments. And they were, unfortunately, in public. Frankie and I," Sofia paused. "We had a complicated relationship."

"Can you elaborate on what these arguments were about?" Ramirez pressed.

Sofia took a deep breath. "The first was about the casino's opening. We were going to celebrate at Carmine's. I don't know. He had worked so many hours that week to prepare for the opening. He was exhausted and had probably already celebrated a little too much by the time we met that evening. It was nothing, really. He just got a little, how do you say, exasperated?"

"Witnesses say *you* were the one escorted out of the door," Marshall stated, checking the back pages of his pocket notepad.

"Yes, well," Sofia said, leaning back in her chair with a calm smirk. "Frankie and Carmine, the owner, go way back. They are friends. Men stick together. I know this. I understand this."

"Mr. Grant fired you as they dragged you out of the restaurant.

Is that correct?" Ramirez asked.

Sofia's posture stiffened in contempt as she turned to sneer at Ramirez. "Dragged me out? Dragged? Really?"

Marshall raised his fingers in Ramirez's direction, his forearm and wrist remaining on the table—a clear signal from the lead detective to tone down his choice of words. Marshall then took over the line of questioning.

"Ms. Ferranero, is it true you also said …" Marshall began to ask as he flipped to different pages in his notepad. "Did you state, quote, 'you'll regret this, bastard,' unquote?"

Sofia turned her chair an inch toward Marshall and away from Ramirez. "I'm not sure, Detective. It got heated. I am unsure of the exact words as I was '*dragged out.*' Like I said, Frankie and I worked very hard for very long hours to get the Casbah opened. Everyone was tired and stressed."

"And the second argument, Ms. Ferranero?" asked Detective Marshall.

"The second incident was about his wife, Evilyn. Frankie told me he was planning to leave her, but he said that in the past."

"And this was at Mary's Café, the morning of the shooting?"

"Yes, that's correct. We had breakfast together."

"That's a personal, intimate conversation for a husband to talk to another woman about, someone he had just fired a week before, isn't it?" asked Marshall. "You were no longer employed at the casino when you met for breakfast, were you?"

"Yes, the conversation was intimate, but Frankie and I worked closely together and shared many things. He asked me to come back. I was a guest in their home just the afternoon before," she continued, addressing her responses directly at Marshall the whole time. "I visited Evilyn, and we had tea. Frankie was there. They both talked about how hard running the casino without me was and asked me to return."

"Why were you and Frankie arguing over his marital problems?" asked Marshall.

"I encouraged him not to do anything rash. You know, for the children's sake."

"Did Frankie mention what the issues were? Why was he considering leaving his wife?"

"Oh, lots of reasons," Sofia replied. "She never liked the idea of the casino. Evilyn hated the hours he was away from the family. She thought the casino put them in too much personal debt. She nagged him constantly." Sofia took a deep breath. "Frankie and Evilyn had been having problems for a while. She thought he was having an affair. It made her furious. Frankie told me more than once that Emily threatened to ruin him if he didn't stop. I'm not sure there was anything for him to stop, though. I think Evilyn was seeing something that just wasn't there."

Marshall jotted down notes, his expression unreadable. "Interesting. Do you have any evidence to support this claim?"

"Proof, no." Sofia hesitated. "Like I said, I was close to Frankie. He confided in me. Frankie was afraid of her, afraid of what she might do."

Detective Marshall looked thoughtful, tapping his pen against the desk. "You realize these are serious accusations. If you're lying or withholding information—"

"No, I'm aware," Sofia interjected, meeting his gaze without flinching. "I'm telling you the truth. As much as I like working with Evilyn, I see now more than ever how strong-willed of a woman she is. When she feels cornered, she lashes out."

Ramirez glanced at Marshall before speaking. "Did Frankie Grant have any dealings with organized crime? We have reason to believe his murder might be connected to something bigger."

Sofia's face took on a look of genuine surprise. "Organized crime? Do you mean Sam Giancarlo and his gang?"

Both Marshall and Ramirez perked up and looked at one another. They knew something Sofia didn't, or at least thought they did.

"Now that's an interesting name just to throw out there," commented Detective Ramirez.

"Not really," replied Sofia. "Everyone in town knows who Sam is."

"And did Frankie have any dealings with Sam Giancarlo?"

"Oh, no. Not Frankie. Frankie was cautious about who he did business with. He wanted to keep the Casbah clean no matter how much Sam pressured him."

Marshall pressed on, "Pressured in what way?"

Sofia shook her head slowly. "I told Frankie to be careful. Sam wanted to buy into the Casbah. 'To invest,' he said. When Frankie refused, Sam made things difficult for us to open. Sam was even at Frankie's funeral service, sitting in the back with a few of his henchmen, snickering and acting rude. Their behavior was disgraceful. Sam even approached Evilyn recently about buying the whole thing. She told him the same thing, and he was just as furious at her as he was before with Frankie." A concerned look came over Sofia's face as she paused, waiting for the full impact of her declaration to register.

Detective Marshall leaned back. "Why didn't you come forward with this information earlier?"

"Come forward with what?" Sofia asked. "You should know as well as I do, Detective Marshall. Sam Giancarlo does what he wants in this town. His hands are everywhere, dirty or clean." Sofia paused again, looking down at her hands to avoid eye contact. "I am scared of him," she admitted, her voice breaking. "Scared of what he did. Or what he might still do," she corrected herself. "I just want to help Evilyn run this place. The Casbah was Frankie's dream."

The detectives stood up and closed their notebooks.

"Thank you for your time, Miss Ferranero. We'll be in touch," Marshall said, his tone softer now.

Sofia watched them leave the room as a security guard escorted them back to the front lobby. Her mind replayed the conversation, and a small, satisfied smile played on the corners of her lips. She had planted the seeds of doubt, and now it was only a matter of time before the detectives would nurture those seeds into a motive.

***

Three days after Detectives Marshall and Ramirez's visit to the Casbah to speak with Sofia, Evilyn walked into Frankie's office, the early morning colored lights from the casino floor filtering through the blinds. Sofia was already there, rifling through papers and documents scattered across Frankie's desk, her face a mix of concentration and anxiety. Sofia looked startled as Evilyn entered, but immediately grabbed the folded morning paper from the desk's corner and sprang toward Evilyn.

"Have you seen this?" Sofia asked impatiently, unfolding the paper to reveal its front page.

"No," replied Evilyn, shaking her head. "I just dropped the kids off at school. What's going on?"

Sofia grabbed Evilyn's elbow and led her to the large desk, spreading the newspaper over the documents she had just been scouring through. "You need to see this. It's all over the front page." Evilyn hardly had time to toss her pocketbook to the guest chair before both women stood at the desk and leaned in to scan the pages together. Sofia read the article aloud as Evilyn's eyes widened, reading the bold headlines herself.

~

Las Vegas Review-Journal

October 5, 1963

Feds Strike Back: Major Mob Figures Arrested in Las Vegas Crackdown

Las Vegas was rocked yesterday by the biggest anti-crime operation in its history as federal agents arrested several high-profile mobsters in a sweeping nationwide crackdown orchestrated by Attorney General Robert F. Kennedy. Dubbed "Operation Big Squeeze," this operation is the latest salvo in Kennedy's relentless campaign against organized crime.

Dramatic Arrests Shake Sin City

In the early hours, federal agents descended upon the opulent casinos and luxury hotels of Las Vegas, executing arrest warrants for numerous reputed members of the national crime syndicate. Among those detained was Sam Giancarlo, a name synonymous with organized crime and illicit operations in the region. Giancarlo, along with several other suspected racketeers, was apprehended in coordinated raids that sent shockwaves through the city.

Giancarlo, long suspected of orchestrating illegal gambling and other racketeering activities, was taken into custody without incident. Federal agents, backed by local law enforcement, meticulously planned and executed the operation, ensuring minimal disruption to the tourist city.

~

"Sam Giancarlo? Arrested?" Evilyn said.

Sofia nodded. "Yes, and it's not just him. It's a huge DOJ

effort."

The women continued to read.

~

RFK's Crusade Against the Mob

This high-profile crackdown is part of Robert Kennedy's broader effort to dismantle organized crime networks that have entrenched themselves in American society. Since taking office as Attorney General in 1961, Kennedy has been unwavering in his pursuit of mob figures, leveraging the full might of the Justice Department to bring them to justice.

Kennedy's aggressive tactics have not only led to numerous indictments and convictions but have also raised public awareness about the pervasive influence of organized crime. His efforts have garnered both praise and criticism, but there's no denying the impact he's had on the fight against the mob.

A Broader National Effort

The Las Vegas arrests are just one facet of "Operation Big Squeeze," a nationwide initiative that has seen simultaneous actions in cities across the country. From Chicago to New York, federal agents have been relentless in their pursuit, targeting major crime families and their associates.

In a statement released yesterday, Attorney General Kennedy expressed his determination to continue the fight against organized crime. "We will not rest until we have dismantled these criminal enterprises that prey on our society," he said. "This operation is a testament to our resolve and a clear message to those who think they can operate above the law."

Looking Ahead

As the dust settles from this latest round of arrests, the focus now shifts to the legal battles that lie ahead. The arrested individuals, including Giancarlo, will face an array of charges ranging from racketeering to tax evasion. The Justice Department's Special Prosecutions Unit is expected to spearhead the cases, drawing on extensive evidence gathered through months of meticulous investigation.

For Las Vegas, a city that thrives on its reputation as a playground for the rich and famous, these arrests mark a significant chapter in its ongoing battle with organized crime. As federal agents continue their efforts, the message is clear: the days of the mob's unchecked influence in Sin City are numbered.

Community Response

Residents and local leaders have reacted with a mix of relief and anticipation. Many see the arrests as necessary for a safer, more lawful city. In contrast, others worry about the potential economic impact on the city's lucrative entertainment industry.

As Las Vegas comes to terms with this dramatic turn of events, the legacy of Robert Kennedy's campaign against organized crime continues to unfold, shaping the future of law enforcement in America.

~

Evilyn slowly sat, sinking into Frankie's chair while exhaling as if she had been holding her breath the entire time she read. At the same time, Sofia collected the newspaper and the documents underneath before sitting in the guest chair in front of the desk. Each quietly considered the implications of the morning news.

Evilyn looked up at Sofia and sighed in relief. "This changes everything," she said. "With Sam out of the picture, things might settle down for us."

Smiling, Sofia replied, "Agreed. We might have a chance to operate without constantly looking over our shoulders. Who knows what they'll find and pin on him?"

As they reread the article and continued discussing the implications, the tension in the room eased. Sam's arrest by the Feds relieved both women, signaling a possible shift in the power dynamics that dictated their lives.

The Check-Out

(Present)

There were few people at the front desk this early in the morning. Flights into Vegas had not yet begun to arrive, and few casino guests took the first departing flights of the day. City residents with jobs requiring travel booked the early flights.

Jack leaned against the counter, rotating his wallet in his fingertips and tapping its corners against the marble as he waited for the clerk to run his card and print his room folio. Each time he glanced at his watch during the delay, he estimated the time for the short ride to the airport, usually ten to fifteen minutes. Clearing security screening shouldn't take long this early, and even a walk to the farthest gate takes only ten to twenty minutes. *Flight 3808 departs at 6:05 a.m.*, Jack reminded himself. He looked at his watch again at 5:03 a.m. He had time but not much to spare.

"Apologies, sir," the clerk stated in an understated tone, sliding Jack's American Express card back to him across the polished, cold marble counter.

Jack initially assumed the apology was for the brief delay. When he realized it wasn't, he shook his head in denial. "No, no, no, that's not possible."

"Perhaps there's another card, Mr. Harper?"

"Just hold on, please," Jack replied, already logging into the account's application on his cellphone by placing his thumb over the biometric scanner to log in. As the page loaded on his screen, Jack saw the status banner noting the freeze on the account. He stared at it, his thoughts scrambling to understand. When Jack hit the refresh button, he glanced at his watch again and decided to figure the problem out later on the flight or at home. He didn't have time to argue with the clerk or call American Express; he had a flight to catch. Jack took his card back and handed his bank debit card to the young man behind the marble counter to replace it.

When the young desk clerk returned, he handed the card to Jack, clearing his throat and regretfully saying, "Apologies, Mr. Harper." It, too, was declined.

Jack glanced around for a rescue and then leaned in. "Come on now," he denounced, his tone firming. "That's our joint checking account."

"Yes, sir," the service agent replied, "it is a debit card, but I'm afraid the charge has been declined. Perhaps there is——."

"I said there's plenty of money in there," Jack rebutted, raising his tone. "It's got overdraft protection, damnit. I have to get to the airport NOW."

"I understand, Mr. Harper. One moment, please."

As the clerk walked behind the counter and through the door, Jack used his phone again to log into his bank's checking account. A feeling of befuddlement swept over him. Jack felt his chest tighten while his mind raced, searching for possible answers for why their joint checking account balance would read zero dollars. It wasn't possible. *Em?* He glanced at his watch again and read 5:17 a.m.. Jack did another quick time calculation.

"I'm sorry, what?" Jack asked, running his fingers through his hair and rubbing the back of his neck, fumbling his attention between his phone and his watch.

"Sir," the front desk manager repeated, turning the two pieces of paper around for Jack to scan before sliding the list of charges toward him. Room rates for two nights, local, state, and tourist taxes, resort fees, service fees, restaurant charges, room service charges, Emily's spa visit and laundry services for preparing her concern dress, and, of course, the charge from the Galleria Jewelers for Emily's earrings. "We must make suitable arrangements to satisfy your room charges and purchases, Mr. Harper."

"Yeah, of course," Jack dismissively snapped back before pausing to regain his composure. "You don't understand. There's been a mistake here. It's obviously an error, and I have to catch my flight. My wife is waiting for—." Jack paused, the courtesy text message from the airline to announce boarding momentarily distracting him. He rechecked his watch – 5:26 a.m. – half an hour from his flight home with his wife. He looked up to see the young clerk and the front desk manager watching him, flashbacks of powerlessness from the night before in front of The Coliseum echoing in his memory until his phone chimed and vibrated again, notifying him of another text message. This time, Emily was texting him.

[You're not here.]

Jack fumbled with his phone, almost dropping it while trying to type a rapid reply. He wanted to tell Emily something before she switched her phone off for takeoff. Jack tried to type his reply, holding one palm up toward the hotel staff, signaling them to give him a second. As he typed, his phone's screen lit up again.

[BTW, the vet texted to say Casey was alright, no thanks to

you, asshole.]

"Sir," the manager repeated.

"Wait, Emily," Jack shouted as if his phone could interpret his panicked words and transmit them to her on the plane. He felt exposed, the fight-or-flight response beginning to overpower him.

"Mr. Harper," the front desk manager stated tersely.

[I never want to see you again, you lying bastard.]

"Just hold on," Jack barked back, handling his phone while the screen went completely dark. The phone shut down; its power was finally exhausted from the last charge Friday night on Emily's charger.

Jack struggled to process the rapid influx of information. He laid the phone down on the cold marble, then pushed his thumb and index finger into his temples with one hand while rubbing the back of his neck with the other. *This can't be happening*, he told himself. Jack's blinking intensified and was now rapid, as was his heart rate. His breathing was shallow, and he could feel the sweat forming on his forehead as he got uncomfortably hot, unlike the lucky chip still in his pocket. It, in contrast, was cold and lifeless; its fortune expended and its value worthless. Jack drove his hand into his pocket to touch it, its icy surface almost burning him like a frostbite-inducing chill, numbing his fingers and searing his skin.

In a sudden and violent moment of rage, Jack heaved the chip, sending it skipping and sliding across the polished marble floor of the lobby. The chip flipped and spun, eventually landing on its narrow ribbed side, slowly rolling into the polished wingtip shoe of the stationary man standing near the lobby's back wall.

THE LOCKED DRAWER

(1963)

A week after reading about the Justice Department's arrests in the *Las Vegas Review-Journal,* Marshall and Ramirez knocked on the door of the Grant residence. Evilyn expected their visit; they called beforehand to arrange the meeting with her. She also appreciated the call, allowing her time to ensure Mrs. Jenkins could watch Richard and Lucy during the detective's visit. Evilyn looked forward to their update on the investigation.

"Would you gentlemen like something to drink? Coffee, or perhaps some fresh-brewed iced tea?"

"Thank you, no," answered Detective Marshall first. His partner politely declined as well. "If you don't mind, we would like to ask you some follow-up questions, Mrs. Grant. May we sit?" he asked, gesturing toward the grouping of sofa and chairs in the living room.

"Certainly. Please," Evilyn replied, sitting on the edge of the sofa while the detectives sat in the upholstered chairs opposite her. "You said questions?" Evilyn confirmed, expecting them to provide information or updates on the shooting rather than ask her more questions.

"Yes, Mrs. Grant," Ramirez quickly confirmed, anxious to get to the questioning as he removed his notebook from his jacket pocket. "What can you tell us about your relationship with Sofia Ferranero?"

"Relationship?" asked Evilyn. "In what way? She works with me at the Casbah. She worked for Frankie, but you already know this."

Ramirez exchanged a glance with Marshall before continuing. "We've learned of a few public fights between Ms. Ferranero and your late husband shortly before his shooting. Can you tell us anything about those, Mrs. Grant?"

"Why no," Evilyn answered. "They worked well together. Frankie relied on Sofia a great deal, as I do now. Frankie thought the world of Sofia. What sort of fights?" she asked.

"Were you aware your husband fired Ms. Ferranero after one of those altercations?" asked Detective Marshall.

"Of course not," she replied, trying to make sense of what the detectives might be trying to say or imply. "Other than her vacation, Sofia's been at the Casbah. Who said he fired her?"

The detectives exchanged glances again, digesting Evilyn's responses and silently debating which questions to ask next.

"Mrs. Grant, I know this is a personal question, and I do apologize," Marshall stated. "But were you and your husband having marital issues?"

Evilyn's hands, politely fixed on her knees as she sat on the sofa's edge, shot up sharply and landed on her chest just below the neck. "Of course not!" she answered, leaning back and away from the detective's offensive question.

"Did you suspect or did you accuse your husband of having an affair?" asked Ramirez, his tone more biting than it should have been.

"An affair? Absolutely not. Frankie would never do that." Evilyn wanted to bolt up and stand to escort the detectives to the door and regain her home's peaceful atmosphere before their arrival. "Where did you hear that?"

Marshall looked at Ramirez and soundlessly regained control of the questioning. "Apologies, Mrs. Grant. Some questions we need to ask."

"How about I ask you some questions," replied Evilyn. "What new information do you have about my husband's shooting? What's being done to find his killer?" Evilyn could feel her pulse quicken. Her arm began to quiver as she pointed toward the front window in the living room, reminding the detectives Frankie's killer was out there somewhere.

Detective Marshall understood Evilyn's frustration and assured her the police were doing everything possible to find the person or persons responsible for shooting her husband. He explained how patrolmen noted Frankie's wallet was missing at the crime scene but later recovered in a nearby alley a few blocks away. Any cash that may have been in the wallet was gone. Frankie's wedding band, as well as his watch, were still on his person when he was found in those early morning hours, lying in the street near death in a pool of blood.

The watch and wedding band were returned to Evilyn after a jeweler cleaned them of residual dirt and blood. She wore his ring on a thin chain around her neck, under her dress or blouse to keep it close to her heart. Evilyn put Frankie's watch away, saving it for Richard as a memento or tribute to his father when he was old enough to wear it. What was curious was that Frankie's wallet was taken, but his jewelry wasn't. Robbers usually grab both cash and jewelry. Robbers also seldom shoot their victims six times.

The police classified the murder a violent robbery for now. Still, for the detectives, the possibility of an organized crime slaying could not be dismissed.

Detective Marshall leaned forward. "Mrs. Grant. Are you aware of any dealings with organized crime by your husband? There might be some evidence connecting his murder to something bigger than robbery."

"Organized crime? Of course not. Frankie was a good Christian man. He was a service veteran. He worked hard to open a clean casino. We have two children. Look around this house, Detective. Does this look like an organized crime household to you?"

"No, of course not, Mrs. Grant. I did not mean to imply—"

Evilyn interrupted Marshall and asked, "Does this have anything to do with the crackdown I read about in the papers last week?"

"Did your husband know Sam Giancarlo, Mrs. Grant?" asked Ramirez.

Evilyn paused, crossing her arms and leaning back to rest her elbow on the arm of the sofa. She glanced at Marshall and then stared at Ramirez, her mind putting bits and pieces of information together, like when you see a cluster of shapes and colors fitting together in a giant jigsaw puzzle.

"Yes, I understand he did," she answered. "He wanted to buy into the Casbah, but Frankie refused. Sam Giancarlo approached me as well after Frankie's funeral. He wanted me to sell the whole thing to him. I declined as well."

The two detectives glanced at one another again, silently

exchanging thoughts and opinions.

"Did he threaten you in any way when you declined his offer?" asked Marshall.

Evilyn brought her fingers up to her ear and lightly tugged at her earring while she thought. "He questioned my ability to run a casino without experience or connections. He said I can't be serious about keeping it." Evilyn paused again.

"Anything else?" asked Ramirez as Marshall jotted notes in his notebook.

Evilyn hesitated. "He claimed he and Frankie had an agreement. He claimed he had already given Frankie $150,000 as an investment. That's not true, though. My attorney and accountants have already reviewed everything. My husband's business has no private investors, just the bank loans and our private funds."

"You mean your business, don't you, Mrs. Grant?" clarified Ramirez.

***

After Detectives Marshall and Ramirez left Evilyn's home, she drove to the Casbah. Tonight would mark the first time Evilyn would venture into the casino in the late evening. Still, with Mrs. Jenkins agreeing to keep the children overnight and knowing Sofia mentioned earlier in the day that she had a dinner engagement, Evilyn did not want to wait until tomorrow. Something was gnawing at her.

It did not take long for Evilyn to find the key. She knew her husband and his habits. He left essential account numbers written on a piece of paper under his desk pad. A few new and crisp large-denomination bills were always kept in the dictionary on the bookshelf under the letter "C" in case of an emergency. Frankie did not memorize phone numbers. Instead, he wrote them in a small black phone directory, the same size as detectives used to jot down investigation notes to store in their jacket pockets. Frankie always wrote the numbers in pencil, knowing numbers sometimes change and the entries occasionally needed to be erased. Like the account numbers, emergency cash, and phone numbers, Frankie had a place where he kept his desk drawer key, and Evilyn quickly found it at the bottom of the pen holder cup sitting on his desk.

When she unlocked and opened the drawer, Evilyn thought she might find fifteen bundles of $100 bills, all wrapped in paper currency straps, indicating $10,000 per bundle. They would likely be in a small metal cash box or a paper bag. She wasn't sure but needed to know. Evilyn wasn't sure what to do with the cash if discovered; she had not thought that far ahead. She wanted to avoid finding the money Sam claimed to have invested in the casino. Evilyn hoped for confirmation Frankie was not involved in an off-the-books deal with Sam Giancarlo. She was not prepared to believe her husband had ties to organized crime. As the new owner of the Casbah, what would happen to Richard and Lucy if their mother was arrested in the next round of DOJ sweeps? What Evilyn found locked away in the desk drawer was even more shocking and unexpected than cash.

Evilyn sat on the edge of the oversized executive chair as she lifted the drawer's contents and placed them on the desk. She opened the small felt box first. Inside, a beautiful set of earrings made of cut aquamarine stones set in platinum and encircled with smaller brilliant diamonds. They were stunning, but not meant for her.

Opened greeting cards were among the drawer's contents: cards professing Sofia's love for Frankie, cards thanking her late husband for flowers or dinners or small gifts, and cards reminding the former owner of the Casbah about his promise to divorce his wife and marry her instead. They were hurtful to read and not meant for her eyes.

On top of the greeting cards and the small felt box of stunning earrings was a large envelope. Evilyn hesitated before opening it, her vision obscured by the sadness. It was like losing her husband and the father of her children all over again. Evilyn wanted to deny what she had already seen and avoid what she had yet not. She dug in her purse for tissues and dried her eyes, sniffing and wiping at her nose. Evilyn's hands trembled as she pinched the metal tabs, keeping the envelope's contents secret. As she slowly pulled the contents out, old photographs and yellowed documents fell into her lap like heavy stones, each the weight of a hidden past she knew nothing of—Sofia's letter to Frankie, pleading for him to help her find *their* son, her remembrance of how and when they met, and black and white photographs of a newborn infant.

With each revelation, the betrayal and heartbreak deepened, leaving Evilyn feeling as if her world had shattered, forcing her to confront a truth more painful than she had ever imagined.

THE SUNRISE

(Present)

As soon as Jack threw the old poker chip across the lobby, he grabbed the extended handle of his carry-on and quickly darted toward the hotel entrance. He could hear the voices of the hotel staff shouting behind him for his return. Still, those shouts became mere fading echoes into the background noise of Jack's anxiety as he entered the revolving doors. The doors spun slowly, mocking his urgency, but he pushed through, his heart pounding.

Clearing the doors, he glanced at his watch and decided what to do next. Twenty minutes. Each second ticked away like a bomb's countdown, each one amplifying his desperation. A few guests passed Jack as they moved toward the hotel's entrance, either just getting in from a long night on the strip or newly arriving in the pre-dawn hours to check in. Whatever their circumstances, they were as blurred a vision to Jack as his choices on what to do next. Their carefree attitudes contrasted sharply with the desperation and turmoil he felt inside, making him feel even more isolated in his frantic state.

When a figure called Jack Harper's name from the direction of the revolving door behind him, Jack bolted from under the hotel's covered portico toward the street ahead. The hotel staffer didn't bother to give chase, though. They had his wallet he had just left on the marble countertop when fumbling with his dying cell phone just before he threw the chip and hastily dashed to the door to catch his flight. As he sprinted away, the staffer's voice drifted into the distance, replaced by the noise of the waking city.

With his single bag rolling behind him, Jack began walking the distance between the mega-resorts and Harry Reid International Airport. The airport's tower and jets waiting their turn to taxi onto the runway were within plain sight of the lively Vegas strip, but the actual distance to the terminal was over two miles, and Jack had no chance of crossing that distance in time. His pace was brisk at first but then slowed to a trudge, each step becoming heavier than the previous. His stride reflected the emotional weight of his failures, each footfall a reminder of his broken promises and missteps. Flight 3808 was due to depart in ten minutes.

Jack had no cash for a cab. He had no wallet, no identification. Hailing an Uber was impossible on his phone; it was as powerless as Jack felt. Alternating between the sidewalk and street pavement, across Tropicana Avenue and down Paradise Road, beyond where pedestrians were meant to walk between the hotel district and the airport, the brightness and increasing heat of a new day starkly contrasted with the dark and coolness of the casino floor. The casino, with its artificial lights and air-conditioned comfort, had been a refuge for Jack. He could escape reality there. But now, reality was unavoidable. What had been so easy to take before became challenging to accept now.

Each of Jack's steps felt like a penance, a slow march through his own personal purgatory. His thoughts churned, a turbulent mix of regret, frustration, and self-recrimination. Jack tried to imagine Emily's calm and reassuring voice to guide him through the chaos as her voice had done so many times before. But Emily was gone now, and there was no calm and guiding voice. Jack was left to navigate this nightmare on his own. The airport, so tantalizingly close, mocked him with its inaccessibility. His dreams of reaching Emily in time and reconciling were slipping away like the minutes ticking down to his flight's departure.

Pre-dawn became dawn as the first rays of daybreak shone through the Sunrise Mountain Range, gradually replacing the artificial lighting illuminating Jack's surroundings and path to the airport. The same sun over the same mountain range illuminated Frankie's path to the hospital sixty years prior.

A GRAVE RECKONING

(1963)

Evilyn's hands shook as she turned the key to lock her car door at dawn. The weight of her discoveries from the night before pressed heavily on her heart, making each step toward the Casbah's entrance feel like a journey through quicksand. She had barely slept, her mind racing with questions and the overwhelming sense of betrayal. The early morning light filtering through the mountain range surrounding the city did little to lift her spirits. Richard and Lucy would be rising soon. Mrs. Jenkins would feed and dress them before driving them to school, while their mother would confront the consequences of other people's actions.

As she passed through the casino floor on her way to the Eye above, the sounds of slot machines and murmured conversations of early morning gamblers were a distant buzz in her ears. She barely registered the greetings from her staff, her thoughts consumed by the contents of Frankie's drawer.

Evilyn knew Sofia would soon arrive at the office, starting her day like any other. The thought of confronting her stirred a mix of dread and determination within Evilyn as she ascended the stairs. She needed answers and wanted to address the shocking revelations immediately. Evilyn had a business to run, children to raise, and a life to live. What was about to happen was essential for her family to move forward.

When Evilyn reached the casino owner's office, she paused outside the door, taking a deep breath to steady herself. Pushing it open, she stepped inside, her gaze immediately drawn to the desk drawer. Evilyn placed her pocketbook on the credenza behind her desk and settled into her chair. She felt the weight of her discovery from the prior night transform into a source of empowerment. She realized there were limits to what one could control, and other people's actions would remain beyond that. Evilyn was ready to harness this newfound empowerment to take action; she refused to play the role of a victim. She sat quietly in her office, the new Casbah Hotel and Casino owner, and waited like a lioness in the brush, poised to protect her newborn cubs.

When Sofia entered the Eye, she was surprised to see Evilyn in Frankie's office so early in the morning. "Good morning, Evilyn," Sofia said with a warm smile that quickly faded when she saw the look on Evilyn's face. "Is everything alright?"

Evilyn rose and walked around her desk, telling Sofia to sit in the guest chair while she closed the door, the click of the latch sounding ominous. She crossed the room and sat behind her desk; the items she discovered the night before spread out on the desktop. Evilyn didn't say anything at first, her eyes boring into Sofia's, searching for any signs of recognition, remorse, or guilt. Finally, she spoke, her voice low and controlled. "Sofia, I need to know the truth. About you and Frankie."

Sofia's expression widened, and she glanced at the papers on the desk, her hands fidgeting nervously. "Evilyn, I—"

"Don't lie to me," Evilyn interrupted, her voice quivering with barely contained anger. She picked up the small felt box and opened it, revealing the aquamarine earrings. "These were in his drawer. Along with these," she added, lifting the greeting cards one by one and dropping them on the desk, each a painful reminder of the betrayal.

Sofia's face turned pale, and she leaned back, her eyes darting to the door as if considering an escape. "Evilyn, please, let me explain—"

Evilyn slammed her hand on the desk, causing Sofia to flinch. "Explain? Explain how you were involved with my husband? How you wrote him love letters? How you encouraged him to leave me, promising him a better future with you?" Evilyn's voice broke as the tears welled up. "How could you, Sofia? I trusted you. How could you do that to my children?"

Sofia's eyes fixed with a cold and dead gaze as she stood and took inventory of the items on the desk: promises, pleas, evidence, and hopes. "Evilyn, it wasn't supposed to be like this. Frankie and I," she paused. "We had a history. It was a complicated history. But I never meant to hurt you."

Evilyn shook her head, her heart aching with every word she heard. "Complicated? It is more than complicated, Sofia." Evilyn reached for the large envelope and turned it over, spilling old photographs and documents across the desk. "You have a child together. A son you kept secret. How could you do this to me? To Frankie? To my children?"

Sofia's expression softened as she returned to the chair and sank into it. "I didn't know how to tell you. Frankie was going to leave you, but he changed his mind. He left me with nothing."

Evilyn's anger flared again. "And what about now? Now that he's gone, what were you trying to get from me? Was this all just a ruse to get control of the Casbah?"

Sofia looked up, her eyes now red and swollen, her tough exterior softened. "It's true. At first, I wanted Frankie. I wanted him to share the Casbah with me. I worked so hard to get us here. But Frankie was weak, and he wouldn't leave you. Then, I just wanted him to help me find our son. He's here, Evilyn, somewhere in this country. I know it. I have proof." As Sofia reached for the pile of documents on the desk, Evilyn quickly bent down to shield them with her hands and arms.

"Don't you touch anything," Evilyn shouted, batting Sofia's hand away. "This was all in Frankie's desk and it's going to the police. They need to figure out who killed my husband."

Sofia's hands grasped the corner of the desk, her eyes narrowed, and she lifted her chin defiantly. "You think I wanted it to happen this way? Do you think I enjoyed sneaking around, living in the shadows of your perfect little life? No, Evilyn. I did what I had to do. Frankie promised me a future, and when he backed out, he left me with nothing but empty words. So, yes, I pursued him, I pushed, but only because I knew what we had was real, and I wasn't going to let him walk away from that—from us—without a fight."

Sofia leaned in, her voice gaining a hard edge. "And don't you dare think I did this just to hurt you. I couldn't care less about you or your precious image of the perfect wife. Frankie belonged to me deep down, and I think you knew that."

Sofia's eyes blazed with anger and pain as she added, "I wanted the Casbah because it was ours. Frankie and I built that dream together. It was never just his, and it certainly wasn't yours. I've been fighting for what's rightfully mine, and I won't apologize for that."

By now, the women's actions and shouting had diverted the attention of the security personnel in the Eye, who were otherwise monitoring closed-circuit television screens to surveil the casino floor below. They had summoned two security guards who were now outside of Evilyn's office. When Evilyn waved them in, they entered.

Evilyn stared at Sofia for a long moment, the silence between them thick with tension. Finally, she spoke, her voice calm and confident. "You've shattered my family, and there's no fixing that. You're no longer welcome here."

Evilyn instructed her security personnel to remove Sofia from the premises and ban her from stepping inside the Casbah again. As they flanked Sofia and walked her to the open door, Evilyn called out to her assistant and asked her to please get Detectives Marshall and Ramirez on the phone. Evilyn watched Sofia leave the office for the last time. She felt both relief and sorrow, letting out a long and cleansing breath.

Although the revelations and events of the past twelve hours left Evilyn tested and shaken, she emerged more resilient for the sake of her children and herself. Sitting back in her chair, she looked at the items on her desk one last time before collecting them and placing them back into the drawer. Evilyn was more determined than ever to move forward and do what needed to come next.

***

The cemetery was peaceful, a gentle breeze rustling the fronds of the old Mexican and California fan palms lining the long, windy path. Evilyn strolled hard-packed gravel respectfully with her children beside her. The weight of the past few months bore heavily on her, but she knew this visit was essential for her and the kids.

When they arrived at Frankie's grave, they saw the newly placed headstone for the first time. Crafted from polished granite, the reddish hue of the stone caught the morning sunlight, adding a touch of warmth and distinction without drawing undue attention. The headstone was etched with Frankie's name, birth and death dates, and the words "Beloved Husband and Father." Richard and Lucy kneeled and placed the flowers Evilyn had bought for them to give their father at its base. Evilyn kneeled between her children and traced the letters of the engraving with her fingertip. Richard and Lucy then did the same to mimic their mother's actions.

"Alright, kids," she said softly, looking first at her son and then at her daughter. "Why don't you tell Daddy what you've been up to?"

Since Richard was the older of the two, he spoke first. "Hi, Dad," he began. "School's been good. I got an A on my math test last week. Mrs. Jamison says I'm doing really well. I," he paused. "I miss you. I wish you were here to see it." Richard reached into his pocket and pulled out one of his prized Matchbox cars. It was the one Frankie always chose first for himself when the two played on the marble floors of their home. The car was a 1962 Lincoln Continental, a model of the stylish American luxury car. Richard placed the die-cast replica on the ground in front of his headstone. "Here, Dad," Richard whispered. "I want you to keep this one. It's your favorite."

Younger and the more emotional of the two, Lucy followed suit, her voice trembling slightly. "Daddy, I drew a picture of us in art class. It's hanging on the fridge now. And I started taking gymnastics in school. Do you want to see me do a handstand, Daddy?" Lucy stood up and took a few steps back before leaning forward to place her hands on the ground. She tumbled forward to land on her back on the first two attempts but successfully held a handstand for a few seconds on her third try. Both Evilyn and Richard clapped when she returned to her feet. "Did you see that,

Daddy? Aren't you proud of me?"

Evilyn smiled through her tears, her heart aching at seeing her children speaking to their father. "That's wonderful, you two. Daddy is so proud of you both." She paused, then gently nudged them. "Why don't you wait in the car for a minute while Mommy has a word alone with Daddy?"

Richard and Lucy nodded, understanding, and gave the headstone a final, lingering look before heading back down the path to the car. Evilyn watched them go, her heart heavy yet filled with love for her children. Once they were out of earshot, she turned back to the grave, her expression hardening as the tears came freely.

"Frankie," she began, her voice breaking. "I found your drawer. The letters, the photos, the secrets you kept from me." She took a shuddering breath, her fingers still tracing his name on the headstone. "It was like losing you all over again. I never imagined you had another life or another child. The pain, Frankie, it's unbearable. Why would you—" Evilyn paused for a long moment and glanced to the left to see her children patiently standing near the car, looking in her direction and giving their mother the time and consideration she asked of them.

Wiping her tears, Evilyn tried to steady her voice. "But I've had time to think. I know you loved us. You loved Richard and Lucy. And despite everything, I loved you too. All that glitters is not gold, Frankie. We had our struggles, but we had something real, something precious. We still do."

Evilyn stood up, brushing any small blades of grass from her dress, and looked down at the grave. "I forgive you, Frankie. For everything. I have to, for the sake of our children and myself. We can't change the past, but we can learn from it. And I know now how important it is to appreciate what we have, to cherish every moment."

Evilyn took a deep breath and felt a sense of peace wash over her. "Goodbye, Frankie. Rest in peace." With a final glance at the headstone, she turned and walked back to the car, her steps lighter than before.

The sun was setting, casting a warm golden glow over the cemetery. As Evilyn approached the car, Richard and Lucy looked up, their faces filled with concern and love. She smiled at them, a genuine smile, and they ran to her, wrapping their arms around their mother in a tight embrace.

Frankie's headstone stood silent, a testament to a complicated life and enduring love. Evilyn glanced back one last time before getting into the car, ready to move forward with her children, appreciating the present and the future they would build together.

Dearly Departed

(Present)

Jack stayed down when his stride wavered, stumbling onto the hard cement sidewalk beneath him. He crawled a few feet to the chain-link fence separating the road from the airport runway and propped his back against it for support. Cars whizzed by, and planes took off overhead, everyone heading somewhere he wasn't. Jack's luck had run out. His luck was as dry as the desert sand and rocks surrounding him. But then again, there was no such thing as luck for Jack. Instead, his fate was merely a product of his actions and decisions. But what was *fate*? Was fate not the events in Jack's life predetermined by a supernatural force beyond his control?

He sat there, feeling the metal of the fence press into his back and the rough texture of the concrete beneath him. The suitcase beside him held all he had left—the clothes on his back, a few personal items, and the remnants of a life that had seemed so perfect. He had no identification, no cash, and a dead cell phone. The world had become a vast, indifferent expanse, and Jack had become an insignificant speck on its surface.

When Jack looked up and saw the planes ascend into the sky, he knew one of them carried Emily. She was heading back to the comfortable home she owned, yet they shared. She was heading back to a life she would recreate for herself. It would be a better life, one without him. Jack had missed his flight. More than that, he had squandered his second chance.

As Jack sensed the motion around him, people moving with purpose and principle, he reflected on what he once had and was now lost. Emily's natural intelligence and beauty, her patience and forbearance when he was not who he should have been, and her strength and resilience when he had none—all gone. Not because of some cruel twist of fate, but because of his choices. The drinking and gambling, the self-indulgence and the lies, the inability to see what truly mattered until it was too late.

Jack thought about the moments he had squandered during the weekend and the opportunities he let slip through his fingers like sand. He remembered the hope on Emily's face each time she thought he had returned to be the man she met and thought he was. Jack remembered the frustration on her face when denied entry into the concert and when he admitted to keeping the old poker chip and gambling. He recalled Emily's anger when she discovered his selfish deception in keeping Casey's illness from her. Most of all, Jack remembered the silent resignation in her eyes when he promised to change for the hundredth time, and she realized then he never would.

It wasn't just bad luck that brought Jack here. He knew it was his insatiable desire for more—the thrill of the next big win, the illusion that he could dismiss his problems if only he had enough money. Jack had focused on chasing his ideas of success and failed to cherish the reality he already had.

Jack sat on the hard concrete in a pool of failures, his regrets bleeding out of him like gaping gunshot holes of consequences. He realized true success wasn't in the fleeting victories or the false security of money. Success was in the love he took for granted, the relationship he neglected, the simple moments of joy he had ignored. Jack now understood all that glittered was not gold, and sometimes, the things he sought most desperately were the very things leading him to his undoing.

At some point, a police officer would stop and ask for identification, which Jack didn't have. He would recount his weekend in Las Vegas with the officer, a familiar tale of luck and loss. Jack knew he would not be allowed to remain on the side of the busy roadway and would likely be labeled a 'stranded traveler' and transported somewhere. The connection between the man calling himself Jack Harper and the hotel charges he ran from was inevitable. The earring purchase, a husband's lovely anniversary gift to his wife, would technically be classified as theft. The rest of the weekend's charges on the hotel folio would have to be paid by Emily. The bill would serve as another painful reminder to her, just one more item in a long list of reminders, like the cost and time of filing the divorce papers or storing Jack's possessions once she removed them from her home. Jack foresaw all these things as he sat there and watched the planes roar overhead, eventually becoming distant specks in the sky.

FOUR MONTHS LATER

(1964)

Four months had passed since Evilyn made the surprising discovery in Frankie's desk drawer and dismissed Sofia. The two had not spoken since. Now, as Evilyn packed the last of the boxes, Richard and Lucy bustled around the living room, wrapping up memories and preparing for the movers' arrival in the morning. The Grant family was moving to Westport to stay with her parents until they could find a new home to call their own. She thought her hometown, with its beautiful beaches and change of seasons, would be a good change for them all and an opportunity for her children to develop a strong relationship with their grandparents. It was about as far as she could get from the sand, heat, and memories of Las Vegas Valley.

Evilyn remembered reading, in Ladies' Home Journal, she believed, a list of life's most stressful events. The Grants were experiencing many of them now: the death of a spouse and father, a significant cross-country move involving changes in schools and residence, and a change of friends, occupation, and lifestyle.

The sale of the Casbah closed just the day before. The transaction had been quick, all cash and for a fair price, to an investment group with principles unknown to Evilyn. She did not need to know who they were. She did not care. Mr. Watkins, her attorney, handled the negotiation and closing, marking the end of one chapter for the Grant family and the beginning of another.

As the children made up challenges for themselves as they packed, who could wrap pictures the fastest or which could pack the most items to make the boxes the heaviest, Evilyn walked into the kitchen and sat at the dinette table. She held the large envelope addressed to 'Evilyn Grant' and stamped with large red letters, 'PRIVATE AND CONFIDENTIAL.' Evilyn had examined the envelope's contents from the Burns International Detective Agency several times over the past week but wanted to review them just once more before packing them in a special box reserved for the most important of her official documents. She read the letter carefully again, mindful of her children's whereabouts in the other room.

~

Burns International Detective Agency

Confidential Investigation Report

Date: January 17, 1964

To: Mrs. Evilyn Grant

Subject: Summary of Investigation Findings Regarding Sofia Ferranero

Dear Mrs. Grant,

After a thorough investigation utilizing a variety of sources and methods, Burns International Detective Agency has confirmed the legitimacy of the documents provided to us by you regarding the paternity claim of Sofia Ferranero.

Based on our comprehensive findings, we can assert with a high degree of certainty that Mr. Francis Grant likely fathered a child with Sofia Ferranero in 1946. That child's legally registered name is Beniamino Giancarlo.

Our investigation was bolstered by the efforts of Mr. Giancarlo himself, who conducted an independent inquiry in search of his birth parents two years ago in Palermo, Sicily. The evidence supporting our conclusion was gathered from several sources, including civil registry offices, US naval and military records, the American Red Cross, church archives, consulate records, and interviews with local civilians in Palermo.

Please note that at no point did any employees or investigators from Burns International have direct contact with Mr. Giancarlo during our inquiry. Furthermore, we cannot substantiate any findings that he may have obtained independently during his personal investigation.

We can also confirm that Mr. Beniamino Giancarlo was granted an F-1 student visa to study in the United States as a foreign national in 1962 and is currently a registered student at the University of California, Santa Barbara.

Our investigative team has diligently reviewed and cross-referenced all obtained information to ensure its accuracy and reliability. We understand the sensitive nature of this matter and have taken every precaution to handle it with discretion and professionalism.

Attached please find copies of relevant records and documents. Please do not hesitate to reach out if you require any further assistance regarding our findings.

Yours sincerely,

Mr. Richard Thompson
Lead Investigator
Burns International Detective Agency

~

Each time Evelyn read the summary letter, one word stood out above all others: the name 'Giancarlo.' Burns International uncovered far more detail than Sofia had provided, including the fact that Sam Giancarlo's family in Sicily had sponsored

229

Beniamino's adoption and upbringing after birth. Was it coincidental Sam and Beniamino shared the same last name? Evilyn knew Sofia distrusted and hated Sam, but did Sofia know about her son's adoption by the Giancarlo family after giving him up for adoption at birth? *She couldn't have*, Evilyn thought.

"Hello, Grant residence," Evilyn answered from the kitchen phone when it rang.

"Hello, Mrs. Grant? Mr. Myers here, down at First National Bank. How are you this afternoon?"

"Yes, Mr. Myers," she replied, gathering the letter and supporting documents to place back into the Burns International envelope. "I'm well, thanks."

"That's good to hear. Mrs. Grant, I just wanted to inform you the funds transfer from yesterday's closing is complete. It is now available in your account."

Evilyn felt the weight of responsibility and anxiety over the decision to sell the Casbah lift from her shoulders. She took a deep, cleansing breath, relieved the financial burden was finally gone. She could now look forward and focus on rebuilding their lives. "Thank you, Mr. Myers. That's excellent news. I appreciate your call to let me know."

"Mrs. Grant, I hope we can schedule something soon to discuss the best way to invest these funds. It's a considerable amount of money, Mrs. Grant."

"Thank you, Mr. Myers. We'll talk soon. Goodbye." Evilyn rested the phone's receiver on her shoulder as she pressed the hook switch to disconnect the call. She paused to give her following action one last consideration, even though she had reviewed the decision a hundred times during the past few days, coming to the same conclusion nearly every time.

With resolve, Evilyn dialed her attorney's number to confirm establishing a trust for Beniamino Giancarlo to support his college education. It was a gesture of closure and goodwill to honor Frankie's memory and set right some of the wrongs of the past.

When she hung up the phone, Evilyn walked around the familiar home in Paradise Palms where she and Frankie started their family. Now stripped of the personal touches that help make a house a home, the rooms became mere echoes of the past. The movers would pick up the furniture and boxes in the morning, leaving the rooms empty. Evilyn felt a mixture of sadness and anticipation for the future. Richard and Lucy would have a fresh start, away from the shadows of the Casbah and the ghosts of their father's mistakes.

Gathering her children, Evilyn stepped out onto the porch one last time. The sun was setting over the desert horizon, casting a warm glow over their departure. She took a deep breath, feeling a sense of closure and readiness for the new beginning. "Let's go home," Evilyn said, her voice filled with subdued determination. Ahead lay the promise of a new life for Evilyn—a life built on forgiveness, resilience, and the enduring love of her family.

The Lucky Chip

(Present)

In that early morning hour before sunrise, Jack threw the poker chip across the lobby, convinced that the unlucky find was to blame for all his misfortunes that weekend. The plastic chip flipped and spun before landing on its narrow ribbed side and slowly rolling across the polished marble floor. The gentleman near the lobby's back wall watched the purple chip slowly roll toward him. When it tapped his polished wingtip shoe, it fell on its side, exposing the familiar Casbah Hotel and Casino lettering and logo.

Benjamin gracefully bent over and picked the chip up, casually slipping it into his pressed bellman's uniform pocket. Shortly after, when the bellman called for Mr. Harper by name, Jack took off running toward the street.

The bellman worked long hours that evening. He usually did. When he arrived at his modest apartment in the late afternoon, the sun was low on the horizon, and the evening desert air was rapidly cooling. Benjamin poured himself a drink, a whiskey neat, and walked to the large window to gaze at the distant mountain range as burnt orange light filled his study through the slats of the wooden blinds. He loved the natural light of the early morning and late afternoon hours. Mountain ranges, sunrises, and sunsets—they all reminded Benjamin of his childhood.

When the sun sank below the desert sand, its light replaced by the waning gibbous of the moon, Benjamin strolled the length of the room and pulled the chain on the banker's lamp atop his desk. He sat and savored the liquid in his lowball glass, sipping the pour casually as he slowly surveyed the items on his desk and those on the wall above it. This evening was memorable for Benjamin. He would take his time this evening, recalling his childhood and admiring his accomplishments. He had nearly eighty years of them, most of them satisfying and a few that were not.

Benjamin often took time for these quiet moments in the evenings after a long day of watching people scurry around, oblivious to life around them as they talked about nothing on their cell phones and stared into their screens with glazed-over eyes, absorbing fake news or fixating on stupid snippets of ridiculously staged mishaps meant to make others they didn't know laugh. The whole world wanted attention, while no one wanted to take responsibility. Everything today was fast and virtual. Everything growing up in Sicily had been slow and true—everything except the identity of his true parents, that is.

Beniamino knew as an early teenager he would find his birth parents. By sixteen, he was actively searching for clues. Beniamino asked people questions and requested records from the Church of San Giovanni degli Eremiti. The Giancarlo family taught their adopted son the value of hard work and determination, and he wasn't afraid to apply those lessons in his quest for the truth. Beniamino harvested lemons and olives from the trees for the churches and convents. He tended gardens for his neighbors. Beniamino helped fishermen on their boats, casting their nets and hauling their catches. He worked for favors, for information, and for leads. Beniamino did all of this with the utmost discretion.

Privacy and anticipating the needs of others while being mindful not to impose were among the first of the great codes he honed to a fine skill and lived by in his profession.

Benjamin poured himself another whiskey neat. He didn't usually have two, but today was a memorable day. Not all memorable days are worth celebrating, but they are nonetheless significant.

Above Benjamin's desk hung a square frame containing four passenger tickets. The first was for the transatlantic voyage from the Port of Palermo to New York Harbor, taking him twelve days to complete. Traveling by plane would have been faster, but the young Beniamino did not mind. The voyage gave him time to study and practice his English for the new life summoning him to America.

The second ticket was for the Broadway Limited from New York to Chicago to meet his uncle Sam. That was the first time Beniamino had taken a train, and the comfortable eleven-hour ride allowed him to see some of the countryside of this vast new country.

The third ticket in the frame was for Beniamino's first travel by jet aircraft, a sixteen-hour American Airlines Flight from Chicago to Los Angeles with stops in Dallas and Las Vegas. His uncle Sam accompanied him on the first two legs of the flight, deplaning in Vegas while Beniamino continued to Los Angeles. The trip gave the two Giancarlos from different eras time to reacquaint themselves and discuss their futures.

Years ago, when Sam moved to the States to establish himself and the operation in Vegas, he ensured Beniamino was well cared for back home. Now that Beniamino was joining him, Sam intended to continue his mentorship in the States. The young Giancarlo would first need an American education, however.

The fourth and final ticket proudly displayed in the frame above Benjamin's desk was for the short three-hour Greyhound bus ride from Los Angeles to Santa Barbara. In those two weeks, the young American-Sicilian traveled over 7,400 miles, retracing much of the route of his mother's exile almost two decades before.

As the polite and unassuming bellman sipped his drink, he gazed at the faded black-and-white photograph of the young girl standing before the cathedral after Sunday service, proudly holding up for the camera her grandmother's gift that hung around her neck. The same Trinacria necklace was now carefully laced around the picture frame, its Medusa head emblem next to the young girl's image. Benjamin slightly gestured to toast the photograph of his mother.

Reaching into his vest pocket, Benjamin opened the small felt box and placed it beside the frame, returning the aquamarine earrings to their rightful place next to his mother's photograph. The earrings had traveled far and passed through many hands yet brought pleasure to none. Crafted to Frankie's specifications for Sofia but never given to her. Discovered by Evilyn and abandoned in Frankie's desk drawer, discarded for the new owners of the Casbah. Worn by Sofia and willed to Benjamin upon her death. Planted in the jeweler's showcase with the help of a salesman, then sold to Jack. A bellman's quick hand in Jack's coat pocket, while he was mesmerized by the roulette wheel, ensured they would never reach Emily.

Benjamin squared his chair up to the desk and opened the scrapbook in the center of the desk pad. Each time he turned a page, tiny particles of dust rose from within the album, dancing and swirling under the illumination of the banker's lamp like minute memories released forever by age and scattered into the silent ether of his past.

In this mystical space, Benjamin's memories resided: newspaper clippings of the Casbah's grand opening, articles detailing Frankie Grant's shooting, his death, the unsolved case that grew cold and eventually faded away with time, and the sale of the casino to a private, unnamed investor group.

The casino only lasted another decade or so until the arrival of the mega-resorts, eventually falling into decay and occupied by prostitutes, drug addicts, and the homeless. The city condemned the property and eventually tore the hotel and casino down, leaving its principal owner in the investment group, Sofia Ferranero, penniless after settling property back taxes and fines owed to The City of Las Vegas.

With backing from the Alliance and Sam in prison, Benjamin's mother fulfilled her dream and obtained her casino. It was short-lived, however. The Alliance dissolved with the crackdown on organized crime, and The Casbah fell into ruin with the arrival of the Vegas entertainment mega-resorts. Sofia succumbed to odd jobs beneath her ambition and poor health. She died being honored by her son without ever really having known who he was or what he did. Sofia became dust in another desert sunset for someone else's Sunrise Mountain Range sunrise.

This space in Benjamin's dimly lit and unassuming apartment is where many of Benjamin's memories floated, untouched and unspoken, yet ever-present, influencing his sense of self, history, and purpose. The old apartment was where Beniamino became Benjamin, as shown in the records and documents in his scrapbook of history. The spot was where, late at night, he admired his mother for her grit and determination and despised his father for abandoning him and betraying her.

Beniamino's adopted family raised him to respect specific values and codes: appreciation for hard-earned gains and gifts, respect for and reliance on family, and unwavering loyalty to those who stood by him, no matter the cost. There was an irreverence for those who broke the code.

Benjamin rewarded himself with just one last pour, lightly clanking his glass against the rim of another whiskey glass on his desk. That glass contained six spent shell casings from a .38 Special fired precisely eighty years ago to the day. Not all anniversaries are celebrated, but many are memorable. The young Sicilian immigrant had been all too eager to satisfy his first assignment as a recruit-in-training in his uncle's organization. Like the sea voyage, train ride, and jet flight, it was Benjamin's first experience executing the values of unwavering loyalty and family code to those who stood by him, no matter the cost.

In this mystical space where memories dance and swirl in the light only to be scattered into the silent ether of the past, Benjamin carefully placed the lucky purple chip into another envelope yellowed with age. Before he did, however, he lit a candle and held the chip close to its flame. The bellman then whispered the La Vecchia Religione chat in the old language. It was the language Sofia's grandmother Nonnina used when she and Sofia walked the narrow streets of Palermo searching for fresh produce and seafood in the local markets. It was the language Nonnina spoke when teaching Sofia how to cook, sew, embroider, and cast enchantments.

Benjamin read his mother's worn note and whispered the charm in his old language, repeating it in English to ensure the token retained the same luck and retribution his mother had imbued within it all those years ago:

~

With true heart and pure intent,

This chip I bless, good fortune sent.

As long as he remains steadfast,

Luck will stay, and riches last.

But should his heart betray his vow,

May fortune turn and bring him down.

By powers old and spirits wise,

This charm I cast, let it be so.

~

Benjamin placed the poker chip in the yellowed envelope and wrote, '*To Sofia. I'm so sorry. Frankie*' on the front with his finest fountain pen and penmanship.

The following morning, the bellman securely placed the yellowed envelope in Room 214 to await its discovery by the next lucky and deserving guest.

END

THANK YOU!

I greatly appreciate the time you took to give my book a read. As a small indie publisher, it means a lot, and I hope you enjoyed the story. You are making a difference in my journey as a writer!

Please consider leaving your honest feedback on Amazon. Your review or rating means the world to me and helps other potential readers decide if this story is right for them. You can still leave reviews on Amazon even if you obtained the book elsewhere. If you are a Goodreads subscriber, you may also leave feedback there. Reader feedback does wonders for the book, and I would love to hear about your experiences reading it!

QR Code for Amazon Rating or Review

Thank you again for your support!

239

ACKNOWLEDGMENTS

Completing this novel would not have been possible without the encouragement and support of the following people, all of which I am deeply indebted to:

To my Beta Readers **Juan Delgado, Jo Ciccarello, Nanc Van Fleet, David Singleton, Michael Casisi, and David Middleton**, thank you for the hours spent reading those early drafts and your invaluable feedback.

To **David Singleton**, thank you for your continued encouragement and reminding me to enjoy the writing process.

To **Juan Delgado**, thank you for your expert proofreading skills and input while developing the story's plot and characters.

To my editor, **Kristin McTiernan**, thank you for your partnership in the developmental editing process. Your advice helps to make my voice and tone consistent and my story structure sound. (https://nonsensefreeeditor.com/)

To my cover designer and artist, **Juan Jose Padron**. Thank you for the countless tweaks and adjustments necessary throughout the production process. (https://jcovers.com/)

To **Paul Myrick**, thank you for designing, building, and maintaining my website. Paul is an amazing creative in many fields, and I appreciate the web development services he provides. (https://pmyrick.com/)

LET'S STAY CONNECTED!

I have many stories in the works to offer you in the future. Please visit my website for a complete list of past and upcoming works. For exclusive updates and announcements about upcoming works, please subscribe by entering your email address (I promise only to send relevant emails.) Thank You!

https://www.djciccarello.com/

Thank you again for your support!

D.J. Ciccarello